RIVER'S SONG

**Center Point
Large Print**

Also by Melody Carlson
and available from Center Point Large Print:

Ready to Wed
Winter Wonders
Limelight

**This Large Print Book carries the
Seal of Approval of N.A.V.H.**

RIVER'S SONG

The Inn at Shining Waters Series

Melody Carlson

CENTER POINT PUBLISHING
THORNDIKE, MAINE

This Center Point Large Print edition
is published in the year 2011 by arrangement with
Abingdon Press.

The persons and events portrayed in this work of fiction
are the creations of the author, and any resemblance to
persons living or dead is purely coincidental.

The text of this Large Print edition is unabridged.
In other aspects, this book may vary
from the original edition.
Printed in the United States of America
on permanent paper.
Set in 16-point Times New Roman type.

ISBN: 978-1-61173-200-9

Library of Congress Cataloging-in-Publication Data

Carlson, Melody.
River's song / Melody Carlson.
p. cm.
ISBN 978-1-61173-200-9 (library binding : alk. paper)
1. Self-realization in women—Fiction. 2. Large type books. I. Title.
PS3553.A73257R58 2011b
813′.54—dc22

                                                    2011025059

River's Song

1

Siuslaw River 1959

In twenty years' time, nothing had changed on the river. Or so it seemed. Although mid June, the sky was gloomy, the color of a weathered tin roof, and the river, a few shades darker, was tinged with mossy green. The surface of the water was serene, barely moving with the ebb tide, and the sounds of birds and a churning boat motor were muffled, hushed by the low-slung clouds. Not a scene that everyone could appreciate, but Anna wished to drink it in, absorb it into her being, and savor it for years to come when she was far from this beloved place.

"So what d'ya think, Anna?" Henry Ackerman shouted over the chugging sound of the diesel engine. "Everything still look all right to you?"

"Yes," Anna assured him. "It feels the same—not much has changed."

Henry nodded as he guided the old boat along, greasy felt hat pulled low over his shaggy brows, peering intently at the water, just as he'd done for decades. Henry, like the river, hadn't changed much. Older maybe, and a little more grizzled if that was possible, but the easy smile and friendly demeanor were just the same. She'd known Henry for so long, he seemed like family.

Something caught Anna's eye upstream. "What's that?" she called out, pointing to a dark smudge in the water.

"Just another one of them dad-burned rogue logs." He spat into the water as he steered the boat clear of it. "Always getting loose from the pilings. You gotta watch out real close when you run the river anymore." He pointed upriver. "I'm telling you, Anna, them logs are like gold nowadays. The lumber mills can't seem to get enough of 'em."

Anna stood in the boat, staring out at the enormous stretch of floating logs around the bend. Laid out like firewood side by side, they were cabled together in large groups, creating a wide, uneven border along the south side of the river—stretching for miles.

"Oh, my!" she gasped. "I've never seen so many logs in my entire life."

"Been like that for years now. Seems they can't get 'em outta the woods fast enough. Then they dump 'em here in the river and leave 'em." He cursed. "And them logs just float there till the mill's ready to cut 'em into lumber. That is, unless there's a storm or a cable busts and them logs break loose and head straight out for the ocean. You don't want to be on the water when that happens."

Anna stared in horror at the deformity on the river. The log barges resembled big ugly scabs cutting into the otherwise sleek surface of the water. Even creeping into the estuaries, like a growing cancer, barge after barge of floating logs seemed to fill up most of the surface of the Siuslaw. She could only imagine what the surrounding woods must look like. Glancing up at a hillside that had once been lush and green, she gasped to see the land scalped bare and brown . . . the stubble trunks of trees the only reminder of what had been. Her dad used to call those men gippo loggers—the reckless kind who came in and clear-cut the trees, took their money, and ran. With no concern for the future, those thieving loggers ravaged the land, leaving it barren and useless . . . dead. A lump of sadness filled her throat to think that while she was gone, the Siuslaw was being ruined.

"How long's it been since you were back here, Anna?"

"About eight years." She spoke loudly to be heard. "I came out for the funeral after Daddy died, back in '52." She wondered why she hadn't noticed this devastation back then. Perhaps she'd been too distracted by grief and guilt . . . or perhaps the river hadn't looked this bad.

Henry slowly shook his head, tucked a pinch of snuff into his cheek, and huffed. "Can't understand you young'uns nowadays. Everybody ups and leaves. My boy James went off to war and never came back."

Anna was shocked—her mother had never written of this. But then Anna had her own problems to tend to back then, her own casualties of war to keep her busy. Perhaps this was just one more piece of sadness that had eluded her. "James was killed in the war?" she asked gently.

"Nah. James made it through the war. He got hisself a GI education grant then landed hisself a fancy job in the big city. James is an *accountant*." He pronounced the word as if it meant something distasteful. "Now he's gotta wear a suit and tie every day. He sits around in a stuffy office building and counts other people's money. Course, he thinks it's mighty important work. Better than running the river every day year in and year out." Henry shook his head again. "Can't understand how a body would choose to work indoors and give up all this." He waved his hand out over the river. Henry looked honestly dumbfounded, and a part of Anna understood his bewilderment. Why had she given up all this?

"Do you hear much from James?" she asked.

"Aw sure, he writes me once in a great long while. He and the wife got two girls that are pert' near growed up now. But they don't hardly come back down here no more. Too citified, I reckon."

"It's hard coming back . . . after you've left . . ." Anna said this quietly, not sure she wanted Henry to hear her words, probably because she was guilty of the same thing as James. To confess it out loud sounded like betrayal. Not that she wouldn't do it all differently now—if only she could. But her chances, like time and tide—and the forests and the river—had come and gone. She would turn forty next year, and she was worn out and weary. It was too late to start over now.

Henry looked out over the water as he guided his boat. "You couldn't pay me to leave this river. When I die, I want them to tie this here anchor 'round my neck and just toss me overboard." He spewed a long brown stream of tobacco into the water, then continued without missing a beat, "right up there at the mouth of the Siuslaw. At high tide, hopefully around sunset."

Anna almost smiled. "My mother loved the river too." She wondered if her mother had felt the same sense of loss that Anna did right now seeing the log barges eating into the water like they planned to swallow the river whole.

"Say, how was the funeral anyway? I'd truly meant to come and show my final respects. You know I thought real highly of your ma. But then Jim Flanders calls me up just as I was heading out and says he needs me to deliver a barrel of heating oil up to their place. They'd run plumb dry and it's been cold this past week. And well, what with their new baby and all—"

"That's all right, Henry. Mother would appreciate you thinking of the little Flanders baby like that. And the funeral was just fine.

There was a nice reception at her church afterwards." Anna felt tears gathering again. "I was surprised at how many people attended. I didn't realize how many friends my mother had."

Henry pressed his lips together and nodded sagely. "Your folks were good people, Anna. And don't you never think otherwise. Most everybody on the river's been helped out at least once or twice by Oscar and Marion Larson; some were helped many a time over. We were all real sorry when Marion had to finally close up the store. A real loss for all of us. Not just for getting milk and eggs either—your mother was a right good woman."

"Thank you." Anna knew Henry spoke from the heart. And the funeral had been a touching reminder to her that most folks in these parts never concerned themselves with the fact that her mother was one of the few Indians remaining from the Siuslaw Tribe. Even now it irritated Anna that she was still overly conscious, perhaps even ashamed, of her Indian blood. And even though Anna's mother had tried to distance herself from her heritage, it seemed disrespectful for Anna to feel like this. But truth be told, Marion Larson, married to a Swede, had lived and worked in the white man's world. She dressed, acted, and spoke like a white woman. And for the most part, she'd been accepted as such. Folks on the river were like that.

Henry guided his boat past another barge of logs, then turned into the inlet that ran in front of Anna's parents' riverfront land. She had expected to see this section, like so much of the rest of the river, clogged with log barges, but to her relief, it was not. When she asked Henry how that was so, he explained that because of the store, back when it was opened and the dock was used frequently, no log barges were allowed.

"Your mama fought to keep this part of the river clear, Anna. And she won." He slowed his engine and another surge of relief rushed through Anna as she spied the familiar stand of Douglas firs ahead. Lined along the muddy riverbanks, about a dozen majestic sentries stood tall and noble, some with trunks nearly four feet wide. She knew from her grandmother's stories that these evergreens were not like those of the ancient forests, but substantial just the same. She also knew the only thing that had saved those trees from doom was the property line.

Like it was yesterday, Anna remembered her father's outrage when loggers, clear-cutting on the adjacent land, dared to raise a saw to one of those trees. Daddy had marched down there and told them in no uncertain terms to keep their hands off of his trees. And since Daddy used to be a logger, he knew how to talk to men like that. It wasn't that he had anything against cutting down trees in general, as long as it was done

13

right, but he just didn't want anybody cutting down his trees without his consent. After the loggers saw that he meant business, they all stood around and shot the breeze for the better part of an hour.

Anna had recently read the term "second-growth trees" in a newspaper column, but she knew better. These tall firs were simply the descendants of generations and generations of evergreen trees that had lived and died before them. Second-growth trees, like so many other explanations about nature, were man-made myths.

The trees were so many you could walk for days and not reach the end. So big they blocked the sun, making the great forest dark like night, and the plants grew so thick beneath the trees that your foot never touched the forest floor. But that was before the great fire. Her grandmother's words echoed in her mind with such clarity that she looked over her shoulder—almost as if the old sweet-faced woman were sitting right next to Anna in the riverboat.

"Say, how come you didn't bring that little girlie of yours along?" Henry asked suddenly, as if he had just remembered that Anna had a child.

Anna forced a laugh. "That 'little girlie' is a young woman now. Lauren will be nineteen this fall."

"You're pulling my leg!" Henry slapped his hand across his knee. "It cannot be! You're not old enough to have a child that big. Just yesterday you were a girl, Anna."

Anna sighed. "Children grow up fast." Too fast as far as she was concerned. Her daughter had only graduated from high school a week ago, and yet Lauren already knew everything there was to know about everything, and she was quick to point out how much her mother didn't know. Anna had begged Lauren to join her on this trip. She thought it might improve their strained-to-breaking relationship. But finally she realized it was useless to force her headstrong daughter to do anything against her will.

At first Anna had felt guilty about leaving Lauren behind. But then she wondered why, since her mother-in-law had made it perfectly clear that she had everything under control—including Lauren—or so she claimed. Perhaps Anna was no longer needed there. And now that she was free to come home, her mother was gone. Blinking back tears, she stared at the shore of her childhood home.

Henry cut back the engine and slipped it into reverse, easing that old boat to the dock as gracefully as a young swan. Anna looked up at the square-shaped, two-story cedar building. It looked like a tall, gray wooden crate that someone had set down next to the river and then simply walked off and forgotten. The windows were blank, with shades drawn; and the big front door to the store, which had almost always been open, was now closed, and a faded sign, painted in white block letters, probably by her mother's hand, was nailed to the door. "Sorry, store closed" it declared with abrupt finality.

Henry tied up to the dock and unloaded Anna's bags, then reached for her hand to help her from the boat. "You have everything you need here at the house, Anna? I can bring you supplies from town, you know."

Still wearing her good suit and shoes, Anna stepped carefully from the boat. "I picked up a few things in town," she assured him. "That should tide me over for a day or two."

"Can I carry your bags up for you?" Henry stood and slowly rubbed his whiskered chin as if he had all the time in the world. And maybe he did. He had to be pushing seventy, but he still ran his boat daily, servicing the river folks as faithfully as ever.

"Thanks anyway, Henry, but I can get these." Anna looked up at the darkening sky. "It looks like it's going to rain again. You'd better head on home before it lets loose."

Henry laughed. "Ain't never been worried about the rain a'fore. Can't live on the river if you don't like rain, Anna."

"I guess not." She forced a smile and picked up her suitcase. "Thanks again for everything, Henry."

"You betcha. Now you take care, ya hear?"

She waited for Henry to untie the rope, waving as his boat began to chug back down the river. She watched the rust-colored craft, followed by a wispy blue cloud of exhaust, growing smaller as it sliced its V-shaped trail through the river. Satisfied that Henry would be home before long, Anna hurried to transport her bags and things from the dock and up the exterior stairs that led to the house, which was situated above the old store.

On her second trip from the dock, she paused beneath the covered porch, where customers used to linger and catch up on the local gossip, and for a moment she could almost hear someone talking about how Tina Flanders gave birth to a baby three weeks early and how her husband, Jim, the same one who'd run out of oil that morning, had been stuck in the woods during the birth and couldn't make it home until the baby was two days old. But then Anna realized she was simply remembering her mother's most recent six-page letter. Marion Larson didn't write short letters. She wrote regular epistles. Anna had always thought that if the river had started up a newspaper, her mother would've made a great society columnist. But thanks to those letters, Anna had stayed fairly well informed on all the local comings and goings of the river folk these past twenty years.

Anna could smell rain in the air now. She hurried back to the dock for the box of food she'd picked up at the grocery store, carried it up the stairs, and set it next to her other bags. Despite his rainy day bravado, Anna knew that Henry had probably cranked up his engine by now. She hoped he'd make it back to his river house before the clouds broke. As she dug in her handbag, trying to find the house key, she wondered how many times she'd sat in Henry's little two-room shanty while he and her father loaded store supplies to take back upriver. She still remembered the smell of that river shanty— old canvas, damp wood, stale coffee, gasoline, and smoke. She imagined how old Henry would soon be stoking up his little potbellied stove and warming a can of pork and beans—or if fishing had been good he might fry up the catch of the day. Not a bad way to live really.

2

The first raindrops began to fall, plunking noisily on the metal roof, as Anna searched in her handbag for the keys that the lawyer had given her that morning. He said the brass key was for the upstairs entrance and the stainless steel one was for the store below, but the brass key looked foreign to her. She couldn't remember anyone locking the door to their house while she was growing up. Sometimes Daddy didn't even bother to lock up the store. Despite a fairly steady cash flow in the store, except during the Great Depression, her parents had never seemed overly concerned about thieves or break-ins. Each night, her dad would stash the day's earnings in an old tin box that he kept tucked beneath his bed. But he had always been more careful when they made their weekly trip into town. Then he would place the cash in a money belt "in case the boat sinks," he'd explain with a broad grin as he patted the slight bulge under his shirt. Of course, the boat never did sink. And the store never made their family wealthy either.

In fact, the store's income barely kept them clothed and fed during the Depression, but that wasn't so unusual; everyone had a tough time in those days. Each night at supper, after Daddy said the blessing, he reminded them how fortunate they were to have food on the table and a roof over their heads. Anna had been aware of Mother's black ledger book, where she recorded customers' cashless purchases, and that a fair amount of credit had been extended to their neighbors during those hard times. She also knew that customers sometimes paid their bills with an exchange of goods—and that could get interesting.

As Anna worked the key into the stubborn lock, she remembered the time Daddy had accepted a beautiful spinning wheel from Mrs. Sawyer. It was to cancel the Sawyers' rather large accumulation of debt. With tears in her eyes, Mrs. Sawyer had explained how her grandmother had brought the delicate item over by wagon train across the Oregon Trail. It was one of the few pieces to make it all the way to Oregon. Daddy kept the spinning wheel in a corner of the store right next to the potato bin, and every time Mrs. Sawyer came in she would head straight for it, running her hands over its polished surfaces. Daddy kept the spinning wheel for several years. He would occasionally get a generous offer from a collector wanting to purchase it. But each time he said, "Sorry, not for sale." Then one day, Mrs. Sawyer came in swinging her tattered purse and wearing a big smile. She made him a cash offer on the spinning wheel, explaining how she'd been saving up since the day she'd exchanged it. Daddy grinned and, refusing to take a profit, he sold it back to her for the exact price that he'd wiped clean from her bill those many years before.

Anna smiled at that memory, and the key turned in the lock. She pushed the door open with her foot and reached for her suitcase. Taking a deep breath, unsure of what to expect, she went inside. It had only been six days since her mother had died right here in this house. She knew that Mrs. Thorne, a neighbor from upriver, had stopped by last week to share a bucket of clams, and had found her mother on the kitchen floor. The doctor said she'd been dead for a day or two, but had in all likelihood died instantly. Probably a stroke or heart attack. No need for an autopsy, he'd said, nothing suspicious about a sixty-nine-year-old woman dying in her own kitchen. Anna swallowed hard and closed the door behind her. She set her suitcase on a straight-back chair and looked around, sighing in relief. Thankfully, all signs of the recent tragedy had been removed. Everything looked scrubbed clean and neat with even a vase of wild snapdragons on the kitchen table, probably from Mrs. Thorne, or maybe Babette. River folks were like that—they looked out for one another.

Anna set the box of food on the kitchen table, putting the perishable items in the old icebox, which was cold as well as recently cleaned. Now she went straight to her mother's beloved piano. She gently ran her fingers over the keys, playing a scale. Still in tune, but the sound was slightly jarring in the otherwise silent house. Daddy had sent for the upright piano when Anna was around four. It was to be a Christmas present for Mother. Anna still remembered looking on in awe as Daddy and three other men carried the enormous crate from the dock and into the house. She stood in the doorway, watching as Daddy used a crowbar to pry big pieces of wood from the crate.

She had been told to keep watch in case Mother came up while he was unpacking it, but Mother had more than enough to keep her busy that day with last-minute holiday shoppers flocking into the tiny store. Anna had hoped that there was a pony inside the big box, and was slightly dismayed when a tall brown piano appeared instead. Mother had cried when she saw it. Then to Anna's amazement she sat down and played—beautifully. It turned out that Mother had taken lessons (in exchange for housekeeping) as a child. And her dream had been to teach Anna to play as well. Consequently, almost every day after the arrival of the piano, Anna was subjected to a long hour's worth of lessons and practice.

She studied a silver-framed photo on the piano. She had seen it hundreds of times, but suddenly it was like seeing it for the first time. It had been Easter Sunday when her family had posed for a neighbor in front of their store before church, all three of them in their Sunday best. Anna must've been around seven or eight, because it was before the Great Depression and the last time she would have pretty shoes like those for a while. The shoes were soft white leather with dainty straps and not a bit practical for life on the Siuslaw River, but Daddy had thought they were pretty and brought them home for her just a few days earlier.

Although the photo was black and white, in her

mind's eye she could see it in color, and her dress was a delightful robin's egg blue with several layers of ruffles on the skirt. Mother had made it for her. Anna's long dark hair was pulled back with an oversized bow that matched the dress. Even as a girl, it was easy to see that Anna would take after her father in build and height, already resembling a gangling colt, and her face taking on angles not normally seen in the Siuslaw people. But her eyes were dark and clear and full of life. Eyes that Anna had not seen in years.

The dark-eyed girl in the photo was smiling happily. Life had been good for them. She was her parents' little pearl, and the world was her oyster. Anna's focus moved to her mother. How incredibly young she looked! Almost like a girl herself. Her mother stood nearly a foot shorter than her six-foot-tall husband, but unlike many of her race, she was neither squat nor heavy. Her facial features were traditional Siuslaw—broad nose, big dark eyes, and full lips with the corners turned slightly up—but her eyes were downcast, as if she were too shy to look straight into the lens of the camera.

In this photo, Mother's sleek black hair had been recently cut into a stylish short bob. Anna could still remember the horrified look on Daddy's face when Mother had come home from town after having her long tresses cut. He had lamented the loss for some time, then must have noticed Mother's somber face close to tears, and he quickly recovered, reassuring her that she looked very nice in her new "boy's" hair. Mother wasn't a beauty, but she was attractive in a wholesome way. Her dress, like all their clothing, had been sewn by her. It was an off-white linen, straight and sensible, not unlike the fashion of the times, and her lace-up shoes were sturdy and practical. Her appearance was exactly what one would expect for the wife of a store proprietor in the late 1920s, except, of course, that she was Indian.

Anna's gaze moved over to Daddy and she smiled. He stood ramrod straight, looking directly into the camera as if he were the proudest man on the river. Not the kind of pride associated with arrogance, but the kind that showed he was happy and satisfied with life. His jacket was slung casually over his arm, and he had on his good suspenders, or braces as he called them. His long, narrow tie seemed to exaggerate his height, but Daddy had never been a bow-tie man. But it was his smile that stopped her. Big and broad and sincere. It was that smile that brought people into the store even if they didn't need to make a purchase. Old Mrs. O'Neil had once commented that "Oscar Larson's smile was just like sunshine." And with overcast days so common to the Oregon coast, a slice of sunshine could be a priceless commodity indeed.

After all these years, Anna would still agree with Mrs. O'Neil. How she missed that sunny smile and those clear blue eyes that crinkled at the edges—Daddy's whole face seemed to light up when he smiled. People used to say that Anna had her father's smile. Certainly, no one would make that claim anymore. Time and trials had worn it away. Just last week her mother-in-law had commented that perhaps the reason Anna was approaching forty without facial wrinkles was because she rarely showed emotion. Anna might have received that as a compliment, but her mother-in-law quickly added, "I guess that's just the way it is with your people. I've always thought that Indian faces look as if they're carved in stone." Anna had wondered if her mother-in-law's heart might also be carved in stone. But out of habit she had held her tongue. She had long since learned that to respond to her mother-in-law's continual barbs only made matters worse.

Anna replaced the photo and moved to the north window that looked out over the river. She slid back the faded blue-and-white gingham café curtains that her mother had sewn before the war. She reached for the string on the roller shades, which were blocking the view as well as the light, probably pulled down by a well-meaning neighbor. As she gave the cord a tug the whole works tumbled down in a loud crash. Not that

Anna cared much. The stiff and yellowed shades had only been put to use on unusually hot summer days to keep the sun out and the house cool. Because Mother, like Anna, had always welcomed the light into the house.

Today, however, was dreary and even with the shades up there wasn't much light. Anna looked out on the dull gray scene before her. This was a day when Anna could've used a small dose of Daddy's famous sunny smile. The late afternoon sun was low in the slate-colored sky, and big fat drops were pelleting the smooth surface of the river, coming faster and harder until she could barely see the river. Anna hoped that Henry was docked by now.

For a long time she stood there, mesmerized by the watery world outside of the north window. Eventually the deluge eased itself into a steady drizzle and Anna continued to stare out across the river. *Her river.* Even on a gray and rainy day, there was a soothing quality to the slow-moving water. It was constant and dependable, ebbing and flowing with the tide, yes, but continually moving westward on its journey to the sea. The Siuslaw had always filled her with a sense of peace, a calm reassurance that life would continue. But how long had it been since she'd experienced that kind of peace in her own life? Was it possible she could ever experience it again?

How many times had she stood in this exact spot, looking out over her peaceful river world, thinking that it would never change? Truly, the river never did change. Outside of its seasonal rhythms and tidal flows, its song remained the same. A timeless melody of blue and green, water and trees, sunshine and moonlight, rain and wind. And for a brief moment she felt as if nothing in the entire world had changed.

And yet, she knew, nothing was the same.

3

With hungry eyes, Anna looked around her childhood home. Thankful that Mother had changed so little in the house over the past two decades, she was relieved to see that even the furnishings were in the same places. Maybe that was Mother's way of preserving the past. Even the smells were the same. Pungently comforting. The ever-present mustiness that came from living near water; the faint aroma of sweet cedar from the wood paneling on the ceiling; the smoky smell from the fireplace that never drafted properly in a windstorm, and all tinged by the lingering fragrance of dried lavender. Mother had always kept a large bouquet of these purple aromatic blossoms in a big white pitcher that sat on top of her old Singer treadle sewing machine. At the end of every summer the bouquet would be replaced by a fresh one.

Mother had acquired this habit from her good friend Babette McDougal. Babette had come from France as a young bride with her first husband, Pierre, just before the turn of the century. Pierre had come over to help an elderly uncle who'd been working an old gold claim in southern Oregon, certain that it was only a matter of weeks before he would strike the mother lode. After several backbreaking years, the mine actually began to pay off, but Pierre's uncle's lungs were giving out. By the time Pierre hit a solid pocket of gold, the uncle was long gone.

Tragedy continued when, shortly after Pierre and Babette began to enjoy the fruit of their long labors, Pierre was killed in a collapsed mine. Babette became a very rich widow, and decided that she wanted to live near the ocean. Anna had been surprised to see Babette at the funeral today, looking not much older than the last time she had seen her; Anna wondered if the French had some antiaging secrets.

Anna had expressed her sympathy for Babette's recent loss of her second husband, Bernard, but Babette had merely smiled and patted her hand, saying, "These things happen, ma chérie. Death is just a fact of life. Please, do come and visit me on the river, chérie. I would love to hear more about how you are doing and about your little daughter." Then tears clouded her faded blue eyes and she whispered, "I will miss your mother, chérie. She was like a sister to me." Anna didn't know why, but Babette's simple words had touched her deeply—more than anything had in a very long time. Her kindness felt familiar and warm. She would definitely spend some time with Babette during her visit here.

All at once Anna was overcome by an unexpected eagerness to relive and relish every single pleasant memory that her old homestead could conjure up. So much of her disappointing adult life had made her feel hard and dry, like a stiff, thirsty sponge deprived of all moisture. But life on the river had never been like that. It had been fulfilling and peaceful, and right now she needed to know and remember that there had truly been such a time.

A selection of baskets caught her eye. They were nicely arranged on the coffee table that her father had created from a burled piece of myrtle wood. She could tell by the intricate weave and geometric design that the baskets were Indian made. Strange. Her mother had never learned the craft, nor had she ever cared much for the traditions of her people.

Anna's mother had been a *modern* woman. She even read modern women's magazines. And theirs had been a *modern* home. Anna remembered the first time her best friend,

Dorothy, had come over to visit. They'd been about eight or nine that summer, and Dorothy had been eager to spend a day with Anna. As soon as Dorothy's dad dropped her off, she'd walked silently around Anna's house, as if she were searching for something she couldn't find. Finally she turned to Anna with a look of disdain and declared, "Why, Anna Pearl Larson, your house is just like mine!"

"Why shouldn't it be like your house?" Anna had retorted as she ran her fingers over the piano keys, showing off for her good friend.

"Because I expected to see *genuine* Indian stuff. Where do you keep it all anyway?"

Anna had been taken aback at first. She didn't even know what Dorothy was talking about. But then she'd just laughed it off and taken Dorothy over to visit Grandma Pearl. She lived in a little cabin about a hundred yards from the store. And although Grandma Pearl liked some modern things, she did many things in the old ways too. That visit had satisfied Dorothy's hunger for some "genuine Indian stuff." In fact, it was partly due to Dorothy's sincere interest and appreciation that Anna began to see Grandma Pearl in a whole new light. Unfortunately, Anna's mother did not share this enthusiasm.

"We live in the modern world, Anna. We do things in the new ways," Mother had patiently explained one day after Anna had spent a long afternoon at Grandma Pearl's little cabin. She'd been learning to twist and roll scratchy river reeds over the top of her knee, making them into long pieces that could be woven into a small sewing basket. As she did this, Grandma Pearl had been working with the more stubborn Sitka Spruce roots, explaining that they were much harder to find as well as to work with. But after Anna mastered reeds, she could move on to roots.

However, Mother questioned what she referred to as "a complete waste of time." Pressing her lips together in a tight line, she sighed deeply. "There are better ways to use your precious time, Anna Pearl," she said in a controlled tone. Anna knew by the blackness of Mother's eyes that she was losing her patience, but since Mother never lost her temper Anna knew that it was safe to persist.

"But Grandma says the old ways have been lost," pleaded Anna. "We need to save them or they'll be gone forever."

"Good riddance then. This is a new age, Anna. The old ways were fine for the old people, but they are useless for our lives today."

"But Grandma said it's possible to weave baskets that can actually carry water," Anna explained with wonder.

That had simply made Mother laugh. She picked up a tin bucket. "*This* can also carry water. And it doesn't take me days and days just to make one. Now, why don't you go fill it up with huckleberries from the woods? That should make you feel like a good little Indian squaw."

Thankfully, Mother didn't forbid Anna to spend time with Grandma Pearl. So for the next few summers, Anna spent hour after hour learning how to do "Indian things," the kinds of things she kept quiet about because, other than Dorothy, most of her friends would not have understood. And she knew that her mother would say it was worse than senseless. Fortunately, summertime was also the tourist season. People from the Willamette Valley and other inland places would journey west to see the ocean or do recreational fishing or camping on the river. This was the busiest time for the store. Daddy would stock the shelves with more colorful and interesting items, including sweets and money-making knickknacks, the sorts of things tourists liked to spend their cash on. Consequently, her parents stayed busy and as long as Anna's chores were done to satisfaction and she had practiced piano, no one seemed to mind having her out from under foot—usually spending time with Grandma Pearl.

It was helpful that Daddy approved of Grandma Pearl. Perhaps he missed the family relationships he had left behind in Sweden, or maybe, like Anna, he just thought that Grandma Pearl was entertaining. Whatever it was, he had great respect for his mother-in-law, and he encouraged Anna to continue spending time with her. He was even known to take his pipe over to her cabin and spend a good portion of an evening just visiting with the old woman. He enjoyed hearing her tales of days gone by, and the old stories of her ancestors.

Daddy often took a little notebook with him and he would attempt to record her stories as she told them. Sometimes at night, if it wasn't too late, Anna got to sit in and listen too, and she would watch in wonder as Grandma closed her big brown eyes and tried to get the stories *just right*. Anna didn't get to hear all of Grandma's stories because, as Daddy explained to her privately one night, some tales were better understood by grown-up ears. "Someday you will hear them too."

Because of this, Anna became even more curious as to what was in Daddy's "legend book." She sneaked it to her room and tried to read from it once, but because Daddy's mother tongue was Swedish, his phonetically challenged spelling was rather strange and difficult to unravel. That was why Mother always kept the books for the store. Anna wondered if Daddy's notebook might still be around the house somewhere, although she doubted she would have any more luck understanding it now than she had back then.

One summer, an anthropologist had stopped by the store for supplies, and Daddy had mentioned that he was trying to record Grandma's stories. At first the anthropologist was very interested, but when he learned that Grandma had become a Christian during a turn-of-the-century revival that had taken place in Florence, he waved his hand in dismissal, saying that Grandma's stories would be tainted with Christianity now and no longer *authentic*. Anna asked Daddy what "authentic" was, and he said it was like telling the truth. That's when Anna decided that the anthropologist was full of beans because she knew that Grandma stories *were* authentic. Grandma Pearl wouldn't lie.

Anna couldn't specifically recall her mother ever taking the path that wound back behind the store over to Grandma's cabin, except perhaps the time when Grandma was very sick and Mother had taken her soup and medicine. Grandma drank the soup, but wouldn't touch the medicine. Instead, she relied on her own herbal remedies. And the herbs must have worked because Grandma was up and well after just a few days. After that, whether it was an extra loaf of bread or eggs or produce from the garden, Mother usually sent it by way of Anna.

By the same token, Grandma Pearl rarely came into the store. And although she was quite old, it wasn't that she couldn't get around easily, because the fact was, most of the time Grandma was as healthy as a horse. She would take a large root basket and spend hours in the woods collecting berries, nuts, and herbs until the basket was heavy and full. Anna suspected the reason Grandma didn't come by to visit was because she didn't feel very welcome at the store or the house. The only time that Anna could recall Grandma stopping by the store, her mother had grabbed up the broom and become very busy sweeping an already spotless floor. At the time, Anna had thought it strange; now she understood it was Mother's way of keeping Grandma at a distance.

Mother didn't approve of Grandma's long gray braids ornately tied with strips of deerskin, or her homemade clothing, often decorated with found embellishments from nature—things like shells, feathers, and carved bone. Nor did she approve of Grandma's smell. Mostly it was kind of a smoky, musky smell. Anna never understood the problem. But when Mother gave Grandma Pearl a bottle of toilette water (Babette's suggestion) Grandma Pearl took it home. But thinking it was something to use for cooking, she sampled it. Naturally, it tasted terrible, so she poured out the cologne and saved the bottle to fill with "good medicine." Later she told Anna, with a sour expression, "The stinky water was no good. *Rotten.*"

Anna remembered a day when she'd been sitting on the old hewn log that served as a bench in front of Grandma's cabin. She and Grandma Pearl had just finished shelling a basket of pea pods that Anna had picked and carried down from their garden. It was one of those flawless summer afternoons, and the glassy surface of the bluer-than-blue river reflected a perfect mirror image of towering trees and cloudless sky. They both sat peacefully, without speaking. The only sounds were the birds' occasional calls and the lapping of water at the river's edge from a fishing boat that had recently passed, and then Anna had spoiled everything by asking Grandma why she and Mother didn't get along very well.

After a lengthy silence Grandma answered, her dark eyes serious, "Your mother, my Marion, lives in moving man's world." Anna knew by then that "moving man" was an old Indian term for white man, assigned to them when they moved to this part of the country from somewhere else about fifty years ago. "Your mother does not know the ways of her people, Anna. She does not want to know . . . she wants to forget. I accept this. I, too, once tried to forget the ways of my people."

"Why would you do that?" Anna asked. "I think your ways are wonderful." She held up a basket recently made by Grandma's old wrinkled hands. "The things you make are so beautiful."

Grandma smiled, revealing uneven yellowed teeth. "There was a time when it was very good to be a Siuslaw Indian. Before my time. When my mother and father were young people, they were free to hunt and fish and live good life. Our people on the Siuslaw were not many, but they strong people—good people. They work hard and they help each other." She pointed to the basket in Anna's hand. "They skillful people too."

"But then the white man—the moving man—came?"

"Yes. Before I was born, the moving man came to the river. Not many at first. Our people welcome them. Our chief share his home. We share food. The moving man hunt our otter, our beaver. Not for food. For skin only."

Anna nodded. She had read of trappers and such in school. History books credited companies like the Hudson's Bay for settling the Northwest Territory.

"First the moving man say this"—Grandma waved her hand in all directions—"all you see from here to the ocean, to Tahkenitch to Yachats; all is your land. Reservation."

"All the land?" Anna was surprised. "All belonged to the Indians?" She had never heard this before.

Grandma Pearl waved her hands more vigorously. "All the land; all you see and more." Now she pointed to her head with a sly look, cunning like a fox. "But moving man, he change mind. He think—no, no, wait, let's see . . . this *good* land. This very good land. Too good for Indian only." She clapped her hands together so loud, so fast, that Anna jumped. "No more reservation!"

"Then what?" Anna waited anxiously for the rest of the story.

"Sickness come with moving man. Our numbers became less and less. I think about one hundred then. My grandparents die of moving man diseases. The others, my mother and my father, they taken from their homes and their land. They herded like horses onto beach. Walking, walking, north to Siletz Reservation. My mother walk for fifty miles up beach"—she pointed to her belly—"with me inside of her! She walk carrying baby. Many, many people walk. Coos, Siuslaw, Alsea, Coquille, Umpqua—all our people from here walk. My mother almost die, but she strong woman. I born on the reservation. Only moving man food on the reservation, bad food. Make us sick. But no one can go gather berries, fish, bring good food. One night, my father worry about my mother and me. He sneak out to gather clams and berries. He never come back. Before she die, my mother tell me, white man chase my father, hunt him like coyote, and kill him because he want to find food."

"How horrible!"

Grandma nodded. "Then one day when I am girl, about as big as you, moving man take our people, the Siuslaw, aside and say, 'You free to leave reservation now.' They say we can have land back, only we must file claim. My mother cannot read, cannot write. Her younger sister, Aunt Dora, she white man's wife. They live in Florence town. Because her husband white, she not go to reservation. My mother say, 'Dora will help us. We go to Dora.' And so we walk and walk and walk. Fifty miles down the beach. But it is a good walk. We are happy. We are free. We gather berries. We catch fish and dig clams. It is a party. But much walking."

Anna had listened carefully, hoping that Daddy had heard this story too, had written it all down. She had no idea that Grandma Pearl's life had been this exciting. It was almost as good as a motion picture. Naturally, Mother had never mentioned any of this to Anna. Most of the time it was almost forgotten that they had any Indian blood. This was the way Mother wanted it. She never said as much, but Anna knew it was true.

"We go to Dora," Grandma continued her tale, her eyes looking far away. "But Dora is unhappy. When her husband at work, she tell us he is mean man, that he beat her like dog. Dora show us bruises and scars. So Mother tell her sister about free land, and when Dora's husband hear about

39

free land, he act nice. He help write claim. He think he get land. After claim is filed Dora leave her bad husband."

"And is that when you came to live here?"

Grandma shook her head. "No. My mother and Dora work in the town. They clean house and wash clothes for moving man wives. I sit on chair for hours and hours waiting for my mother to finish her work. And sometimes the white woman yell and call my mother bad names. But my mother does not fight back. I ask her why. She say it is only way for us to survive. Then white man say I must go to mission school. I must learn to read and write. I must learn white man ways. To talk right. I go and I begin to forget the ways of my people. I learn that life is easier when I look and talk like the white people."

"That must have been sad."

"Yes. Then I get older and my mother send me to Indian school up north. I ride train by myself. I am frightened. I learned more white men's ways at their school. I unhappy there. But I meet John." Now Grandma smiled, once again revealing her yellowed teeth.

"Is that my grandpa? John?" Anna knew she had heard the name before.

"Yes. John was also at Indian school. His mother was Siuslaw, a friend of my mother. John's father was from Alsea Tribe, but he die on the reservation like my father. Most men die on reservation. Only women and children live. John promise to marry me when we finish school and return to Florence town. And he keep promise. John build this house." Grandma set down the bowl of peas on the rough-hewn table outside of her cabin, looking proudly at the little two-room wooden house. "My mother and John's mother live here too. John was logger. He be in woods for two, sometimes three weeks before he come home again. We women only at home."

"And were you happy then?" asked Anna. She had been reading fairy tales lately, and liked the ones where everyone lived happily ever after the best.

Grandma smiled. "We were happy. The mothers knew old ways. They remember how to gather what we need from the land. John's mother know how to make medicine with plants. My mother know to make baskets. They teach me their ways. I know to sew because I learn at Indian school and I make clothes for us, for Marion too. Living on river is good medicine, Anna. River make us well again." And just then, Anna's mother had called, saying it was supper time. It had been like being pulled out of a storybook, but it was a good place to end. It wasn't until many years later that Anna had heard other parts of Grandma Pearl's story, and much of it was not so happy.

When Anna was almost twelve, Grandmother

Pearl died suddenly, taking all of her Indian ways with her—or so it seemed at first. But to everyone's surprise, especially Mother's, the coastal newspaper ran a special obituary, noting that Pearl Martin might have been the last of the full-blooded Siuslaws. Anna had proudly clipped it out and read it aloud with tears choking her voice. For the next few weeks, she spent many hours in Grandma's little cabin mourning her absent friend. It was the first time she'd ever lost a loved one and it hurt deep inside of her, like a stomachache that wouldn't go away.

At first, Anna held it against her mother that she hadn't been kinder to Grandma Pearl while she was alive. Later Anna became confused and even rankled at the way Mother seemed to slip into a deep depression over the death of her mother. Anna couldn't understand. If Mother had cared so much about her mother, why hadn't she spent more time with the old woman? It just didn't make sense. Now she understood the sorrow only too well.

Anna picked up another basket, running her hands over its smoothly woven surface. This one was probably watertight. She traced her fingers over the dark, triangular design of the intricate weave. It seemed familiar, and suddenly she wondered if Mother might have saved some of Grandma Pearl's things after all. At the time of Grandma's death, her mother had dismissed

Anna's questioning about Grandma's things, saying that they were all old and worthless and "probably full of bugs." For the first couple of years, Anna had maintained Grandma's little cabin, almost like a shrine. But then as time passed and she grew older, with more distractions at school and in her social life, she went to the cabin less and less.

It wasn't until she was sixteen that she realized that everything had been cleared out of the small cabin. Anna had assumed it was her mother's doing and she feared that everything had been dumped. In fact, she punished her mother with the silent treatment for nearly a week as a result. She later learned that several years after Grandma's death, Daddy had decreed that nothing should be thrown away. Just stored. And he told her that he'd very carefully boxed up some of the more special things, like trade beads and a ceremonial dress and some old beaded baby moccasins . . . things he thought Anna might appreciate when she was older. As far as she knew, these were still safely stored somewhere in the attic.

But by far the best thing that Daddy had saved was the *River Dove*. Apparently, Grandma Pearl had told Daddy that the little dugout canoe was to go to Anna. Grandma Pearl had told Anna about how she'd acquired this sound little boat. Her husband—not John but the second one,

Crazy Bob, the one who drank too much—had brought it home quite late one night. It was only a "squaw canoe," only big enough for one small person, and Crazy Bob could barely squeeze in or out of it. He told her he'd won it gambling, and since no one ever showed up to reclaim it, she figured it must be true. She was glad to have the canoe and happily used it for many years.

Daddy told Anna that dugout canoes had been fairly common before the turn of the century (and the reservation woes) and that many Indians had used them as their primary mode of transportation, traveling up and down the river to follow fish and food wherever it was to be found. "But," he explained quietly, probably so that Mother wouldn't overhear, "nowadays the old craft of making the dugout is nearly lost, like so many of the Indian ways. Lucky for you, Grandma Pearl told me all about it, and I'll explain it all to you too someday."

That summer, Daddy made Anna prove her aquatic ability by swimming all the way across the river while he paddled the little canoe alongside her. "Grandma told me that no self-respecting man would use a canoe like this," he called out as she swam. "But I kind of like it so if you change your mind and decide to swim back, I won't mind." The twinkle in his blue eyes told her that he was just teasing.

And Anna showed herself to be a strong

swimmer that day. She couldn't remember a time when she hadn't been able to at least dog-paddle, but she had never actually swum all the way across the river before; in fact she'd been forbidden to even attempt such a thing. But she had always accepted her parents' extreme caution when it came to river safety because she knew they had lost their firstborn child, a brother she'd never even met, when he apparently toddled off the edge of the dock and drowned. No one had witnessed the tragedy, but the theory was that the child had been tempted by Grandma Pearl's canoe, which had been tied to the dock at the time. He had been begging for rides in the canoe, but Mother had been afraid it was too tippy for a small child.

Daddy had spotted him from the store, floating just below the surface of the water. Dropping a bottle of fish oil, which shattered right behind the counter (the stain remained after all those years), he'd dashed out to rescue his son . . . too late. Little Eric Joseph, named after a grandfather in far-off Sweden, never saw his third birthday. It had been the one dark shadow of sadness on their otherwise rather blissful little lives, and they rarely spoke of it. But because of losing little Eric, Daddy had made certain that Anna could swim even before she could walk.

Anna could still remember the look of sheer joy on her father's tanned features when she triumphantly reached the other side. She would never forget how he had pulled the canoe onto the shore and handed her the paddle. Then, to her surprise, he stripped off his shirt. "It's your canoe now." Then he jumped in the river, swimming next to her this time, as he shouted instructions and she clumsily paddled back across the river to their own dock.

After that day, the canoe became her ticket to freedom on the river. And before long, at least during summer and on weekends, she took to wearing her dark hair in two long pigtails, just like Grandma used to do. And as she paddled along the river, she imagined herself to be a Siuslaw Indian princess. Like her grandma before her, Anna called her little canoe *River Dove* because of the bird's head that was carved into the bow, but unlike her grandma (at least she'd assumed) Anna secretly called herself the "Indian Princess of Shining Waters." Because in her mind, she ruled the river—or at least the portion directly in front of their store. Customers seemed to acknowledge her reign as they smiled and waved to her, careful not to rock her in their wake as they docked their boats and went into the store for supplies and the latest news. Life had been so sweet and simple then.

Anna sighed. If only it were so simple now. She looked out the window again. At the present moment, her river didn't look any more like the

Shining Waters than she felt like an Indian princess. She set the woven basket down and sank onto the old, familiar camel-hair sofa, pulling a shabby pink and green knitted afghan over her legs. She fingered the crocheted throw with sadness. Already it was falling apart, whether from moths or too much use, and it would soon be a useless pile of pink and green yarn bits. And yet her mother's own hands had meticulously hooked each loop on this blanket. Anna still remembered how, so many years ago, after several months of crocheting each evening, her mother had draped the pink and green fruit of her labors over the back of this very sofa with such pride—a white woman sort of pride. And now the blanket looked so shabby and pathetic and stringy. Compared to the beautiful Indian baskets on the coffee table, the afghan seemed rather silly . . . and useless . . . and sad.

And for the first time, in a very long time, Anna cried.

4

When Anna awoke, the house was dark and silent and, feeling cold and disoriented, she had to take a moment to remember where she was. Then relief washed over her as she realized that she was home. *Really home.* Now if she could only remember how to start up the old generator.

It had obviously been turned off by the neighbors to save fuel while the house was unoccupied. And although it was late June the air was cold and damp today, not unusual for this region, where the summer could be windy and cool and autumn could be balmy.

Stumbling through the darkness toward where she thought the fireplace lay, she inched her fingers along the mantle until she located the ever-present kerosene lamp and a box of matches. They were always ready for those unexpected moments when the generator would shut down. Soon a warm golden glow illuminated the room, and she soon found several other lanterns, which she lit and placed strategically. She found kindling and wood and before long had a crackling fire burning. Perhaps she wouldn't need any electricity tonight after all.

She stepped back and held her hands over the flickering flames, admiring her handiwork, and then admiring her father's. He'd designed and built this fireplace himself. He had shown her the very spot where he had collected the big smooth stones from a bank up the river, telling how he'd made dozens of trips in his little rowboat until he finally had enough. That was long before Anna, or even Eric Joseph, had been born. Anna knew it had taken them nearly five years to conceive their first child. And then four more after Eric's death to conceive Anna. As a child, she occasionally wondered why she didn't have any other siblings, although Grandma once alluded to some health issues that occurred during Anna's mother's childhood.

Just the same, Anna enjoyed the attention lavished on an only child. The first time she heard the term "only child," it had come from Babette. With Babette's thick French accent, Anna had thought she'd said, "You are a lonely child," and Anna had answered, "I'm not a lonely child. I have lots of friends, and Grandma Pearl, and Daddy and Mother." And then Babette had laughed the way that only Babette could laugh, deep in her throat until her bosom shook like a small earthquake. But when she regained her composure, she kindly explained to Anna what "only child" meant, and that she had only just learned the term herself.

It wasn't until Anna was about to become a mother herself that her mother explained that the reason they didn't have more children wasn't that they didn't want them, but a result of some "female problems" that prohibited her from conceiving. "But we've always been thankful to have you," she told Anna a couple of days before Lauren was born. "And we hope you and Adam give us lots of grandchildren. Nothing makes me happier than to see you happy, dear."

As a result, Anna had always gone to great effort to ensure her parents remained oblivious to

49

her troubled adult life. She sent cheerful letters and photos of Lauren wearing the fancy store-bought clothes her mother-in-law provided. Sheltering her parents from the realities of her miserable existence, she wrote about how Lauren took dance classes and excelled in school and anything she could think of to fill a page and a half of a letter. Sometimes she simply wrote the words larger, taking care to use perfect penmanship, filling the blank space with lovely cursive letters. It seemed the least she could do for them. Her parents had already survived their own troubled childhoods. Besides the hardships her mother had endured, Anna knew that Daddy had been orphaned as a young teen, and that he'd snuck out onto a freighter from Sweden, traveling halfway around the world to make his own way in life. Anna hadn't wanted to push her parents out of her life; she'd simply wanted them to be happy.

Her mother had been so pleased and proud when Anna had caught the eye of the strapping young lumberman who had been tearing up and down the river in a very impressive motorboat. Adam Gunderson, fresh out of college, had been spending time at one of the larger mills along the river. Not as a worker, but as a member of a prosperous Northwest logging family. His uncle owned the mill on the Siuslaw. And his father owned a similar but smaller mill on the other side of the coastal range mountains in Pine

Ridge. Adam had come to the coast to observe some of the new technology and machinery his uncle had recently installed in his mill. He'd also spent some time observing and being observed by the local girls.

Barely out of high school, Anna had been helping out at the store and making plans to go to teachers' college in the fall. Of course, Adam had changed all that. First she'd ignored the flirtatious behavior of the handsome young man—imagining him to be a spoiled, rich brat, which wasn't far from the truth. But he seemed to take her standoffishness as a personal challenge and by the Fourth of July he had talked her into going on a picnic and to the fireworks show with him. Naturally, she only agreed to this after he promised to let some of her friends come along as well. It was quite an exciting day and evening and, as Dorothy said, the boy was smitten. And when Adam called Anna his Indian princess a few days later, she was equally smitten.

One thing led to another and by the summer's end they were officially engaged, with a wedding date set for the following June. Adam went back to Pine Ridge to run his family's mill and Anna continued with her plans of continuing education at the teachers' college in Monmouth. Her mother tried to talk her out of this, saying that she should use the year to prepare for the wedding by learning to cook and preparing a trousseau. But Anna imagined herself to be an independent young woman. A fan of Katharine Hepburn and some of the other take-charge sort of popular young actresses of the day, Anna had seen a variety of movies, and she liked to imagine that she too was like that—a capable, confident, modern sort of woman. Going to college seemed the way to prove that.

When Adam showed up on campus shortly before Christmas break, he declared his undying affection to Anna, insisting that he couldn't live another day without her, convincing her that their only solution was elopement. Flattered and excited, not to mention somewhat homesick and thoroughly disenchanted with her lackluster college classes, she agreed. And since they were both of age, he drove them to Reno where they were quickly and quietly married. Anna's parents sounded understanding when she placed the collect call to the store, but she could tell that her mother was disappointed. She had wanted to sew the wedding dress, prepare a trousseau, and host a lovely wedding by the river—all things that Anna would've enjoyed as well. But now she pushed those thoughts from her mind, telling herself that being married to Adam was all that mattered.

"The house isn't much," Adam told her as they returned from their honeymoon three days before Christmas. "I've been so busy at the mill that I haven't had time to keep it up." He parked his roadster in front of a sweet looking little cottage with cedar shingles and white shutters and flower boxes.

"I love it," she told him as he picked her up into his arms. She laughed as he carried her over the threshold. Of course, once inside the cottage, she realized that it did need some work. But, never mind, she was a hard worker. The next morning, Adam went off to the mill and Anna tied her hair in a bandana and put on a pair of Adam's dungarees, belting them tight to keep them on. She rolled up the sleeves of one of his old flannel shirts and went right to work. Cleaning and scrubbing with an intensity that surprised even her, she intended to make that cottage sparkle and shine before Christmas!

It was mid-afternoon when she opened the front door to throw out what must've been her tenth bucket of blackened mop water when a well-dressed middle-aged woman walked up the brick-paved walk. She had a brown crocodile handbag on her arm and wore shoes that matched it. "Oh, my!" Anna cried, stopping herself from dousing the woman with the filthy water.

"Who are *you?*" the woman asked with narrowed eyes.

"Excuse me?" Anna set the bucket aside, studying the slightly built fair-haired woman. Her eyes were pale blue and cold.

"Oh, I see." The woman nodded with a relieved

expression. "Adam must've hired a cleaning woman. Yes, it's about time. That cabin is appalling. I've told my son a pig wouldn't live there."

"Your son?" Anna wiped her hands on the back of her dirty pants.

"That's right. Adam Gunderson is my son. I am Mrs. Gunderson." The woman turned to leave then stopped abruptly. Turning back around, she wore a curious expression. "You *are* a cleaning woman, are you not?"

Anna was speechless. *Hadn't Adam told his mother about her—about their marriage?*

As Mrs. Gunderson came closer, her arched brows drew together and she looked very worried. "Please, answer me, young woman. You do speak English, don't you?"

Suddenly Anna was aware of her Indian heritage. "Yes, of course, I speak English," she said quickly.

"Did my son hire you to clean his house or not?" she demanded.

Anna's heart was pounding so hard, she could feel it in her throat. This was Adam's mother! This woman had no idea that Adam was married! Anna took in a deep breath and made a forced smile. "I'm so sorry to meet you under such awkward circumstances, Mrs. Gunderson."

"Who are you?"

"I am Anna Larson. Actually, that's not quite right, I'm—"

"What are you doing in Adam's house?" she demanded. "Did you *sleep* here?"

Embarrassed, Anna lowered her gaze to the ground. "Adam and I—we were married—about a week ago in Reno."

"You are lying!" she shrieked.

Anna looked back up to see that Mrs. Gunderson's face was even paler than before and she was clutching her chest as if in pain.

"Are you all right?" Anna ran over to help her.

But the woman backed away, holding up her hands as if she thought Anna might hurt her. "Keep your filthy hands off me."

Anna just stared in horror as Mrs. Gunderson turned and hurried over to where a shiny black sedan was parked on the other side of the street. It took her a few moments to get inside and start the car, but once the engine turned over, the car's tires squealed as it roared down the quiet street. Sickened by what had just transpired, all Anna could think was that she wanted to go home. She wanted the familiarity of the river . . . her parents . . . and peace.

Anna stood and walked over to the fireplace, tossing a couple more logs onto the still-red embers. So now she was home with the familiarity she had longed for. Although her parents were gone . . . and that sense of peace felt elusive . . . but at least the river was still here. That never changed.

5

Anna slept soundly that night. She wasn't sure if it was from pure exhaustion, the comfort of the bed, or the lulling sound of the flowing river, but when she awoke, she felt refreshed and ready to face the day. To her delight the clouds were gone and the sun was shining. And when she looked out toward the river, the water glistened and sparkled—just like diamonds—and she felt a rush of excitement that reminded her of childhood.

Unexpectedly hungry, she lit the gas stove and soon had eggs sizzling and coffee perking. She still hadn't turned the generator on to use the electric toaster, but using a fork she toasted a slice of bread over the gas flame. Then she took her breakfast outside and, sitting on the steps of the porch in front of the store, ate it while watching the river. Several fishing boats passed by. One of the people in a boat waved.

She was just going back inside, wanting to get the generator started when she heard a woman's voice calling out to her. "Hallo! Hallo!" Knowing by the accent that it must be Babette, Anna set her plate and cup on the porch and then went out to the dock to greet her.

"Hello, neighbor." Anna smiled as she helped her tie the little motorboat. "You're up bright and early this morning."

"Ees such a beautiful day! How can I resist?" Babette handed Anna a paper bag. "I brought you provisions."

"I have coffee in the house," Anna told her.

"Fantastic!" Babette linked her arm into Anna's. "Ees so good to see you, ma chérie." She reached up and held Anna's chin in her hand. "And you are still beautiful. But your complexion, chérie, you must use care."

"What do you mean?" Anna asked as they went up the stairs.

"You are beautiful now, but you will look like old woman before your time."

Anna laughed as she opened the door to the house. "I'm not sure that I care what I look like."

"Of course, you care!" she scolded. "You are a woman—you must always care."

As Anna poured them each a cup of coffee, Babette carefully removed some delicate pastries from the bag she'd brought. "I made éclairs," she told Anna. "I remember how you loved them as a little girl."

They sat at the small fir kitchen table together, sharing coffee and pastries and the latest river news. Anna was surprised at how good it felt. "This would be absolutely perfect," she said with regret, "if only Mother were here too."

Babette made a sad smile. "Oui."

"I wish I'd come home more. . . ."

"Why did you not?"

Anna thought about this. "Do you want to know the truth?"

Babette's dark brows arched. "Oui, chérie. As your mama would say, the truth, she set you free."

So for the first time Anna told someone what her life had really been like. She started with her first encounter with Adam's mother and her sharp disapproval of Anna. "In retrospect, I almost wish I'd let that slop water go," she confessed.

"Perhaps it would have been better." Babette shook her head. "Then she would know she could not walk on you."

"I never knew, before we got married that is, that Adam's mother was vehemently opposed to our marriage. As soon as she'd heard news of our engagement, she had insisted he call the whole thing off."

"Why was that, chérie?"

"I thought it was because she found out I was half Indian, but Adam swore that had nothing to do with it. You know that Adam was her only son and, after being widowed when he was only fourteen, Eunice had come to depend on him to be the man of the family." Anna shook her head. "I don't think that was the best way for a boy to grow up. Besides being spoiled, he became quite stubborn. He was used to getting his way. As a result, it seemed that the more his mother put her foot down on the marriage plans, the more bound and determined Adam became to marry me. Sometimes I wonder if he married me simply to spite his mother."

"But he loved you, Anna. We all could see that."

She nodded. "I suppose you're right. And, truly, we were happy. For a very short while we were very happy. As long as Eunice kept her distance."

"Then, just one year after your marriage, your baby came." Babette smiled. "Your mama, she was so happy. And such a beautiful little girl." She pointed to a framed baby photo of Lauren sitting on a side table. "I have photos of her at my house too."

"And I had actually hoped that Lauren's arrival would improve my relationship with my mother-in-law."

"But it did not?"

"It seemed to at first. Eunice would come to visit the baby, always bringing expensive and somewhat useless presents. It was obvious she loved Lauren, and I'm sure Eunice was immensely relieved that she didn't come out looking like me."

"Oh, Anna." Babette shook her finger. "You are a very beautiful woman. Everyone says so."

"Not my mother-in-law. Eunice made it quite clear that she did not like Indians."

"I think that Eunice would not have liked you no matter what you were."

"Maybe so. No matter how hard I tried to please her, I was never good enough. Nothing I did was right in her eyes and she was never afraid to let me know. It was bad enough with Adam still home, but after he went to war, it became worse. She often called me the Squaw Woman—right in front of Lauren too. I asked her to stop, but she would just laugh and tell me not to be so sensitive."

"Sounds like she is the one who needs to be more sensitive." Babette frowned.

"It got so bad that I was ready to bring Lauren back here. I wanted to come home to the river. I decided I would set up housekeeping in Grandma Pearl's little cabin until Adam came home from the war."

"But Adam came home sooner than expected."

"I had already phoned Daddy, saying that I wanted to come home. And I had just started to pack my bags when the telegram arrived. Naturally, I was relieved that Adam had not been killed in the line of duty, but was upset that he'd been severely wounded in Normandy. The telegram said he would arrive in Pine Ridge in less than three weeks. It was no time to be running back home to my parents. I needed to stay put, preparing for the arrival of my wounded soldier. I felt guilty for how thankful I was that he was coming home. But I figured I needed him more than the army did. I just didn't realize, not until some time later, that Adam's mind had been more severely injured than his body. Even now, after he's been gone for eight years, it's hard to grasp what the horrors of war did to that man. I doubt that I ever will."

"War is horrible, horrible." Babette frowned. "But I did not know this . . . about Adam's mind being injured. Your mama, she never speak a word."

"Because she didn't know. I never told her. I always referred to his physical injuries, not the mental ones."

"But why, chérie? Your mama, she would understand. She knew of hardships."

"Yes. And if she knew I was unhappy . . . she would be unhappy. And Daddy too."

Babette nodded. "Oh . . . I see."

She told Babette that it was after Adam came home, missing an arm and a piece of his heart, that Anna's campaign to protect her parents from the harsh realities of her own life became intense. "Daddy was determined to go up to Pine Ridge and fetch us. He wanted to bring Lauren and me back to the river to live. He suspected something was very wrong. But I assured him we were fine and that I needed to be there to help Adam recover. Looking back, it might have been best to have come home then." But at the time, she thought if things couldn't get worse, then they could only get better. "And so my letters to my parents were written from a very positive perspective." She smiled. "Oddly enough, I usually felt better after I wrote one."

"Your mama loved your letters. She saved every one, you know—reading them again and again. She said they were like medicine. Good medicine."

"It wasn't that I saw the world through rose-colored glasses, but it didn't hurt to hope for better days. My letters became so convincing that I almost believed them myself by the time I sealed up the envelopes and stuck on the stamps. And there seemed no reason to think my parents ever suspected anything different. Then, after Daddy developed his heart condition, it had seemed best to keep up my charade. No need to add stress to his life."

"But after he died?" Babette tipped her head to one side. "Why not tell your mama the truth then?"

"Mother was so overwhelmed with grief, she needed me to be strong for her."

"Then why not stay here then? You and Lauren could've lived right here—very happily."

"I still had Adam to care for. His mother had made it clear from the moment he came home from the war that he was my responsibility. And Lauren had school and her friends and activities by then. I thought she'd enjoy seeing where I grew up, but she seemed to hate it. She'd already been influenced by her other grandmother. She wasn't quite eleven and she was already turning up her nose like a spoiled teenager. She thought everyone here was backward and she called the Siuslaw a backwater. Thankfully, my mother never heard her say these things, but I know Lauren is ashamed of her Indian heritage. She is ashamed of me."

"Oh, Anna." Babette had tears in her eyes now. "I am so sorry, chérie." She got up and gathered Anna in her arms, squeezing her tightly, smelling of sweet French perfume. "So very sorry." Babette went over for the coffeepot, refilled their coffee cups, and sat down again. Retrieving a lace-trimmed handkerchief from the bodice of her dress, she daubed her eyes.

"And now I've made you sad." Anna stirred a bit of sugar in her coffee.

"Because I love you, I am sad. Now, please, tell me the rest of your story."

"There's really not much else to tell. I took care of Adam and Lauren and did all the housekeeping in Eunice's house—"

"You kept house for that wicked woman?"

"I had no choice. She and the doctor insisted that Adam needed to live in her house to receive adequate care. He was taken immediately to his old bedroom." She shook her head. "And that's where he remained for the next seven years . . . until he passed." Anna didn't have the strength to say that Adam took his own life. No one had ever spoken those words before, but Anna knew in her heart it was true. She suspected Adam had saved up several weeks' worth of pain pills, the ones she carefully doled out daily. His lack of medication would explain his horrid meanness in the last weeks of his life. And, really, on so very many levels, she didn't blame him for doing it. It would be up to God to sort that one out.

"But why did you not come home then?"

Anna sighed. "Lauren."

"Oh. . . ." She nodded sadly. "I see."

"How could I drag her away from everything she loved? And even though I could see my mother-in-law turning my daughter into a brat, how could I abandon my own daughter? I suppose I hoped that I would still be able to influence her . . . that she would grow up and see that Grandma Eunice has her faults. But I'm afraid all Lauren sees is that Grandma Eunice has a fat pocketbook. And I have nothing. And so I kept my troubles bottled up inside and continued writing my sunny letters to mother. And now she is gone." Suddenly Anna was crying again. As if all that she had lost came rushing at her like a tidal wave. "Oh, Babette!" she cried. "She is gone. Truly gone!"

Now they both cried. Flooded with regret,

Anna wished with all her heart that she'd come back to her mother sooner—before it was too late. Why hadn't she simply packed up Lauren and brought her back here? Eventually, Lauren would've gotten used to the slower-paced life. She would've made friends. Perhaps she would've grown to love the river eventually. And now she never would.

"I wish I'd been honest. I wish I'd told Mother all about my life," Anna said through her tears. "All about Adam's problems, how it felt having my mean mother-in-law breathing down my neck all the time, putting me down, calling me names. I wish I'd confessed to Mother that I was letting my daughter push me around—the same way I allowed Eunice to bully me. I should've told her everything."

"Maybe not, chérie."

Anna blinked, blotting her eyes with her own handkerchief now. "Why not?"

"I think it would have crushed her."

"Oh."

"Your mama she was a wise woman in her way."

"Yes." Anna nodded.

"She knew things about Adam . . . things she never told anyone except me."

"What?" Anna waited anxiously.

"Your mama saw a weakness in him. She hoped it was only youth. But when you called her to say you were married—so quickly—your mama, she was worried."

"I know . . . I could hear it in her voice."

"Her worry . . . it make her sick . . . such stomach troubles." Babette shook her head. "All from too much worrying."

"Poor Mother."

"So your letters come . . . and the sun it comes out . . . your mama, she happy. Her stomach is well. Like I said, your letters were good medicine."

Anna thought about this. Perhaps her pretense at a happy life had prolonged her mother's life. Maybe it had all been for the best. At least for her mother. "Do you think she knows the truth now, Babette? That all wasn't as it seemed in my life?"

"I do not know about that, chérie. But I do believe she is in heaven and to be in heaven is to be happy, so I think this—if your mama knows your story, the sad story you have just told me, then she also knows the other part of your story."

"The other part?"

"The part that is not yet to happen!" Babette laughed. "And I am sure it will be the happy part."

Anna sighed. "I hope you're right. You know, if Mother was here right now, I would tell her everything. I would admit that her concerns about marrying so quickly were justified. I would confess that the weakness she saw in Adam was correct, and that I was blinded to it at the time. It was just like that song Lauren listens to on her record player."

"What's that?"

"The words go something like this: *when you're heart's on fire, smoke gets in your eyes.*" She shook her head. "But what the song fails to mention is that sometimes when your heart's on fire you get badly burned."

Babette laughed. "Oh, I could tell you that, chérie."

"But Mother never told me much about love and romance while I was growing up. I watched it in the motion pictures at the Saturday matinees, but the silver screen was always filled with heat and passion and fire."

"Oh, Hollywood, they are expert at making it sizzle."

"But for the most part the characters didn't get burned in the movies, not in the ending anyway." At least that was true in the movies she'd liked. "I remember they got singed from time to time, but in the end they usually wound up with their true love, presumably living happily ever after."

"Except for *Casablanca*," Babette reminded her. "And *Gone with the Wind*."

"That's true. Perhaps I should've paid closer attention to those films. Maybe I would've learned something useful."

"You had your parents' marriage," Babette pointed out. "They were happy."

"Yes, they had a few squabbles, but for the most part they made it look fairly easy. Nothing like what I experienced in my life."

"Just remember this, chérie." Babette stood. "Your life is not over."

Anna gave her a weary smile. "It feels like it is."

"It is only beginning, chérie. Trust Babette." Now she touched Anna's cheek. "But you do not want to look like it is over. You must take care!" And now she promised to bring by a special facial cream on her next visit. "Before it is too late for your pretty face."

Anna walked her back down to the dock, untying her rope and handing it to her. "Thank you for coming by," she said. "And remember what you said about how my letters were good medicine for my mother?"

"Oh, yes." Babette put on her broad-brimmed straw river hat, tying the ribbons beneath her chin. "Very good medicine."

"That's what you were for me today. Good medicine. Thanks!"

Babette grinned. "There ees lots more where that comes from!" She leaned over and reached for the cord to the motor, pulling it out with surprising strength. Impressive for her age, which Anna guessed must be more than sixty now, although she wasn't sure. The engine roared to life and Babette waved. "Adieu!"

"Adieu!" Anna called back, watching as the small boat sliced a path through the glass-like surface of the river.

Suddenly, Anna had an idea. She would take out the *River Dove*. Hopefully it would still be seaworthy, or at least riverworthy. Hopefully she would be as well.

6

Anna felt slightly silly as she went to get her canoe. Not for wanting to take a boat ride. There was nothing silly about that. But she felt slightly silly because she'd taken her long hair out of its customary "old lady bun" as Lauren liked to call it, and divided it into two long braids. This was something she would never dare do back in Pine Ridge. Between Eunice and Lauren, the teasing would be unbearable. However, here on the river, it felt perfect. And because she'd brought no casual clothes, she went through her parents' closet to discover some of her dad's old work clothes. Finding a pair of corduroy pants and a tan work shirt, she outfitted herself for a nice little row on the river. And if she fell in, which she hoped would not happen, she would not be the worse for wear. However, she knew that if someone like Eunice or Lauren spotted her

69

looking like this, they would probably laugh. "Well, let them laugh," she said with determined resolve as she tugged the canoe out from where it had been stored back behind Grandma Pearl's old cabin. She'd brought rags to wipe out the canoe with and, naturally, it was full of spiderwebs and such. But before long, it looked as good as new—or as good as when it had been given to her. The oar was in good shape too. Obviously, someone had made this canoe to last.

She slipped the small vessel into the water next to the dock, then carefully—very carefully—she stepped one foot into the center of the boat and, holding both sides with both hands, she slipped the other in as well. The canoe tipped back and forth a bit but she resisted the urge to leap out; instead she took in a slow, deep breath and, still holding to the sides, she held her torso erect and slowly squatted to a sitting position. She released the breath and smiled at her accomplishment. Now, picking up the oar, she used it to give herself a gentle shove from the dock, which rocked the canoe even more, but once again she took in a deep breath and resisted the urge to overcorrect. Instead, she waited, slowly releasing her breath, and just like that the canoe stopped rocking. Holding itself evenly in the water, the canoe now glided out onto the river, almost as if it knew exactly what it was doing. Maybe it did.

Canoeing came back to her—perhaps in the way people said riding a bike would do, except that Anna had never learned to ride a bike. There was no place on the river to ride to. Boats were the way to travel. Although she'd heard there was a gravel road running out behind the property now, and that it supposedly connected to town, it would take two to three times as long to drive as to go down the river. And most folks thought it was a waste of taxpayers' money.

Anna felt like someone else as she peacefully paddled along—or maybe she was finally just her old self again—but it felt amazingly good . . . and right . . . and true. Even so, she finally got to the place where she knew she should turn back. Really, what was she doing here? Out paddling around the river like she was twelve. And here she had a daughter back home, probably wondering when her mother was coming back. And Eunice was probably piling up the household chores, making a new to-do list, just waiting for her "squaw" to get back to put the place in order again. "It's how she earns her keep," Eunice would tell anyone who was bold enough to inquire about the curious arrangement between the two women.

Anna had no doubts that Eunice shelled out a fair amount of money on account of them. At least on account of Lauren, since Anna lived simply enough. But between her daughter's expensive taste in clothes and her appetite for social activities, not to mention the convertible Eunice had gotten Lauren for graduation, well, there was no way Anna could afford such luxuries. Working for Eunice was her contribution.

"You do realize that you're entitled to some of your husband's assets," the family attorney, Joseph P. Miller, had told her once when she'd run into him at the hardware store not long after Adam had passed. "Why don't you come into my office sometime?"

Of course, when Anna had set out a week or so later, planning to walk into town to pay Mr. Miller a visit, Eunice had stopped her even before she got out the door. "Where are you going all dressed up today?"

"To town."

"What for?"

"To attend to some business." Anna reached for the doorknob, wishing she'd timed her getaway a little better, or perhaps hadn't bothered to wear her good gray suit, one she had sewn for herself and felt looked nearly as good as the ones Eunice spent far too much money on.

"What sort of business?"

Anna had looked directly at her mother-in-law then. Really, it seemed pointless to attempt to keep anything from her. She would find out eventually. Nothing Anna did in this town, and it wasn't much, ever escaped Eunice Gunderson's notice. So Anna told her the truth.

"Well, that's ridiculous." Eunice waved her hand. "Adam's assets ran out ages ago. In fact, if I wanted, I could probably charge you for all the assistance I've given to Lauren and you all these years. But, of course, we're family. I would never dream of doing that. But if you feel you must go see Joe, I'm happy to drive you there myself. Did you make an appointment?"

"No, I, uh . . . well, I just thought I'd drop in."

Eunice laughed. "Drop in? Don't you know he's a very busy attorney? He handles all of the mill's business and I happen to know that this week he has quite a bit on his plate. In the future, I suggest you make an appointment if you care to see him. And keep in mind his hourly rate." She made a tsk-tsk sound. "And it just went up too. Scandalous what lawyers imagine they are worth these days."

Naturally, Anna didn't go see Joseph Miller that day or any other day. She had long since accepted that the only two things Adam left to her were a wedding ring, which she had safely tucked away, and Lauren. She looked at the canoe beneath her, realizing it was probably worth more to her than her wedding ring and, although she didn't love it more than her daughter, it had probably given her more pleasure. Sad—but true.

"Hello over there!"

Anna looked up in surprise. She hadn't heard any other boat motors, but now saw that this was a rowboat, with a gray-haired woman waving from it. "Hello," Anna called back. She didn't recognize the woman, but then it had been years and people, including her, could change.

"Do you live around here?" the woman called as she clumsily rowed over with an eager smile.

"Sort of. Anyway, I used to."

The woman got closer and peered curiously at her. "I couldn't help but notice your dugout canoe. It seems authentic. Are you a native?"

"Native?" Anna frowned as she recalled an old Laurel and Hardy movie about African headhunters. Hadn't they called them natives?

"I mean a Native *American?* An American Indian? *Are you?"* The woman looked excited now, as if she'd just made an unusual discovery and might suddenly whip out a camera to document it by snapping a photo of Anna. Or perhaps she planned to trap Anna and carry her back to a Ripley's museum as an exhibit—they might title her cage "the last of her breed."

Anna knew she was being slightly ridiculous, but just the same she did not answer this strange woman.

"I'm sorry." The woman looked deflated now. "In my enthusiasm, I've made it sound all wrong. It's just that I'm so *happy* to see you today."

Anna remained silent, studying the woman, trying to figure her out. Dressed for the outdoors, almost as if she was going on some kind of safari expedition, she looked fairly normal, although her words sounded a bit nutty.

"You see, I'm an anthropologist. I'm doing my doctoral thesis on coastal Indian tribes and their customs. And, well, they are just so hard to find these days. And I saw you in your beautiful canoe and you looked like you could possibly be a descendant of an American Indian tribe. Please, I beg you, excuse my bad manners. Just attribute it to my age and my passion for Indian history. I am sorry to have offended you."

"Well, at least you didn't say *'How.'*"

The woman laughed. "Thank goodness for that. Let me start over. My name is Hazel Chenowith. I'm from the University of Oregon and I'm spending my summer on the Oregon coast, doing research and writing. Today I'm exploring on the river."

"I'm Anna Gunderson," she said politely. "My parents owned what used to be a small general store over on the river. I'm staying there for a few days."

"Oh, yes. Someone told me about that the other day. A man from town gave me a tour of the river in his speedboat, but he went too fast. However, I did see the place, the gray square building with a faded General Store sign?" Hazel maneuvered her rowboat adjacent to Anna's canoe now, close enough for the women to shake hands if they wanted to. Not that Anna wanted to.

"That sounds right."

"And your mother descended from the Siuslaw Tribe, correct?"

"Yes."

"I'm sorry . . . I just heard of her passing the other day. The man in the speedboat mentioned it. Please accept my sincerest sympathies."

"Thank you."

"I was so disappointed to hear of her death. I know it sounds terribly self-serving, but I had sincerely hoped to meet her and speak with her about her heritage."

Anna shrugged. "Well, you shouldn't feel too bad. I doubt my mother would've told you much."

"Why is that?" Hazel removed her wire-rimmed glasses and, pulling out a man's handkerchief, paused to wipe them clean. "That is, if you don't mind me asking."

"My mother was one hundred percent Indian, but she lived out her life as a white woman. Other than her skin, which she guarded religiously from the sun, you would not have known about her heritage."

"So many Indians went that route. And I don't blame them a bit. In fact, I blame the white man." Hazel scowled as she put her glasses back on.

"You do?"

"Of course. Thanks to *assimilation,*" she said the word with disgust, "most Indians were robbed of their language, their art, their culture, their families, their dignity . . . even their lives in many cases—almost everything was stripped away from them. And those who tried to return to the old ways were usually chastised, sometimes by their very own people."

"That's true." Anna remembered how frustrated her mother became over Grandma's return to the old ways . . . how she resented Anna's interest. If not for Daddy, she never would've tolerated any of it.

"And that is what fear and oppression does to people. Such a shame."

Anna simply nodded.

"All I'm trying to do is to preserve what I can while there is still something left to preserve." She frowned. "But I swear it's getting harder and harder to find people who can remember anything. And then—eureka!—you find someone with a memory and that person shuts up tighter than a razor clam."

"It sounds like frustrating work."

She nodded. "And I'm afraid that the true history of the Native American people is going to just disappear altogether. Other than the Hollywood version anyway. And they almost never get that right."

"But they do better than cartoons." Anna winced to think of some of the images her own daughter had seen and laughed at on Eunice's television. Even when Anna attempted to set Lauren straight, it was useless with Eunice around to defend her granddaughter's sense of humor.

"You're probably right. I don't watch much television, but I have seen some degrading advertisements using Indian images as comical characters."

"Why is that, I wonder?" Anna frowned. "Why, in this enlightened age of science and technology, would an Indian still be the brunt of a joke?"

"That's a very good question." Hazel reached for a little notebook, writing something down. And now she brightened. "But when I saw you out here today, with your glossy black braids and your lovely dugout canoe, well, I suppose I thought I'd finally gotten lucky."

"How so?"

"You just looked like the real thing to me." Her gray eyes grew wide. "Do you know that for an instant I thought you were an apparition or ghost?"

Anna laughed. "I'm not ready for that yet."

Hazel leaned forward in her boat, peering curiously at Anna. "You are very beautiful, you know. You would photograph nicely."

Anna frowned.

"Oh, dear, there I go again. I probably sound like a silly tourist." Hazel laughed. "Again, you'll have to excuse my enthusiasm. Forgive me."

"As long as you don't start snapping photos of me."

Hazel patted a bag at her feet. "I do have a camera, but I wouldn't dream of taking a picture without your permission. And now I assume that since your mother lived like a white woman, you were raised as a white child and you probably know next to nothing about your Native American heritage."

Anna straightened her spine, holding her head high. "Don't be too sure of that."

"*Really?*" Hazel leaned over so far that Anna expected her to topple out of her boat. Hopefully the old woman could swim. "Why do you say that?"

Anna thought carefully about her response. Part of her disliked this woman's intense and intrusive curiosity. Really, it bordered along rudeness and almost reminded her of her pushy mother-in-law. But another part of Anna respected what it seemed this woman was trying to accomplish—to preserve some authentic Indian history. Still . . . she was unsure.

"Do you know *anything* about your ancestors?" Hazel persisted.

"My mother's mother, my grandmother, was Siuslaw. And her mother as well. My great-grandmother was born here on the river and lived a normal childhood. But as a young woman she was forced to the reservation. She was with child at the time. My grandmother was later born on the reservation. I understand that in itself was rather unusual since most of the people died from disease or starvation. My grandmother's father was killed for trying to find food for his family."

Hazel looked surprised, perhaps more by the fact that Anna was telling her things than by the actual information. "You're referring to the Siletz Reservation in the mid to late 1800s."

"Yes. And unlike many of her people, my great-grandmother actually survived the atrocities and returned on foot, walking back down the beach from the reservation with her child. She and her sister somehow claimed this land where the store and our home are located. And now that land . . . it belongs to me."

"That land actually came from an Indian allotment? From the government?" Hazel looked astonished. "And you still have the same land?"

"I have my grandmother's half of it. I understand that it was originally eighty acres, split between my great-grandmother and her sister. The other half was sold long ago."

"That is most unusual that you still have possession of allotment land."

"It isn't something my parents, particularly my mother, ever spoke of. However, according to the lawyer, the land had legally belonged to my mother after her mother passed."

Hazel nodded. "That makes sense."

"And although my grandmother and my mother went through assimilation, as you put it, my grandmother returned to her old ways, the ways of her ancestors."

"Really?" Hazel looked like she was about to burst now. "Did she teach you any of the traditions of her elders?"

"She taught me things that she wanted me to know." A bit of current was taking the canoe back downriver now, as if to gently nudge Anna home.

"What sorts of things?" Hazel maneuvered her bulky rowboat closer to Anna, as if fearful that Anna might slip away.

"Lots of things." Anna picked up her paddle and began to gently row, going with the current, downriver, past the log barges, back toward the house. She wasn't sure why, but she just felt the need to move. She wanted to get her feet back onto the ground. Onto her own land—*her own land.* Those words seemed to reverberate with her as she slowly rowed. Truly, the forty acres on the river belonged to her now. It was her own land. The attorney in Florence had said so.

Hazel continued to follow. With her boat like

an awkward goose trailing a sleek mallard, she continued to pelt Anna with questions. But Anna refrained from answering. It was as if her grandmother was cautioning her. *Go carefully. Do not be reckless with your knowledge. Take your time.* And so she did.

7

Back at her own dock, Anna carefully climbed out of her canoe. Holding onto the rope, like a leash on a dog, she walked her canoe next to the dock, leading it to the shore. Pulling it out of the water, she dragged the canoe up onto the shore so that even if the tide rose high, the *River Dove* would be safe.

"Anna, dear," Hazel called from where she'd paddled her rowboat right up to the dock. Still sitting in the boat, she looked hopeful, expectant. "I'm sorry if I frightened you away in my exuberance."

"Don't worry. I'm not afraid," Anna called back as she returned to the dock. Shoving her hands into the pockets of her father's old trousers, she squinted into the sun now, trying to decide what to do about this stubborn woman. *What would Grandma Pearl do?* She recalled the time, not long before Grandma Pearl passed, when Daddy brought home a man in a tweed suit, some sort of scholar from back East who wanted to use a machine to record Grandma's stories. Anna and Daddy sat in the shadows of Grandma Pearl's smoky little cabin, listening as the man began to question Grandma Pearl about her age and history and such. But when this man learned that, as a girl, Grandma had been baptized into the Christian faith, he turned off his fancy machine. "The old woman's stories are not ethnically accurate now," he told them with disdain. "They will have been tarnished with Western religious undertones. Her words have lost their authenticity." Then he packed up his machine and demanded to be taken back to town.

Grandma Pearl had been hurt and confused by the man's words. When she asked Daddy to explain the meaning, he told her in simple terms that the man questioned the validity of her stories. That's when she became angry. "My stories are the stories of *my* people and *they are true*. I would not lie." She had looked at Anna then, cupping Anna's chin in her bony fingers as she stared into her eyes with an intensity that Anna could still feel burning inside her today. "It is through you my stories live, child. I write them on your heart." Anna sighed. Where were those stories now?

"I know I can come on too strong," Hazel said abruptly.

Anna turned back to the old woman, almost surprised to see she was still there, still waiting patiently in her little rowboat, her hands on the oars, looking up with a hopeful almost childlike expression. Her glasses had fogged up again.

"My father always told me that my enthusiasm would get me into trouble," she said a bit woefully. "And I must admit that it has from time to time. But enthusiasm has its benefits too. In fact, it has helped me to reach this stage in life. Not many women, especially those born in the previous century such as I was, have achieved their doctoral degrees. I plan to have mine by winter. Then you can address me as Dr. Hazel Chenowith." She chuckled as if this was amusing.

Anna considered this. To be fair, it was rather impressive. Anna knew few women with that much education. She herself had only made it through one semester of college and she never even took her last final exams. Oh, it was true that she read—almost insatiably. Just one more thing her mother-in-law liked to tease her about. However, Anna felt it was her only way to enlarge her world, and the small public library in Pine Ridge had been a welcome refuge from Eunice's sharp tongue and constant complaining.

"Why are you so interested in Indians?" she asked Hazel. "Specifically the Siuslaw?" Anna watched her carefully as she answered, almost as if this was a test.

"Oh, didn't I mention it? My grandfather was

half Suquamish and that makes me one-eighth. Of course, I never heard a word about this until I was a grown woman. Even then, my mother—it was on her side—denied it a few times. But I did my own research and discovered that it was actually true. Suquamish means 'clear salt water.' My ancestors, similar to yours, were coastal, dwelling near the Puget Sound in Washington. They are most famous for their Chief Seattle."

"Of course, I've heard of him."

"You and plenty of others too. When it came time to do my dissertation, I found that numerous academic papers and books had already been written on the Suquamish and Chief Seattle. Information on my people isn't nearly as scarce and untraceable as it is with yours."

"Why do you think that is?"

"It has to do with geography. This area, the Siuslaw region, was very difficult for early settlers to get into. With the rugged Coastal mountains on one side and no easily accessible port on the other side—since the jetties around the river weren't in place back then, your people were somewhat protected, at least for a while. As you probably know, when the white man finally did get here, in numbers, things changed quickly."

Anna said nothing now, just studied Hazel, trying to discern her true motives.

"Perhaps that still doesn't answer your question . . . why I chose this topic. Because I'm completing my doctorate through the University of Oregon, I wanted to study a tribe nearby. Also, I absolutely love this part of the country—where river meets ocean with forest and mountains nearby. I find it enchanting. Don't you?"

Anna nodded.

"So here I am. Although I must admit it's been most frustrating trying to connect with people who might be of help. I was about ready to give up." She looked longingly at Anna now. "Is there any way I could possibly entice you to speak to me, just for a bit? You must understand that anything you tell me will be highly valued and esteemed and I will see that it is well preserved in history—something for your children and grandchildren and all the future generations of your family to look back upon someday."

Although she liked the sound of that, Anna shook her head. "I'm afraid my daughter has as much interest in Indian history as my mother did. However . . ." She remembered her grandma's baskets on Mother's coffee table . . . *what did that mean?*

"However?"

"Well . . . perhaps I was wrong about my mother. I wonder if she was starting to appreciate some of the old ways after all." Anna smiled at Hazel now. "Would you like to see something?"

"Oh, yes!" Hazel was already fumbling for the rope. "Most definitely yes!" Anna knelt down, helping to secure the boat to the dock, and extending her hand to steady the old woman, she helped her climb out. "I'm just so pleased!" Hazel exclaimed as they walked down the dock. "So very pleased and excited!"

Anna had to admit that Hazel's enthusiasm was rather contagious. As she led the eager woman up to the house, Anna felt a solidness inside of her, as if she was doing the right thing. She realized that Grandma Pearl had entrusted her with something precious, something Anna didn't fully understand or perhaps even completely respect . . . as of yet. But suddenly it felt very important to do whatever she could to preserve her grandmother's stories and traditions. It didn't matter that Lauren, or even any future generations, might have no interest in the old ways of their ancestors. Anna realized that she had interest. She was doing this for Grandma Pearl . . . and for herself.

"Oh, my! Oh, my!" Hazel held the first basket in her hands as gently as if she were holding a freshly hatched bluebird. "This is absolute perfection. Beautiful." She went on to describe the design and the materials with such expertise that Anna's confidence in her grew.

"I made this one myself." Anna held up the sewing basket.

"You made this?" Hazel peered at her through her slightly fogged lenses. "Yourself?"

"My grandmother taught me."

"Exquisite." She carefully set the basket back on the coffee table. "Do you know who taught your grandmother?"

"Her mother, of course."

"Of course." Hazel nodded, taking this in.

"Please, sit down."

"Yes, thank you, don't mind if I do." Primly, Hazel sat on the edge of the couch, folding her hands in her lap and watching Anna with an uncertain expression.

"Would you like something to drink? I haven't much to offer. Water, milk . . . or I could make coffee or tea."

"Oh, I don't want to put you to any trouble." She was wiping her glasses again.

"It's no trouble."

"Water would be lovely."

Anna filled them each a glass and returned, handed one to Hazel, and then sat down in the old rocker adjacent from the couch. It had been Daddy's favorite chair and just sitting in it now brought back a wonderful sense of him. She could almost smell the tobacco from his pipe.

"Thank you," Hazel murmured, taking a dainty sip. Then she looked up at Anna with her mouth partially open, looking rather strange. Almost as if she were unwell.

"Are you all right?" Anna leaned forward.

"Oh . . . yes, I'm perfectly delightful, dear." She made a sheepish sort of smile. "I think I have been rendered nearly speechless. And, for me, well, that is highly unusual."

Anna chuckled. "I see."

Hazel pointed to the baskets on the coffee table. "Those baskets—oh, my—they are like discovering a treasure chest." She peered intently at Anna. "Do you get my meaning?"

"Not exactly."

"So unusual . . . so exquisite." She shook her head. "I am almost afraid to handle them."

"Oh, they're very well made. They can even be used for—"

"Yes, yes, I don't doubt that. It's just that they are so rare—more valuable than precious jewels—at least in my opinion. They should probably be in a museum."

"Oh." Anna frowned.

"Not that I'd try to take them from you, dear. I'm just saying—"

"I appreciate that."

"You will take good care of them, won't you?"

Anna smiled. "Yes, of course. They're like a treasure to me too."

Hazel sighed. "That's a comfort. Thank you for allowing me to see them."

"My grandmother told me that her mother and

aunt taught her how to make these kinds of baskets while they were on the reservation."

"Oh? I'm surprised that was allowed."

"She did mention that they did it secretly." Anna smiled. "In fact, when Grandma Pearl taught me, we did it in secret too."

"So your mother wouldn't know?"

Anna nodded.

"You were very fortunate to have a grandmother like that, Anna."

"I'm beginning to appreciate that more and more."

"I'm curious about your canoe. Would you mind telling me about it?"

So Anna told her about how it was won in a card game and Hazel laughed. "I have no idea how old it is, but I think my grandma's second husband, Crazy Bob, died about ten years before I was born. So that means it's been in our family for close to fifty years."

Hazel looked confused. "Fifty years? How old are you, if you don't mind me asking?"

"I'll be forty this fall."

Hazel looked shocked. "No, that's not possible. I thought you were a girl when I first saw you. Even now I would've guessed you to be in your twenties."

Anna chuckled. "Well, thank you! But I have a daughter who would beg to differ with you. She is always telling me how old—and how old-fashioned I am." Anna flipped one of her braids. "Although I don't usually wear my hair like this."

"But, really, you look quite young for almost forty." Hazel smiled. "Not that forty is so old, mind you. It's been nearly twenty-five years since I was forty and I'm still fairly spry if I do say so myself. I wouldn't be surprised if I was still around forty years from now. My grandmother recently passed and she was 103."

Anna nodded, absorbing this. "You're making me feel almost young."

"Well, you *are* young!" She laughed. "And don't let anyone convince you otherwise."

"I feel like I can trust you," Anna told her. "And not just because of your flattery."

"I am not a flatterer, my dear. I simply speak my mind. Besides being given over to exuberance, I am also known as a highly opinionated woman. Some people can simply not abide me." She shook her head. "Including my ex-husband, Herbert."

"Ex-husband?"

She nodded firmly. "Yes. I am a divorcée. I have been so for nearly thirty years now and am not the least bit ashamed of it. Never married again. Not that I wouldn't consider it, if the right man came along."

"Do you have any children?"

"My daughter lives near Seattle with her

husband. She has two grown children, both girls, going to college in Washington. And I have a son who lives in Eugene, and a teenaged grandson as well. They're what attracted me to the university there. I wanted to be near my boys." She sighed. "And you say you have a daughter. Any other children?"

Without going into all the details, Anna explained she was a widow with only one child. Then she stood. "As I was saying, I trust you, Hazel."

"That means more than I can say to me." Hazel stood as well. "And I'm highly appreciative of your hospitality and your time."

"Because I trust you, I'm going to let you see where my grandmother lived."

Hazel looked surprised. "I thought she lived here."

"No, my parents lived here. My grandmother had her own cabin. Would you like to see it?"

"Yes, yes, of course!"

As Anna led Hazel out of the house and over to the cabin, she explained about how Grandma Pearl's first husband, John, built this house for Pearl and her mother. "My grandma's aunt lived in town. Her name was Dora. She was married numerous times. Mostly to white men. My grandma sometimes called white men 'the moving men' because they had moved here from someplace else. She usually called them that when telling stories."

"She told you stories?" Hazel stopped walking, placing her hand on Anna's arm, her eyes lighting up. "Do you remember any?"

"Oh, yes. And my father wrote many of them down."

Hazel fanned herself with her handkerchief, almost as if she felt faint. "Oh, my! Oh, my! I feel as if I've just stumbled into a diamond mine."

Anna laughed. "Well, I have heard the town of Florence described as 'The Diamond among the Pearls.' And the Siuslaw River sometimes sparkles like diamonds. But I'm afraid that's the only diamond mine you'll find in these parts. And even those diamonds have become dulled by all these logs crowding in from all directions."

"As they say, it's all in the eyes of the beholder." Hazel smiled at Grandma Pearl's little cabin. "Oh, my, this is perfectly charming." She touched a rough-hewn log. "Wonderful!"

"I haven't actually been inside since I got here. It might be full of spiders and mice by now."

"Don't worry, I've lived all over and those creatures don't scare me."

Anna reached above the door frame to feel for the key. "My father put the padlock on the door shortly after Grandma passed—it was during the Great Depression and he was worried that transients might try to use it. There had been some incidents in the area." She pulled down the grimy key, wiped it off on the back of her trousers, and then, after several tries, managed to unlock the door. The door stuck a little, but she used her foot to push it open. She went inside first, brushing the cobwebs with her hands, and went to the windows and pulled the threadbare curtains open to let in the light. "It's just a two-room cabin, but my grandma was happy here."

"Oh, it's delightful." Hazel was going around now, examining everything and making oohs and ahs and exclamations over every little detail. "It's like a little museum."

"My father boxed up most of Grandma's things. The things he thought we should save, that is. I think they're still in the attic."

"You have *more* things?" Hazel looked as if she'd died and gone to heaven.

So Anna explained how her dad had lost his family, and come from Sweden on a freighter. "And family and history meant a lot to him. He was fascinated by Grandma. That's why he was writing down her stories and—"

"You still have those too?"

"As far as I know. But they're hard to read." Now she explained the language problem.

"Oh, don't worry about that. Linguistics is another area of expertise for me. I'm sure I can decipher them." She stopped and turned to Anna now. "That is, if you will allow me to."

Anna felt she'd already made her decision and she felt certain that Grandma Pearl would approve. "Yes." She nodded. "I would like you to record my family's history. I would consider it an honor."

Hazel grabbed both of Anna's hands now. "Oh, thank you, thank you! It is my honor and privilege." She released Anna's hands and was practically dancing now. "Oh, I'm so excited—I hardly know where to begin."

Anna thought for a moment. "I do feel that I should keep everything here—on my property— for the time being anyway. It's not that I don't trust you, Mrs. Chenowith—"

"Please, dear, call me Hazel."

Anna nodded. "Hazel . . . it's not that I question you. I just feel I'm the protector of these—uh, these diamonds, as you say—and I'd prefer to have them here. Until I have time to figure everything out. Does that sound acceptable?"

"Yes . . . yes . . . I understand and respect that. I suppose I could commute up the river from town each day." She got a thoughtful look now. "That is, unless you'd consider renting me a room . . . or even this little cabin." She looked around the dim room with eager eyes. "Oh, I would be so delighted to stay here—right here where your grandmother lived. It would be such an honor."

"You would stay here?" Anna was shocked.

Her own mother wouldn't have stayed in here. She rarely set foot in here.

"Yes, I can understand how you wouldn't be comfortable with that—"

"I wouldn't think you'd be comfortable."

"Oh, yes! I would. I am a wonderful camper. And I would think of this as camping. I would make a fire in the fireplace and—"

"I don't know." Suddenly Anna was unsure. "I really need to think about this. You see, there's my daughter to consider . . . I left her home . . . and I really only planned to be here for a week or so."

Hazel looked deflated. "I see—"

"But perhaps I can arrange to be here a little longer."

"Oh, could you? I'll gladly reimburse you for any expenses. And I'll pay rent for the use of this cabin."

Anna couldn't imagine charging anyone to stay in the cabin. Not in the shape it was in. But Hazel was walking about the main room now, saying how she'd use the table as her desk, perhaps move it by a window for light. "Oh, I know it needs a bit of cleaning, but I can do that."

"When do you think I could come out and get set up?"

Again, Anna felt overwhelmed. What was she getting herself into? "There's still my daughter . . . and I'll need to go to Babette's to use a telephone."

"You have no telephone in your house?"

Anna made an apologetic smile. "I'm afraid it's quite rustic there as well. There was a telephone in the store, but my mother had it disconnected when she closed the store. She said she didn't need it, but I suspect it was to save money."

"I see."

"And there's no electricity in the house either. Although we do have a reliable generator. And, of course, there's no electricity in here."

"I did notice power poles along the river. I assume it's not difficult to get power, if one wants it."

"Yes . . . if one can afford it. At the time it was being connected my mother felt it was beyond her means."

"If you let me stay, I would gladly pay to have your utilities installed," Hazel said suddenly. "If you didn't mind, that is. It's not that I wish to foist all the modern conveniences of the twentieth century upon you; it's simply that it would make my work so much easier to have some electricity and access to a phone. It's selfish really."

"It is tempting." Anna smiled. "Can you give me a couple of days to figure all this out?"

"Certainly."

"Is there a telephone number where I can reach you?"

"Yes. The Siuslaw Hotel in Florence." She frowned. "But you have no telephone."

"I do have neighbors."

"Oh, yes, of course."

So it was settled. Anna would telephone Hazel as soon as she'd made her decision. But the truth was, Anna felt she'd already decided. She simply wanted to clear things with Lauren . . . and that meant she'd probably have to speak to Eunice as well. She was not particularly looking forward to either of those conversations. However, she felt stronger than ever today, and more like her old self than she'd been in years. Perhaps she would be up to the task after all.

8

Anna returned to the house, got the generator running, washed up the dishes in the sink, cut up an apple and some cheese, then sat down on the front porch of the store to eat. As she ate her miserly lunch, she thought hard. Was she being foolish or impulsive or irrational? Was she shirking her responsibilities at home? *Home,* she ran the word through her head. Had Pine Ridge ever been home? More like a prison or work farm. Never, after the first year or so, had it seemed like a home.

Finally, feeling like a dog chasing its tail, she pushed her ruminating beyond merely thinking and actually prayed for guidance. This was a big decision and she wanted to make sure she was doing the right thing, and doing so would require divine direction. Or, as Grandma Pearl would say, "a nod from the Spirit in the Sky."

When Anna finally stood up, she felt a rush of excitement, or perhaps enthusiasm, as Hazel liked to say. Whatever it was felt slightly foreign and incredibly good. She was going to do this thing—and she was going to do it right. But first she had to call Lauren.

It was close to three when Anna reached Babette's house and asked to borrow the telephone. She hated to place a collect call, but not as much she hated to charge a long-distance call to dear Babette. "Please reverse the charges," she told the operator. Then, waiting anxiously for the phone to ring, she rehearsed the words one more time. There was a good chance Lauren would be in the house at this hour. Too late for tennis and too early to be out socializing with her friends. But to her dismay Eunice answered, accepting the charges in a pompous tone. "Hello?"

"Hello, Eunice. This is Anna."

"Yes, so I gathered."

"Is Lauren there?"

"She is outside right now. Susan and a couple of the other girls were here for lunch. They are out playing croquet just now. When are you coming home, Anna?" Her tone was now a mixture of agitation and desperation. Quite likely she was not happy to have the household chores to herself. And Anna knew she was too cheap to hire someone else to come in. Not when she could get Anna for free.

"That's why I'm calling, Eunice. I have decided to stay on here."

"What?" Now her tone had moved into aggravation.

"I plan to remain in my parents' home and I would—"

"Have you lost your mind, Anna?"

"No, I feel more sane than I've felt in years and I'd—"

"But Lauren has told me about that backwater place. It sounds barbaric. No electricity or phones or water—"

"I have water. And I'll soon have electricity and a telephone as well."

"How can you possibly afford that? Did your mother leave you money? And if she did, what are your responsibilities to Lauren? Surely, you realize her college tuition is quite expensive and she'll need new clothes and the sorority dues are quite steep and—"

"In answer to your question, no, my mother left me no money, Eunice."

"Then how can you afford to put in those improvements?"

"It's a long story and I realize long distance is costly, so will you please get Lauren so I may speak to her?"

"What do you want to say to her? Perhaps I can give her a message."

"You mean you won't call her to the phone for me?"

"She is busy."

"Playing croquet?"

"What do you want me to tell her, Anna? Please, get to the point. This phone call is expensive."

"I wanted to invite Lauren to come out here and stay with me this—"

"I do believe you have lost your mind, Anna." Eunice laughed loudly. "Are you quite serious?"

"I am. I thought we could spend time at the beach and go fishing and—"

"*Fishing?* Honestly, Anna, can you imagine Lauren baiting a hook?"

"Actually, I can."

"And perhaps you can imagine her living like a barbarian out in the sticks. I believe Lauren calls your family home the backwater or the backwoods or something backwards." She laughed again. "Oh, I think I'm seeing the picture now, Anna. You want to turn Lauren into an Indian squaw— like you. Perhaps you'll teach her to tan hides by chewing the leather with her teeth. And then you can show her how to string beads and make moccasins. Oh, perfectly delightful. I can hardly wait to tell Lauren the lovely plans her squaw mama has made for her summer vacation."

Anna was seething now, but determined not to lose her temper. "I'm sure if Lauren would give it a chance, she would discover that the natural beauty of the river and the ocean make for a wonderful place. Tourists abound here. People pay to come see it."

"Oh, yes, I'm sure they do. Poor old souls without good sense pay to do all sorts of ridiculous things. No, I'm sure I can speak for Lauren. She is much happier here. And if you want to see her, I suggest you come home."

"I am home."

There was a deadly silence now. "My patience is wearing thin, Anna."

Anna didn't respond. When had Eunice's patience been anything but thin?

"I mean what I said, if you want to see your daughter, Anna, you better come home. And if you want a home to come to, you better pack your bags now. Otherwise, you can consider yourself an unwelcome stranger under my roof from now on."

Anna took in a deep breath. She wanted to tell Eunice that was what she had always been. But more than that, she wanted to exercise self-control. "Thank you for making your position clear to me, Eunice. Please, tell my daughter I called. And tell her I will write to her."

No response.

"And I'm sure you're aware that tampering

with another person's mail is a federal offense, Eunice."

"Well, I!" And Eunice hung up.

"Oh, dear." Anna shook her head as she replaced the receiver in the cradle on the wall with a loud clunk.

"How did eet go, chérie?" Babette called from the living room.

Anna walked in a daze from the kitchen out to where Babette was sitting by the window doing some needlework. "Not well."

"I tried not to overhear—" She smiled weakly. "But eet ees a small house."

Anna filled Babette in on the details of the unfortunate conversation. "She never even let me speak to Lauren."

"Oh, the evil woman!" Babette tossed her needlework aside. "Eef I could get my hands on her!"

Despite herself, Anna laughed. "I wouldn't want to see that. Eunice looks small and wiry, but I've felt her grip. She's strong and feisty like a ferret—and with sharp teeth too." Now Anna told Babette about Hazel.

"Ah, yes, I heard there was a strange woman going up and down the river searching for Indians. She spent some time at the Olsons and then at the Blacks, but apparently did not find what she was looking for."

"Not until now." Anna smiled. "She's a little

bit odd, but I like her. And I've invited her to stay on the property with me while she does her research. I'm going to go back and clean up Grandma's cabin." Her smile faded. "I hope it's not too rustic for her. She said it would be OK. But it was pretty grimy in there. Maybe I should let her stay in the house with me."

"No, no." Babette stood. "The cabin will be fine for her. And I will come and help you clean it."

"Oh, I can't ask you to—"

"I want to do it!" Babette frowned. "I am tired of sitting around. Let me come and help."

"If you really want to."

"I know." She stuck a finger in the air. "I will make fresh curtains. And I have extra linens too." She gently pushed Anna toward the door. "You go on home and get started. I will follow."

"But first, may I use your phone again?" Anna asked suddenly.

"Oui, oui, but of course!"

Now Anna called Hazel's hotel, leaving a message that she would be welcome to stay with her while she continued her research. "There," she told Babette as she replaced the receiver, "now I'm committed to doing this. I better get home and get things ready."

"And I will be coming right behind you, chérie!"

• • •

Working on the cabin was a good remedy for pushing unpleasant thoughts of the conversation with Eunice from Anna's mind. She started by removing everything from the cabin. First she carefully put anything made by Grandma—items that Hazel could examine more closely later—in a special wooden box. Next she took out all the things that time and critters had destroyed, including the curtains and bedding. She made a big pile that she hoped might burn if she put some dead branches and a dousing of kerosene on it. She'd seen Daddy do that before.

Next she set out all the furnishings, not that there was much besides a few chairs, a small dining table, and a dresser. But before long the cabin was cleared, everything except the hand-hewn wooden bed frame that was strung with rope to hold a mattress. It was too heavy to move. Anna's grandfather had made that from cedar logs, probably more than fifty years ago. Anna also left the kitchen cabinet in place. Daddy had built that from fir and it was attached to the wall, but she did remove the few dishes and pots that were still in it.

She piled all the contents of the house and washed them all down and let them air in the sun. Then she returned to sweep down the cobwebs and scrub down the log walls. She was just attacking the floors when Babette showed up.

"Hallo, hallo," she called as she came into the cabin with a large basket in her arms. "Help is here." She peered inside. "Oh, my, chérie, you have already made good progress."

Anna pushed a strand of hair away from her face. "I've had lots of practice in the science of cleaning," she confessed. "Although I'm not accustomed to cleaning anything this rustic, the basics of soap and water and elbow grease are universal."

Babette's brow creased. "Universal?"

Anna laughed. "They work everywhere."

"Oh, oui. I comprehend." She reached into the basket and pulled out some red and white gingham cloth. "What do you think? For curtains?"

"Perfect!" Anna nodded eagerly. "Thank you so much!"

"I will measure first then I'll go inside the house and use your mother's machine." As she measured the still-dirty windows, she told Anna that she'd brought over fresh sheets and blankets too. "And a pillow. I set them on the porch for now."

"I think I'll bring the mattress down from my old bed," Anna said as she swabbed the fir floorboards. "Grandma's old one was ruined by mice."

"You know what this is like?" Babette said as she put the measuring tape back in her basket. "It is like playing house. You know? When I was a girl my papa made a petite house with petite furniture and my sister and I played house. This is what this is like, Anna. Thank you for letting me play with you." She giggled.

Anna laughed. "I see what you mean. But thank you!"

After the house was as clean as she could get it, including the windows, Anna went into the store to see what kinds of things might still be down there. It was the first time she'd been in the store for years—since before Daddy died—because she couldn't bring herself to go into it after the funeral, too many memories. But she knew that Mother had continued to run the store up until a few years ago when another store not too far down the river opened up, one that catered to outdoor sportsmen and carried a bigger variety of merchandise.

Naturally, Anna didn't expect to find any food or perishable items down there, at least she hoped not. But she was surprised to discover there was still a fair amount of merchandise on the shelves. Like the cabin, it was covered in dust and cobwebs, but there were all sorts of odds and ends, everything from a pair of children's red rubber rain boots to a garden hoe to a yellow pitcher. She felt sure that some of these things had been here since her childhood. As she picked up a blue and white speckled enamel coffeepot, she wondered why her mother hadn't attempted to have some kind of clearance sale to get rid of these things. And yet, at the same time, Anna was relieved that she hadn't. Something about seeing them again was comforting.

She went upstairs and into the house where Babette had opened up the old treadle machine and was happily sewing away, humming to herself as she worked the cheerful fabric through. And for a moment, Anna expected to see her mother coming around a corner, saying something to Babette about what they were making. They had often done sewing projects together.

"How many quilts do you think you and Mother made over the years?" Anna asked as she washed her hands in the sink, where, thanks to an elevated holding tank Daddy had set up years ago, she did indeed have running water, although the generator was required to make the pump run to fill the tank.

"Oh, my, chérie." Babette shook her head. "I do not know."

"I know there must be five or six in this house."

"Oui. And as many in my house. And we have given away many, many more than that."

Anna looked at the old clock above the fireplace. She had used her watch to reset it this morning and it seemed to be keeping good time. But she was surprised to see that it was already past six. Of course, summer was like that. The days were longer and everyone always kept later hours. "Shall I fix us some dinner?" she called to Babette, looking in the refrigerator to see what the possibilities were. "I didn't bring in much food, but I'm sure I could fix something."

"Look at the stove, chérie."

Anna turned to see that already there was a cast iron stewpot on the stove with the gas turned on low beneath it. Using a hand-crocheted pot holder she lifted the heavy lid to see what looked a lot like chicken and dumplings and smelled delicious.

"Where did that come from?"

"Mr. Danner dropped by while you were working in the cabin."

"Dorothy's dad?"

"Oui. He said his wife made it especially for you."

"She remembered how much I loved their chicken and dumplings!"

"Oui. And Mr. Danner say Dorothy ees coming to visit in late August and they wonder if you will still be here. I say I think you will be here. Oui?"

"Oh, I hope I'm still here by then. I would so love to see her. I can't believe I haven't seen her since I got married." Anna was actually dancing around now. "Oh, sweet Dorothy! I wonder if she's changed much."

Babette laughed and turned back to her sewing. "Oh, it is so good to see this house filled with life again, chérie. Your mama—she would be glad."

Later, as they sat and ate dinner together, Anna knew that Babette was right. Mother would be glad to see her house filled with life again. But she would be even more glad to know that her daughter had finally come home. Perhaps even to stay. At least Anna hoped so. If only there was a way to entice Lauren to come.

9

Anna got up with the sun the next morning. She had so much to do, she couldn't wait to get started. And unless she was mistaken, she thought she'd seen a gallon of paint on one of the store's shelves. She wondered if that would be enough to paint the interior of the cabin—or if it would be any good. She remembered the time she'd helped Daddy to repaint the interior of the store. He'd used old paint, mixing it with paint thinner until the consistency was just right. She hoped she could do that today and the paint would be some nice light color. She wanted to brighten up the cabin before she put the furnishings back inside.

The paint turned out to be a milky white and,

other than some gunk on the top, it seemed in fairly good shape. She went into the backroom of the store now. This had also been where Daddy stored his tools and things, and she was pleased to see that there was still a paintbrush and a drop cloth put neatly on a shelf. Before long, she had cleaned up the paint, used turpentine to thin it to a good consistency, which looked like it might make the paint go further, and she took everything over to the cabin.

With a stepladder in place, she was ready to go to work. Starting on the biggest wall—the one with no windows, doors, or fireplace—she started to paint. She was thankful she'd thought to use the drop cloth to protect the nice fir floor. But after a few slops and drips and misstarts, she slowly got the hang of coating the logs with a thin layer of white. Eventually, the wall was finished and she stepped back and smiled. Not bad. She continued to work around the room, being careful not to splatter paint on the fireplace rocks, the wooden kitchen cabinet Daddy had made, or the windows. She was just finishing up when she heard Babette calling to her. "Hallo, chérie, your playmate is back to play."

"In here," Anna called out. "Come and see what I've done."

"Oh, chérie, trés bon! What a difference you have made. So light! So lovely!" Babette clapped her hands. "You are expert painter, no?"

"I did my best." Anna held up the empty paint can. "But I don't have enough for the bedroom now."

Babette waved her hand. "Oh, the bedroom ees not a place for bright light. Eet is good just like that."

"That's probably true."

Babette nodded with approval. "I must hire you to paint for me."

Anna grinned and rubbed her right arm. "Let me think about that."

"I have brought more things for your little house." Babette grinned. "I hope it ees all right."

"Sure. I want to make it a nice place to stay."

"Come and see." Anna wiped her hands on a rag then followed her out.

"This picture—eet always remind me of your grandmamma, and maybe you too. What do you think?"

Anna looked at the depiction of an Indian maid by a pool of water. It was romanticized but very beautiful. "I think it's lovely. Do you really want to hang it in this cabin?"

"Oui. It will be perfect."

"Maybe in the bedroom."

Now Babette showed her some things she'd brought for the kitchen, as well as a couple of large rag rugs. "These were only in storage. Better they are used."

"Those will be perfect in there."

Babette pointed to Anna's paint-covered hands and frowned. "Oh, chérie, you must go clean up so we can play house." She went over to a basket she'd brought and pulled out an amber-colored jar. "Here is some lavender cream. I make it myself. Use it on your hands—and your face— but *after* you are clean. Then come and help Babette play house."

Anna laughed, but after she cleaned up her painting things, she took the cream back to the house, where she followed Babette's instructions. And the cream was actually very nice and soothing to the skin. "You really made that lavender cream yourself?" she asked Babette when she came back.

"Oui. From my own blooms." Babette touched Anna's cheek. "You see? How nice eet ees to have soft skin again. Use this each morning, each night, you will stay young forever." She made a sly wink. "Maybe not that long."

"I think you could sell this cream, Babette."

Babette just laughed, then returned to where she was putting some teacups in the kitchen cabinet. "I am careful not to bump your paint," she told Anna.

"Maybe we should work on the bedroom while this dries," Anna suggested.

"Oui! I have something special for the bedroom."

They finished filling the cupboards and Anna

washed out the sink, another amenity her father had put in, even though Grandma Pearl had protested. She soon grew to appreciate running water inside her house, even if it was only cold. But when he offered her a gas stove, she drew the line. "Fire is the way to cook," she told him, proving it again and again with a bowl of delicious clam soup or fish stew. Her cooking skills were a mix of Indian and what she'd learned while working in the kitchen of a white family when she was a girl. But the results were satisfying and Anna wished she'd thought to write down the recipes.

With the kitchen cupboard filled, Anna and Babette now worked to haul the mattress from Anna's old bedroom. Worried that Babette might fall and hurt herself, Anna tried to carry the bulk of the weight, but by the time they reached the cabin she realized that Babette was in very good shape for her age, which made her wonder, not for the first time, how old Babette was. Carrying it like a dead body, they gingerly maneuvered the floppy mattress through the doorway, and without bumping any of the wet paint, safely into the bedroom. "I hope this will be comfortable enough for Hazel," Anna said as she patted the mattress. "Although she was willing to stay in the cabin like it was."

"Like eet was?" Babette looked appalled. "What kind of woman ees this Hazel?"

"Very outdoorsy. She likes to camp."

"Oh . . . like Betty Moller?"

Anna laughed. "Maybe so. A shorter, stockier version of Betty Moller—and much more talkative." Betty was a legend on the river. No one would ever say it to Betty's face, but everyone knew she wore the pants in the family. Literally, since she'd been wearing pants for decades now. Besides that, she towered over her slight husband, Edmond, who spent most of his time indoors. Some people said he wore an apron and was clever with a needle. Meanwhile, Betty fished and hunted and chopped firewood. They were quite an unusual couple.

"Now for my surprise," Babette said with a twinkle in her eye. "You wait here, chérie."

Anna remained in the bedroom, giving the window another good wiping, although the glass was so old and bubbly that it would never be much clearer than it was now. Babette returned with a box in her arms. She opened it and pulled out a beautiful blue and white and yellow quilt. "Voilà!"

"Oh, Babette, it's gorgeous. Did you make it?"

"Your mama and me, a few years ago. Sunburst pattern. Ees eet not cheerful?"

"Very cheerful. And very pretty. You really want it to be in here?"

"Why not?" Babette frowned. "Ees eet not good enough?"

"Of course, it's good enough. It's far too good for this humble room."

"No, no, not too good. Eet make this room sing."

They spread it over the mattress just to see how it looked. "It's so beautiful. It makes this seem like a real bedroom," Anna said as she smoothed her hand over the fabric.

"And that ees not all." Babette pulled something else blue and white from the box. "Matching curtains!"

"Perfect!"

"Très chic, no?"

"What?"

"Very stylish, you think?" Babette asked.

"Yes." Anna tried to remember the words. "Tray-sheek."

"Oui!"

Even the rag rug had shades of blue and yellow. By the time the room was put together with all the bedding and curtains in place, the Indian maiden picture on the wall over the bed, and one of Mother's hand-crocheted doilies on the dresser with a freshly cleaned kerosene lantern all ready to light, it looked very sweet and inviting.

"I wouldn't mind sleeping in here," Anna said wistfully.

"Eet ees charming."

"I think Hazel will be pleased," Anna said as they closed the door.

Because the paint was still wet and because Anna suspected that Babette was tired, she suggested they call it a day.

"I only go if you agree to let me bring you by an early supper tonight," Babette told her. "I look inside your refrigerator, Anna." She shook a finger at her. "You must get some food in your house."

As they walked toward the dock, Anna promised she'd make a trip to town as soon as she got everything ready for Hazel. She glanced over to where Daddy's old boat was securely tied to its usual place on the dock, covered in an old canvas tarp. She wondered if the engine would even work, or if her mother had ever taken it out. Mother had never been very comfortable in boats.

"When will your guest arrive?" Babette asked.

"I think she might come tomorrow."

"Tomorrow? Then I will telephone an order of groceries for you today. Oui?"

"That's probably a good idea." Anna gave Babette her hand as she climbed into her boat. "Thanks, Babette. I don't know what I'd do without you." She knelt to untie the boat, tossing the rope inside and waving as Babette revved the boat's motor, deftly turning around and roaring across the water.

Of course, after Babette zipped away, Anna realized she should've given her a spending cap for the grocery order, especially knowing that

Babette enjoyed extravagant things like tenderloin steaks and fine French Burgundy. And certainly, Babette could afford those luxuries. Her husband's success in the gold mines had been keeping Babette comfortable for years now and would probably continue to do so even if she lived to be a hundred.

However, Anna's situation was not so comfortable. She had a very limited amount of cash on hand and not much more in her meager savings account back in Pine Ridge. Even with the prospects of a paying guest, she wasn't sure what kind of a budget was required to keep things running here . . . or for how long. But there wasn't time to think about that now.

Anna had noticed some packets of seeds in a cupboard of her mother's kitchen yesterday. And that reminded her of Mother's old garden plot. She'd seen it overgrown with weeds, a sign that Mother hadn't planned to put in a garden this year. Perhaps she'd known her health was failing, or maybe she'd been too weak to use a hoe, but Anna had decided last night that if she was going to try to stay on here—and that was still a big if—it wouldn't hurt to grow some of her own food. Despite the fact that June was nearly over, it wasn't too late to plant in this moderate climate. But that meant she had to do some weeding first. While the paint dried, she would remove weeds.

Anna had plenty of experience with weeding. From the earliest age, she could remember helping Mother in the garden and her job was usually to pull the weeds. At first it had been fun, grabbing a big green leafy plant and jerking it out by its roots. With the loose, damp soil, the weeds always came out easily. Child's play. Then Mother would praise her efforts and Anna would happily toss the weed onto a slowly growing pile. But as Anna became older, she liked weeding less and less. It changed from play to work, and it was one of her least favorite chores. However, it often fell upon her to do it. And she remembered the last year she'd weeded for her mother's garden, shortly after high school graduation, and how she told herself that she would never, never have to do this again.

Yet here she was, weeding, and by choice.

She worked for about an hour and was surprised at how much she enjoyed seeing her weed pile growing taller. Slowly, the rich brown soil became exposed, as if had been lying there expectantly, hoping to be awakened to grow things. She imagined how it would look to see squash and pumpkins and carrots and cucumbers growing. Perhaps it wasn't even too late for tomatoes if she found some starts in town. She stood and surveyed her work, thinking this was actually fun. Perhaps this was why her mother enjoyed it so much. But suspecting her paint might be dry, and feeling her back needed a break, she left the happy brown patch of earth behind. With the plot nearly weed-free now and almost ready for seeds, Anna would come back soon to plant.

After scrubbing her hands and utilizing more of Babette's wonderful cream, she returned to put the main room of her grandmother's cabin back together. The paint was nearly dry and she gingerly hung the new gingham curtains, careful not to let them touch the slightly tacky paint. Then she moved the scarred cedar table over by the window. She knew her grandpa had hand-hewn this table ages ago and, although the legs were uneven, if you turned it just so (since the floor was uneven too), it would stand sturdily. She put the two mismatched chairs in place. She wasn't sure where they had come from, but they were charming in a folksy sort of way. Then she laid the larger of the two rag rugs in front of the fireplace, which made the room look even homier. And she set the old wooden rocker with the cracked leather seat nearby.

Borrowing a few items from the house and a few more from the store, she added all the little touches she felt would make the humble cabin comfortable for Hazel. Finally, she picked a large bouquet of wild flowers and put them in the yellow milk pitcher she'd taken from the store. Then she stepped back to admire the effect.

Shaking her head at the transformation, she vaguely wondered what Grandma Pearl would think of her efforts. Her grandmother had loved her little cabin exactly as it was. But she wasn't here anymore. It was up to Anna to make this work—and if renting this space to Hazel allowed Anna to remain on the river a little while longer, she felt certain that Grandma Pearl would be glad for her.

For all Anna knew, Grandma Pearl might've liked these fresh white walls. The color reminded Anna of the inside of an oyster shell and Grandma Pearl loved oysters. Anna chuckled at the image of Grandma Pearl living inside an oyster shell. That was when it occurred to Anna that she should name this cabin. She would call it Pearl's Oyster Shell.

Anna found an old board and while painting the words in white, she realized that Grandma Pearl was similar to a real pearl. Her grandmother's early life had been full of hardships, just like the rough sand that sneaks into an oyster, irritating and rubbing against it. But like an oyster pearl, her grandmother had been polished smooth by her challenges. Anna had never known a sweeter, kinder, more generous soul than her grandmother. She had been a pearl!

10

When Babette arrived, Anna hurried down to meet her at the dock. "I'll take this up to the house," Anna said as she lifted the covered basket from Babette's arms. "You go and see the cabin."

"Oui! I cannot wait."

They went their separate ways and Anna felt eager to hear Babette's reaction to the completed project. Anna had been nearly unable to tear herself away from the cabin after she'd put the last bit into place. She'd just wanted to stand there and stare and stare, as if she could absorb its sweetness into her being. For some unexplainable reason the accomplishment of transforming that cabin into a usable space was very fulfilling.

As Anna went into the house, she smelled something delicious waft up from the basket. Babette was one of the best cooks on the river. In fact, she often gave Anna and Dorothy cooking lessons when they were in high school. But Mother never wanted much of Anna's help in the kitchen, so it wasn't until Anna married that she was able to attempt some of Babette's recipes again. Of course, Anna's meals never turned out quite like Babette's, but there had been a brief period of time, before their lives were permanently interrupted by the war, that Adam had appreciated her efforts. "Not only is she beautiful," she'd heard him brag to his buddy Earl once, "but she can cook too!" Back then, she had brushed off his praise and compliments. Had she realized how limited those words would be, she might've welcomed them more.

"Oh, chérie," Babette gushed as she burst into the house. "It is so sweet! Delightful! Your friend Hazel, she will be pleased." Babette removed her hat, hanging it on the hook by the door. "And the flowers you put in the pretty yellow pitcher on the table. *Perfect!*" She came over and kissed Anna on the cheek. "You respect the value of beauty. You make good French girl."

Anna laughed. "I'm too old to be any kind of a girl."

"Non!" Babette held up her hand. "Do not say such a thing. You are as young as you feel *inside*." She smiled. "And you will get younger each day if you stay here on the river with me. I will personally see to it."

Anna laughed even louder at that. "I almost think you would."

Babette came closer, peering into her eyes. "That mother-in-law—she maybe try to steal the beauty of your soul, but she no get eet. I see . . . eet ees still there, chérie."

As Babette put the covered baking dish in the oven to warm and saw to some other preparations, Anna started to set places on the humble kitchen table, then changed her mind. Instead, she decided they would eat in the dining room, which wasn't exactly a room, but an open area where a table that could seat up to ten people was situated by a large window that looked out onto the river. And since her guest was Babette, and because Anna felt festive, she opened the china hutch that Daddy had made when Anna was small, carefully removing her mother's good china.

"Ooh, how lovely," Babette said when she saw the table. "I feel very special."

"Good." Anna smiled at the ivory dishes trimmed with narrow strips of gold and black. "You should." Now she told Babette about her first year of her marriage. "I thought about you a lot during that year," she confessed.

"*Moi?*"

"Yes. I remembered the way you cooked and kept your home—you know, with things like fresh flowers on the table or candles burning just because you liked the light they gave out, not because you needed them, since you already had electricity."

Babette chuckled. "Your mother, God bless her soul, thought I was wasteful."

"I'm sure she simply wished she could've afforded to be wasteful too."

"Life ees too short not to enjoy. My first husband, Pierre, the miner who died too young but left me my fortune, he never got to enjoy much. When I marry Bernard, I tell myself that each day I enjoy ees gift from God . . . and Pierre. Ees good way to live, no?"

Anna nodded as she set the butter dish on the table. "If you can do it, it's very good. But once Adam came home, well, in the condition he was in . . . it seemed impossible to enjoy much of anything."

Babette tapped her head. "His mind . . . ? Eet was unwell, no?"

"Very unwell. He blamed himself for the deaths of the men serving under him. So many died. And I know Adam felt he should've died too. I'm not even sure why he didn't. Besides losing his arm, he had some injuries from shrapnel that should've killed him."

"Oh, my."

"It was due to his education and age that Adam went into the army as an officer—although I still wonder why his superiors felt he was qualified to lead young boys into a bloody battle like that. It still mystifies me."

"Nothing prepares a man for war. Nothing."

"But before the war, Babette, we were happy. I never realized at the time how short-lived our happiness would be."

"That ees why the Good Book say—live today for all eet ees worth, for we do not know about tomorrow."

"At least I can say that I lived like that for awhile—before the war stole it all away. After that, well, it seemed to take all my strength to simply make it through a single day. I'd go to bed and almost wish there wouldn't be another one." Anna went to the drawer where her mother used to keep "emergency" candles now. She pulled out a couple of old yellowed ones then got out the silver candelabra that Daddy had given Mother one Christmas. It needed some polishing, but that could come another day. She stuck the candles into place and lit them, and, setting the candelabra in the center of the dining table, she smiled. Too bad she hadn't thought to pick a bouquet of wildflowers for the house. Although, that could come later too.

Babette removed the baking dish and soon they were seated at the table. "Very beautiful, chérie. You like I say blessing?"

"Thank you."

They both bowed their heads and Babette asked a sweet simple blessing and then they began to eat the tartiflette casserole Babette had prepared. Once again, Anna felt sad to think how much her mother would've enjoyed this . . . but perhaps she was smiling down from heaven.

"Everything was delicious," Anna told Babette as they cleared the table. "Just like I knew it would be."

"Merci."

Anna was aware this wasn't an economical meal. The cheeses and wine were not cheap. She could imagine her mother commenting on this extravagance—after Babette was gone, of course—but this reminded Anna about her own concerns over finances. "Did you have time to order my groceries yet?" she asked as she carefully rinsed a plate.

"Oui. Your order ees placed and will be delivered the next time Henry comes upriver. Maybe tomorrow even."

"Oh. . . ." Anna was disappointed, wishing she'd planned this better. "I just hope you didn't order too many groceries for me, Babette. It's embarrassing to say this, but, well, my funds are rather limited."

Babette's brow creased, as if confused, or perhaps she assumed Anna had the same kind of assets that she did—unlimited. "Oh . . . I am not sure of the total cost, chérie." She cocked her head to one side with a curious expression. "You know about the teapot, no?"

"The teapot? Oh, did you want some tea?"

"No, that ees not what I mean. I mean the teapot with the pink rosebuds?"

Now Anna was puzzled. "You mean the teapot with the bad crack in the back?"

"Oui. That ees eet."

Anna nodded, but now felt more confused.

"You mention money. Do you know about the teapot?"

"What do you mean? Is it valuable?"

Babette laughed. "No, no, not on the outside, chérie."

"What?"

"Go—go and get." She pointed to the china hutch. "Eet ees on top, left-hand side, hidden behind cups and saucers."

Anna opened the left cabinet door, carefully moving the dainty teacups until she spotted the old teapot. Anna and Daddy had gotten this teapot at the mercantile in town one year, a surprise for Mother's birthday. But it had cracked the first time Mother put hot water in it. Daddy had wanted to take it back, but when Mother heard it was the only teapot like that in the store, she wouldn't let him return it. Mother adored pink rosebuds—and so she decided to keep the teapot around just to look at, using her old white crockery one to make tea. And sometimes she used the cracked teapot as a vase.

"Here it is." Anna carefully pulled it out. But she could tell by the solid feel of it that there was something inside.

"Open eet!"

Anna set it down on the table and removed the lid to see what looked like a large bundle of bills. "Oh!"

"Your mother's secret savings account in the First National Bank of Teapot." Babette laughed. "She told me of eet a few years ago, after she closed the store. In case there was ever emergency. I almost forgot."

Anna unrolled the bills to see mostly twenties and tens and a few fives. "There must be several hundred dollars here."

"Ees that all?" Babette sounded disappointed. She came over to look more closely. "Oh, I thought the bills would be bigger. Still they are good, no?"

Anna laughed. "I'm not complaining, Babette. This might not be that much to you, but it will help me a lot."

"Très bon! Now for dessert."

As Babette served two dishes of chocolate mousse, Anna complimented her on her culinary skills again. "You're an inspiration to me."

"Merci."

"I want to improve my own cooking abilities. I used to try to imitate you in the early years of marriage, but then life changed and I lost the desire to do more than just the basics. So I've never really mastered French cuisine."

"I will teach you."

Anna nodded eagerly, but then realized it was probably useless.

"Why unhappy? You no want Babette to teach you?"

"That's not it. I just imagined cooking something like this for my mother-in-law. She'd probably complain about it."

"Oh, no, no, no!" Babette waved a warning finger in the air. "I will no teach you if you cook for that nasty witch woman. Babette's food too good for her."

Anna laughed. "I agree."

"Do you really cook for her—every day?"

"Cook, clean—you name it, I do it—every day."

"And now? You are not there? Will she starve?" Babette's tone was skeptical.

"I've tried to teach Lauren to cook. Between the two of them, they'll get by. But it won't be anything like this." She waved her hand over the table. Now she told Babette about how Lauren liked to have friends over and how Anna worked hard to make it nice when she did. "Although it's a bit like running a boarding house. Or a small inn." She chuckled. "In fact, my mother-in-law sounded a bit distressed when I spoke to her yesterday."

"Good. She should be distressed. Maybe she appreciate you."

"I hate to imagine what the kitchen must look like by now. Or the bedrooms. You know there are six bedrooms in that house and sometimes when Lauren has her friends over, every single bed will be slept in. And then there are the bathrooms—three of them. And the towels. Do you know how much laundry that makes?"

"Oh, my." Babette just shook her head. "If I have my way, chérie, you will never go back to that workhouse. *Never!*"

"What about Lauren?"

"She will come here." Babette made a firm nod, like it was settled.

Anna sighed. "I don't know—"

"If she love her mama, she will come."

Anna was planting the last of the seeds, tucking the fat pumpkin seeds into the small hill mounds just like Mother used to do, when she heard the sound of a boat engine chugging along. She paused, listening to see if it was simply passing by or stopping at her dock. And then she realized it was the sound of a larger engine. Maybe it was Henry.

Henry's boat was just pulling alongside her dock as she came around from behind the house. And there, waving from the stern, was Hazel. "Hello-hello!" she called cheerfully. "I'm back!"

Anna waved, returning her greeting, as she went out on the dock.

"Anna Pearl," Henry called back. "You look almost like your same old self today."

She laughed as she caught the end of his rope, holding it while he helped Hazel out of the boat.

"With them pigtails and coveralls, why I'd

swear you was just a young'un when you was running out to meet us. I think our sweet river air is good for what ails you, girl."

"Thanks, Henry. It sure is great to be here."

He went back into the boat now, returning with a wooden crate that he passed over to her. "I brung your grocery order 'long with me. Greeley said he put it on your bill and you can settle up with him later." He nodded to Hazel. "And the missus here covered the delivery fee, so if you don't need nothing more, we'll get this stuff unloaded and I'll keep moving along. Lots of deliveries to make today."

Anna stood next to the boat, just like Daddy used to do, as Henry handed out boxes and luggage and some heavy cases, and she set them on the dock.

"Reckon that's everything. If'n it's not, you'll see me back here again 'fore the sun goes down."

"Thanks, Henry." She threw him back the rope.

He nodded toward Hazel now. Already loaded down with suitcases, the older woman was already on her way. He winked at Anna. "Now that one there, she be a talker, that's for sure."

Anna grinned and nodded. "You have a good day, Henry."

"You too, Anna Pearl." He tooted his whistle then slowly backed out, turned around, and chortled on up the river.

Anna picked up the heavy box of groceries. No

longer feeling so fearful over finances, although she knew last night's unexpected teapot treasury wouldn't last forever, she was curious to see what kind of goodies Babette had ordered for her.

"Let me set this food in the shade," Anna called out to Hazel, "then I'll help you get your things to the cabin."

With the box on the covered porch, she hurried back to get some of Hazel's things. "I cleaned it up a little," she said as caught up with her.

"I hope you didn't go to any trouble, dear. I'm perfectly capable of cleaning."

"It was actually kind of fun. I'd never seen the place very cleaned up before. My grandmother was a good old soul, but housekeeping was not her strong suit."

Hazel chuckled. "Nor mine. I think your grandmother and I would've been great friends." She stopped by the door. "In fact, I hope we shall be—I believe friendship can transpire generations." She nodded to the sign above the door. "Pearl's Oyster Shell?"

Anna chuckled. "I thought I'd name it . . . in Grandma's memory."

"Did I hear Henry calling you Anna *Pearl?*"

"Pearl's my middle name." She set down a bag to free her hand.

"For your grandmother."

"I heard later on that my mother hadn't been

too pleased. It had been Daddy's choice. Mother picked my first name and Daddy picked my middle one, it was already on the birth certificate before Mother could change it." She turned the doorknob.

"Your father certainly must've thought highly of his mother-in-law."

"Oh, he did." She swung the door open wide. "Here you go."

"Oh! My! Word!" Hazel dropped her bags to the ground and walked into the cabin as if entering into a fine palace. "What on earth happened?"

"I hope you don't mind." Suddenly Anna was worried. Perhaps she'd ruined the authenticity or history of the place. Would Hazel be upset?

"Of course, I don't mind. This is absolutely wonderful. Goodness gracious, you may never get rid of me now." She walked around examining every last detail, exclaiming and gasping as if the entire place was made of silver and gold. Now she turned and clasped both of Anna's hands in hers. "My dear, you are a wonder. A delightful wonder. How in heaven's name you accomplished all this in just a couple of days." She shook her head. "I am dumbfounded."

Anna laughed. "My friend Babette helped me. You'll have to meet her."

"I should say so."

"Make yourself comfortable and I'll have some lunch ready for us in about an hour. Does that sound all right?"

"That sounds like pure perfection."

Anna's feet felt light as she walked back to the house. It had been so long since anyone had appreciated her like this. It was like a tonic for the soul. She wondered how things might've been different if her mother-in-law had been more like Hazel or Babette. Perhaps Anna would still be happily slaving away for her mother-in-law now. However, she was thankful not to be back there today. She could imagine the household with dirty dishes and musty laundry piling up, dust and clutter growing, tempers rising. No, she sighed, she would much rather be here on this bucolic stretch of the peaceful Siuslaw River. And the longer she could stay here, the happier she would be.

11

Nosing around on her parents' property—no, she reminded herself, it was her property now—felt a bit like a treasure hunt. Whether she was browsing through the random merchandise in the store, picking through the attic, or even going through a closet in the house, she found all sorts of unexpected things—some familiar, some not. However, one thing became quite clear—her mother never threw anything away. Whether it was old letters, old clothes from when Anna was small, a broken phonograph—it was still here.

Anna supposed this kind of pack rat tendency was a result of the Depression years, and although there were some things that really needed to be tossed or burned (and that pile was growing steadily), there were many other items that she was hugely relieved to see preserved. Also, it gave her a very good excuse to remain here for a week or two longer than originally planned. She had work to do in regard to her parents' estate. Even Eunice wouldn't be able to argue about that. And, as everyone knew, these things took time.

Also there was her guest to care for. After Hazel's first night in the cabin, Anna had felt a bit concerned. Because it was summer, staying warm enough hardly seemed a problem, but what if the bed was uncomfortable?

"Did you rest well?" she asked Hazel as they sat down to breakfast. For Hazel's first breakfast, Anna had gone all out with eggs, bacon, and even sourdough pancakes (thanks to the starter Babette had left in her refrigerator yesterday).

"Oh, my, yes. I don't know when I've slept so well. Certainly much better than I slept at the hotel. So quiet and peaceful. I have absolutely no complaints. Pearl's Oyster Shell is divine."

"And you don't mind using the outhouse?" Anna asked with hesitation.

Hazel chuckled as she poured syrup. "It's a very nice outhouse. It even smelled clean."

Anna smiled. "I did give it a scrub down. And I honestly don't think my grandmother ever used it. Or if she did, it was rarely. And, of course, feel free to use the indoor bathroom anytime you like."

"Thank you, but that won't be necessary. Now, tell me, why did your grandmother never use the outhouse?"

"She had several places back in the woods that she preferred. It had been my mother's idea that she needed an outhouse. Naturally, Daddy didn't argue. We'd switched over to indoor plumbing by then, but there was still an outhouse for the store customers to use, the one out back. And Daddy didn't mind making one just for Grandma, but she always thought it was silly."

"And bathing?" Hazel picked up a piece of bacon.

Anna shrugged. "I honestly don't know. But anytime you want a shower or bath, please feel free to come to the house. In fact, if you'd be more comfortable staying in the house, there's plenty of room, as you can see."

"No, I'm perfectly comfortable in the cabin. I'm afraid you'll have a hard time prying me out of there. You know how stubborn an oyster shell can be if it doesn't want to be opened."

Anna laughed as she filled their coffee cups. "Well, Daddy did put on a wooden bolt to lock the door from inside, so I guess you can barricade yourself in there if you want to."

Hazel stopped with her fork in midair. "You know, Anna, I think I heard a bear last night."

"Not surprising. There are lots of black bears around." She buttered her pancakes. "I hope that won't worry you. My dad always said they were more afraid of us than we are of them. That is, unless you come between a mama and her babies. Then you need to watch out."

"Yes, I know all about that. And having bears around does not bother me in the least. I thoroughly enjoy all forms of wildlife. In fact, I hope to see one before I get done here." She took a bite of eggs. "What a lovely, lovely breakfast, dear. But you better be careful."

"Careful?"

"You treat me too well and I will never want to leave this place." Hazel got a thoughtful look. "You know this location would be a wonderful spot for an inn. Have you ever considered that?"

Anna felt a surprising rush of excitement run through her. "An inn?"

"Yes. I'm sure you'd have no problem finding customers. The east coast is full of little B and Bs."

"What's that?"

"Bed-and-breakfast." Hazel paused to sip her

coffee. "An inn of sorts, where only the morning meal is served. However, out here, you might need to do more than just one meal. Perhaps you'd be a B and B and D. Let your guests fend for themselves for lunch."

"But I'd only have the cabin," Anna pointed out. "It would be a rather small inn."

"Unless you rented rooms up here in the house as well. Or perhaps you'd make rooms in the lower level, where the store used to be. Or you could always have more little cabins built. Wouldn't that be lovely, come to think of it? A line of sweet little cabins, just like the Pearl's Oyster Shell, right along the river. I think I would become a very regular customer here." She forked a piece of pancake. "And I would tell all my friends."

"That's a very interesting idea." Anna's mind was beginning to whirl now. "And it would be a way for me to bring in some income and be able to keep this place."

"You were considering selling it?"

Anna frowned. "I'd hate to sell it."

"I should say so. But if you do consider, please, let me know. I wouldn't want to see something like this getting into the wrong hands."

"Like some of the other places around here." Now Anna confessed her fears over the timber industry and what it was doing to the land and the river and the delicate estuaries. "So many of the birds I used to see around here . . . I have no idea where they've gone."

"That is sad. But this unfortunate phase won't last forever."

"You think this is a phase?" Anna felt a small surge of hope.

"I hope so. That's usually the way it goes. After the lumber people move on—and I suspect they will—it will be up to people like you to help the land and the river to heal again."

"To heal again—" Anna rolled those words around in her mind. "I like the sound of that."

Hazel smiled. "I suspect you have a healer inside of you."

"What do you mean?"

She waved her hand over the cabin. "You took something that was ailing and in need of help . . . and you made it better. You, my dear, are a healer."

Anna felt a rush of pride and wonder. "I hope that's true. I usually think of the river as having the power to heal me. I wish I could help it to heal too."

"You will if you remain here."

Suddenly Anna remembered what Henry had said about her mother fighting to keep the log barges off this part of the river, how having a business along with a working dock may have helped her cause. "But if I did as you said, if I made this place into an inn, I wonder how much money it would bring in. Would it be profitable enough to support me?" She knew she was thinking out loud now and, feeling embarrassed, she tried to brush it off. "Really, it's not your concern, Hazel. You've given me something to consider."

"I don't see why you couldn't open up an inn, Anna. This land belongs to you. I assume it's paid for—unless there are liens or additional mortgages. Are there?"

"No. The lawyer told me it's free and clear . . . and all mine."

"In that case, I do hope you'll hold on to it, Anna. I think the land would serve you well—just as you would serve it. Speaking of innkeeping, we need to settle on the rent for the cabin."

"Oh—" Anna waved her hand. "You're my guest here, Hazel. I don't want to be paid."

"Nonsense!" Hazel frowned. "You're a businesswoman now. And I gave it some thought and I believe the cabin should be worth at least as much as the room I had at the hotel—"

"But you don't even have a real bathroom."

"No matter. It's a much nicer place. And then I'd add on to that the cost of three meals a day, that is if you plan to serve three meals—I don't want you to feel that—"

"I'm used to cooking three meals a day. And I'd be fixing for myself anyway. Really, it's no trouble."

"In that case, would you be willing to accept ten dollars a day?"

"Oh, no, that's too much!" Anna was shocked.

"You obviously don't go on vacation much."

Anna laughed. "Vacation?"

"I'll tell you what, how about if we agree on a weekly rate of $65. I will not settle on a penny less. Otherwise, I will not sleep well at night, Anna. And I would expect your dear grandmother to come back and haunt me for attempting to cheat her granddaughter."

"But I—"

"Please, Anna." She set down the box and stuck out her hand. "As my father would say, we're burning daylight here. Let's come to an agreement on this so that I can get to my work."

Anna shook her hand. "OK . . . then I agree."

"And I will write you a check for the first week in advance."

Knowing it was useless to argue with this woman, Anna simply nodded. As Hazel left, Anna realized that Hazel's check, combined with the teapot savings, was more money than Anna had ever had in her possession before. For a brief time, she'd hoped to inherit a little something after Adam's death—just enough to get her and Lauren on their own, to break free of Eunice's iron grasp. And while some insurance money had gone into a college savings account set up for Lauren, there had been nothing left for Anna.

At least that's what Eunice had claimed. She'd even shown her a stack of paperwork, after discovering Anna's plan to meet with the lawyer. But Eunice had gone to great trouble to lay it all out, showing Anna line after line of Adam's expenses in the final years of his life, as well as the expenses associated with Anna and Lauren. On top of that had been his funeral expenses. There was no denying that it appeared that anything Adam received from the government had been eaten away down to the last cent (and more, according to Eunice). "Just be thankful that I'm willing to keep a roof over your head," she had told Anna, "and that I can provide food and clothing for both you and Lauren and myself. All I ask in return is a bit of housekeeping. I'm sure you must agree that is more than fair." Naturally, Anna had to agree. What other choice did she have? By then, Lauren was accustomed to living in a large comfortable home, wearing the fanciest clothes, going around in the nicest cars, and having friends from the "best" families, not to mention the prestige of being part of an influential lumber family like the Gundersons.

Hazel asked Anna to pass the butter, stirring Anna out of her private reveries. "You probably already knew that many of the coastal tribes, including yours I'd guess, were matriarchal societies."

"Matriarchal—doesn't that mean mother or maternal?"

"Yes. A matriarchal society is one where the women not only have equal rights to the men, but the line of heritage goes through the women. For instance, when property passed, it went from mother to daughter."

"Really?" Anna warmed up Hazel's coffee for her.

"I guess you could consider your family a matriarchal one as well. It sounds as if your grandmother passed this property to your mother and she passed it on to you. You, Anna Pearl, are part of a Siuslaw matriarchal society."

Anna grinned as she picked up her coffee cup. "Well, to think of that."

After breakfast, Anna showed Hazel the box of things her father had saved from Grandma's cabin after her death. "I'm not sure what all of these mean or if they're valuable, but feel free to take them back to the cabin to go through if you'd like."

"Oh, my!" Hazel's face looked luminous. "I feel like a child on Christmas morning! Oh, my, oh, my!"

"And if you learn more about these things, the uses or the origins, I'd enjoy knowing more about them myself."

"And you shall, my dear. Do you mind if I take photos of them? I'll be very careful with them.

And I'll make sure to mark all my photos as to the ownership of the actual artifacts. I can even give you copies if you like."

"Yes, I'd appreciate that. Then if I decide to give anything to museums, I'll have something to remember them by."

"Oh, I can't wait to get to work." Hazel wrapped her arms around the box as if it were a fragile infant.

"Do you want me to carry it down for you?"

"Oh, I'll be very careful with it, I promise. Don't worry; I'm used to handling valuable pieces. And I've even got some museum gloves with me."

"Museum gloves?"

"To ensure that oil or dirt from my hands doesn't harm anything."

Anna had to laugh. "Well, I remember my grandmother's hands and, trust me, they were usually not terribly clean."

"No matter. I will treat these pieces with great care—with the respect that is due to them."

"And I'm still looking for the stories my father wrote down."

"Oh, yes, I can't wait to see those."

"We can be thankful my mother never threw much away. Although it does make it a challenge to find things now."

"Well, I do appreciate all your efforts." Hazel's eyes lit up. "And I almost forgot. I called up someone to give us a hand with the electricity and telephone. I figured you wouldn't know any more about these things than I do."

"Thank you, Hazel." Anna felt worried now. Even though Hazel had offered to help with these expenses, she couldn't expect her to cover everything.

"Now I see those little frown lines creeping onto your forehead, dear. And I do not want you to be concerned about the cost of these improvements. As I already told you, it's the least I can do for your hospitality. Besides, I'm the one who needs the benefits of these silly modern conveniences. Both my electric typewriter, which I must admit is a timesaver, and my recording machine require electricity to operate. And without those tools, I am greatly challenged. To have access to a telephone is probably not an absolute necessity, but I would appreciate being able to reach the university library should I need anything sent out here."

Anna sighed. "All right, I won't worry about that anymore."

"Thank you."

"But I will go look for those stories."

"Perfect."

It was close to noon by the time Anna unearthed two of her father's notebooks containing Grandma's stories. Stuck in the middle of a box of old store ledgers, they would've been easy to overlook and possibly dump. She was thankful that hadn't happened. She peeked into the first one, trying to make sense of the odd spelling. But since she'd promised to have lunch served by one, she knew there wasn't time to decipher the words. So she just dusted the black notebook covers and set them on the table by the door. She couldn't wait to see Hazel's face when she saw they'd been found.

Anna was just stirring up some tuna salad when she saw Henry's boat coming to the dock again. Perhaps he had mail for her, although that would be surprising. But before she could get down there to see, a man jumped out of the boat and onto the dock, and Henry took off. Unsure as to who this tall stranger walking down her dock might be, she felt a little uneasy. Certainly, he didn't think the store was open. Henry would've told him that much.

"Hello?" she called out with hesitation. "Can I help you?"

"I'm Clark," he called back, as if that should explain everything.

She continued walking toward him. He didn't seem dangerous. In fact, he was rather good looking. Tall and broad-shouldered. Wearing a blue-plaid shirt, tan corduroys, and sturdy walking shoes, he might be a fisherman, although he had no gear or anything besides a jacket slung over his arm. On his head was a brown felt hat. As she got closer, she could see a ruffle of brown hair, the same shade as the hat, under the rim. But it was his eyes that gave her pause—a surprisingly intense shade of blue. The color reminded her of the Siuslaw River on a clear autumn day.

12

Still wondering why this gentleman was standing on her dock and looking all around him as if he were trying to figure out the same thing, she decided to introduce herself.

"I'm Anna Gunderson," she said cautiously. "This is my dock and my property." She felt worried. The lawyer had assured her this was her property, and had promised to send the paperwork. But what if something was wrong— what if there really was some sort of lien or something that could take it from her? Perhaps that was why this stranger was here now. This thought alone made her feel slightly sick.

His brow creased. "Gunderson, you say? I was supposed to be dropped off at the Larsons'. Is that around somewhere nearby?"

"This is the Larson place. I am Anna Larson. Gunderson is my married name." She waited, almost afraid to breathe. What did he want?

"Oh." He nodded. "I see. And I'm Clark

Richards. I'm here to take a look around the place."

She frowned. "May I ask why?"

"Oh, I'm sorry. I thought you knew I was coming. I'm here to get an idea of what you might need in order to get connected to power and telephone."

"Oh, yes." Relief washed over her. "You're the man Hazel mentioned."

He made a lopsided grin. "Right. Hazel."

"My goodness, you got here quickly."

"Well, she called me several days ago, when she was still at the hotel." He removed his hat and rubbed his forehead, revealing slightly messy hair, but it seemed thick for his age. Her guess, based on graying temples, was that he was older than her. "I understand she's staying here now." He glanced over to what used to be the store. "Is this a hotel?"

"Not yet . . . but it might be someday," she said wistfully.

"So do you mind if I just poke around, get the lay of the land, and figure out what will be needed before we get the utility guys out here? That will save everyone time and money."

"That sounds good to me. I was just fixing lunch. Would you like to join us?"

"I'd appreciate that. If it's no problem."

"No problem at all." She pointed to the stairs up to the house. "It's up there. I told Hazel to come up about one."

"Where is Hazel anyway?" he asked with a curious grin.

Anna pointed over to the cabin. "It's rustic, but she seems to like it."

"I think I'll go over and say hello."

Anna just nodded, then hurried on back to the house to be sure there was enough lunch for three people. As she opened another can of tuna, she wondered how Hazel had met this Clark person and what he normally did when he wasn't helping in this capacity. She also wondered if he was from Florence and if so, was he a newcomer, since the name Richards was unfamiliar. She was just getting lunch on the table when she heard their voices. The way they were talking sounded like they were old friends.

"Hello in the house," Hazel called. "Are we too early for lunch?"

"Not at all. Come on in." Anna set a pitcher of lemonade on the table. "Make yourselves comfortable."

"Oh, my!" Hazel exclaimed as she picked up a notebook. "Are these what I think they are, Anna?"

"Yes, I found them."

"Oh, Clark, Anna's father actually wrote down stories from her grandmother—and these are the actual books. I'm so tickled, I can hardly stand it."

"You've probably noticed by now that my

mother is given to enthusiasm," Clark said to Anna.

"Your mother?" Anna stared at him, then at Hazel. They looked nothing alike.

"Oh, didn't I mention that?" Hazel asked absently, her eyes fixed on the first page of the open journal. "Yes, Clark is my son . . . has been for quite some time."

He laughed. "My whole life, as a matter of fact." Now he gently removed the book from his mother's hands. "I'm sure that will wait, Mom. Remember your manners. It seems that Mrs. Gunderson has fixed—"

"Please, call me Anna."

He smiled as he pulled out a chair for his mother and then one for Anna as well. Surprised at his courtesy, she sat down. Then she realized she hadn't put everything on the table yet. Embarrassed, she stood. "Go ahead and sit down," she told him. "I forgot something."

Clark and Hazel chatted about his trip up the river while they waited for Anna. Then she rejoined them and Clark offered to say grace. Hazel smiled in what seemed a tolerant way. "My son always likes to pray before he eats," she said as if apologizing.

"My father always did that too," Anna admitted. "I sometimes miss it."

With the blessing said, Hazel explained that Clark had driven over from Eugene yesterday afternoon. "I really didn't expect him so soon, but I'm certainly glad he came."

"And I've already talked to the power and telephone people in town," Clark explained. "Hopefully, we'll get them out here as soon as possible."

"I don't recall if I mentioned that Clark is a building contractor," Hazel told her. "Of course, it's taken me a while to get used to that." She sighed sadly. "You see, Clark graduated top of his class in law school, but then decided it didn't interest him."

Clark shook his head. "Someday I'm hoping she'll get over it too."

"Oh, I am over it, Son." She grinned and patted his hand. "Mostly anyway. I suppose I just like bragging about my boy's impressive education. Despicable, isn't it?"

"Understandable," Anna told her. "And forgivable."

"Bless you."

"The problem was that I went to war," Clark directed this to Anna, as if that should explain the whole thing. And maybe it did.

She nodded as she passed him the pickles. "That was a problem . . . for a lot of people."

"For me, going to war, well, that just changed everything."

She peered curiously at him as he buttered a piece of bread. "I can understand that," she said quietly, hoping he might elaborate more. "It changed things for a lot of men . . . women too for that matter."

Now he seemed to be studying her. "You seem to know something about this yourself?" There was a question in his voice. "Were you in the service?"

"No, not really. Although I suppose I felt like it. You see, my husband was severely injured . . . in battle . . . I cared for him until he passed . . . about eight years ago."

"I'm sorry." Clark's blue eyes looked genuinely sympathetic too. "So I'm sure you do understand how war changes things."

"If women ruled the world there would be no war," Hazel stated.

Clark laughed. "Don't be so sure about that, Mom. I've known some pretty feisty women, some that started a few small battles too."

Hazel chuckled. "I suppose that's true."

"I'm still curious how the war made you decide not to practice law," Anna said to him.

"Ah, yes. I suppose that doesn't make sense." He took a sip of lemonade, and, with a thoughtful expression, continued. "I was a bombardier in the Army Air Corps. At the time it was highly necessary, and it helped us beat Hitler. But now I feel a sense of sadness to think of it . . . all the death and destruction those bombs caused. It's hard to even speak of it now."

"You were simply doing your job, Son."

"I suppose."

"I can understand how that would be hard on a person," Anna told him. "My husband witnessed some horrors that took a toll on him too."

Clark nodded. "So when I got home I was so sick of destruction that I decided I wanted to build things. I wanted to use my hands and my mind and my body to create homes—good solid homes. At first I thought it was just a passing fancy—sort of a phase that I needed to get out of my system. But the more I built, the more I loved doing it."

"And people love Clark's homes too," Hazel gushed. "Every single one of them is unique and wonderful, but without being terribly expensive. He's always got a waiting list of customers too. But just the same, he refused to go with tract housing like some developers do. He only builds one or two houses at the same time."

"And right now I'm between houses," he told her. "Which is why I could come out here and spend some time with you."

"I'm so glad you did, too. I wish you could've brought Marshall with you."

Clark frowned. "I asked him to come, Mom, but as usual, he had something else to do."

"Marshall is Clark's son. Seventeen and he's been a bit of a handful."

"He's with his mother," Clark explained.

"She's the pushover. Lets him have his way if he throws a fit." He shook his head. "But I won't go into that." He looked at his empty plate. "Thank you for the delicious lunch, Anna. Now if you ladies will excuse me, I'd like to go see if I can make myself useful outside." He removed a stub of a pencil and a little notebook from his shirt pocket. "If all goes well, we'll have you powered up by the end of the week."

"It's hard to imagine what it will be like to have electricity around here," Anna said as she started to clear the table. "Although I won't miss the noise of the generator, or having to keep an eye on it, fill it with gas, start it up, or any of that."

"I'd think it might simplify your life considerably." Hazel picked up some things from the table.

"No, no," Anna took the dishes from her. "This is my work, Hazel. I know you can't wait to start reading those stories my father wrote down. Now, off with you."

Hazel chuckled. "Well, I am anxious." But before she left, she called out, "Now, you did mention to Clark that you might turn this place into an inn, didn't you?"

"What do you mean?"

"For the electrical and telephone. It might be best if they knew about that up front, might save you some time and money on down the line. I'd recommend you run down there and let Clark know so he can keep it in mind."

Anna nodded. "Yes, that might be wise. Thank you for thinking of it." She rinsed the plates then set them in the sink, dried her hands, then went out to see if she could find Clark.

"Hey, I was just about to come looking for you," he called out when he saw her.

"Did you need something?"

He asked her about the boundaries of the property and she pointed them out. Then she explained the idea to possibly turn the place into an inn. "It's probably a far-fetched idea. Your mother actually suggested it. And I thought it might be worth looking into."

"I think it's a great idea. And this is a beautiful piece of property. I can imagine people wanting to pay to stay here. With your dock, you could probably entice fishermen at the very least."

"Well, it might be a way to help me to stay here." She looked out over the river with a longing. "And I'd like that."

"Say." He grinned. "If you decide to turn it into an inn, you might need a contractor."

She laughed. "I'm sure that I would. The problem is I couldn't possibly afford one."

"You never know. Anyway, it doesn't hurt to dream big, Anna."

She smiled at the sound of him saying her name with what seemed genuine affection. An unexpected warm rush swept over her—instantly followed by an icy blast of guilt that extinguished it. Good grief, what had come over her just now? Clark had a wife and a son at home. What was she thinking?

"Well, thank you, Clark. I'll let you get to it." She abruptly turned to leave and, feeling her cheeks heat up with embarrassment, she hurried up to the house. She hoped he hadn't noticed anything. Really, when had she become so silly?

She spent the rest of the afternoon sorting through things in the attic, but by the time she needed to quit, she felt fairly certain that she'd found just about anything that would be of use to Hazel. Still, it was interesting going down memory lane, and it would probably be helpful that she'd piled several useless boxes of old store ledgers and papers by the window to be tossed out later, when she was ready to make a big bonfire outside.

But right now, she needed to get herself cleaned up and dinner started. Her only question was, What about Clark? Did he intend to stay for dinner? And if so, did he intend to spend the night? And, if so, where would he stay? She could offer him a cot down in the store. Or maybe he'd want to stay in the cabin with his mother, although that would be rather cozy. She wasn't comfortable offering him one of the bedrooms in the house. That was too cozy for *her* comfort.

So after she cleaned herself up—taking the time to pin her hair up, which wasn't nearly as comfortable as the braids had been—she went to see Hazel, asking her if she knew what Clark's plans were.

Hazel looked up, in a blurry sort of way, from where she'd been peering intently at one of the story notebooks. "Clark?" she asked absently.

"Yes, your son. Remember?" Anna smiled. "Will he be staying for dinner? And if so, does he plan to stay overnight. I realize he's rather stuck here without a boat or car and—"

"Oh, Clark is gone, dear." Hazel waved her hand in a dismissive way. "Don't concern yourself with him."

"Gone?" Anna blinked. What had he done, floated down the river?

"Yes, didn't you hear the boat? That nice Henry fellow picked Clark up, just like he'd promised, on his way back to town. Clark is probably back in the hotel by now."

"Oh." Anna nodded. "I see."

"So when did you say dinner would be?" She looked at her watch. "Six-thirty?"

"Yes." Anna stepped out of the doorway. "I'll see you then."

As she walked back to the house, she felt disappointed that she hadn't been able to tell Clark good-bye. And at the same time she felt silly for feeling disappointed. It was probably best that he'd left just like he'd come—suddenly and without ado.

Hazel was flushed with excitement when she came to dinner. "Oh, I just translated the most wonderful story of your grandmother's." And as they ate, Hazel went on to tell the story of why the river sparkles like stars. Of course, the tale was very familiar, but Anna didn't say anything because she could see how much Hazel was enjoying herself.

"Long, long ago," Hazel launched into the telling, "the tribe on one side of the river owned all the stars in the sky, and naturally the tribe on the other side wanted the stars for themselves."

"Naturally." Anna smiled as she passed Hazel the peas.

"Fortunately, neither tribe was particularly warlike, but they were not opposed to sneaking over in the middle of the night to quietly steal the stars from each other." Hazel chuckled. "And these moonlight raids went on for some time, the two tribes stealing the stars back and forth until I suppose even the stars were confused. Then one time, the tribe who were the original owners of the stars had the stars back in their custody again, and they didn't want to lose them. So that night they all stayed awake—waiting for the star thieves to arrive."

Now Hazel lowered her voice, very much like Grandma Pearl used to do. "And they watched from behind the trees as the thieves once again stole their stars. Only this time the original owners followed the thieves, finally stopping them at the river. Well, the original owners must've been quite fed up because on this night, a great battle arose with both tribes fighting over who rightfully owned the stars." Hazel paused to catch her breath.

"And the stars were caught in the middle of the battle," Anna continued for her in a dramatic voice. "And they didn't like to see the fighting, so hundreds of the stars leaped from the sky, plummeting right into the river. And the rest of the stars spread themselves out so there would be enough for everyone and so the people would quit fighting. And to this day, that is why the river sparkles like there are stars in it."

Hazel grinned. "That is right!"

"I used to love that story." Anna split open a biscuit. "It was my favorite bedtime story. I loved that the stars would do that just to bring peace."

"It's a lovely story. And one I've never heard before." Hazel reached for the butter. "And it reminded me of Clark and Roselyn and Marshall."

"Is Roselyn Clark's wife?"

"Ex-wife." Hazel frowned. "But when she left Clark for Larry back when Marshall was only six, there was a custody battle for Marshall.

Naturally, the mother won—mothers almost always do. But the problem was that she and Larry wanted to move down here to Oregon for his work, which seemed unfair since Clark was building homes up near Seattle."

"That does seem unfair."

"So Clark was like the stars in your grandmother's story—he made the sacrifice, sold his business, and moved down here and started all over again, just so he could still be near his boy." She chuckled. "And then I followed him. That's why I'm at the university, you know."

Anna was nodding, trying to take all this in.

"And now . . . poor Clark, after all he's done, his sacrifices, now his boy is treating him like the enemy."

"I'm sure his son will grow out of it," she said quietly.

"Yes, you're probably right. At least I hope so."

"Did Clark ever remarry?"

Hazel sadly shook her head. "No. I tease him about that sometimes, telling him that he'll never find a good woman as long as he stays married to his job. That's one of the reasons I asked him to come over to the coast. I thought it would force him to take a little break. Of course, I'm a fine one to talk since I'm somewhat wed to my job too. I suppose it runs in the family. But I do wish he'd slow down, take time to smell the roses so to speak."

"Yes. That's something I'm just learning to do myself."

"What an enchanting place you have to do it in too."

And that was absolutely true. This was a wonderful place to slow down and live life more fully. Anna reminded herself of this very fact as she sat outside watching the moon rise over the river later that evening—it was enchanting. It was just that this part of the river could be a very lonely place too. Of course, she reminded herself, she'd rather be lonely here on the beautiful river than back in Pine Ridge. Because the truth was, that had been lonely too.

13

Energized by Hazel's praise and encouragement and the inspiration that she might actually turn her property into a profitable inn, Anna worked harder than she'd ever worked before. Yet at each day's end, she never felt as bone-tired as she'd been while working for her mother-in-law. "I suppose that's the difference between freedom and slavery," she told Hazel one evening as they relaxed in the wicker chairs on the front porch of the store—or rather what used to be the store. Anna was starting to call it the inn now.

"It is surprising how industry is impacted by ownership." Hazel patted the rocking chair arms.

"You did a lovely job on renovating these old chairs, Anna."

Anna had found the pair of old rockers in the attic a few days ago. After cleaning them up, she'd used her basket-weaving skills to repair the seats, then sewn cushions from old pillows to pad them even more. "I remember when I was little and my parents would sit out here in these chairs." She looked out over the river, which reflected the colors of the sunset—rose and peach and lilac. "And sometimes it would just be Daddy, Grandma, and me. And sometimes she would tell a story."

"Do you think all of her stories were from ancestors? Or is it possible she created some of them herself?"

Anna thought about it. "To be honest, I thought she made up all of them herself. As a child, I didn't really understand how stories were passed on from generation to generation. And I knew that so much had been lost. I feel sad now thinking of all the things I never thought to ask her. All the history I might've gotten from her, things that would help you too."

"You were a child, Anna. How would you know? Besides, your father did a lovely job of saving things. He must've loved you and his mother-in-law a lot. That's quite a heritage, if you ask me."

"Daddy was a very special man."

"You mentioned that he came from Sweden, but not much else about his history."

"It's funny, isn't it? I know less about my own father than my grandmother. Although I have found a box of letters and things of his in the attic. Some are from Sweden, although I can't read them since they're in Swedish, at least I assume that's what it is."

"You could get them translated."

"Maybe I will someday when I have time. But Daddy never spoke much of Sweden. I got the feeling he wanted to forget about it."

"What brought him way out here, I wonder."

Anna laughed. "The gold, of course. He'd heard there was still gold to be found down in southern Oregon. But he soon realized he wasn't cut out to be a miner. So he came up here to work as a logger. Daddy was young and big and strong, and he used to fell trees with a diameter wider than he was tall. And not with power saws either. But he hurt his back and had to look for another line of work. And then he met my mother and they decided to open this store."

"I wonder how they could afford to start it up. A young couple like that—he being an immigrant, she being an Indian."

"Oh, that was because of Babette." By now, Hazel had met Babette, and the two had gotten along wonderfully. "Her husband, Pierre, had been a good friend of Daddy's and Pierre had struck it rich down on the Rogue. After his death, Babette came up here. My parents were already married and Daddy wasn't logging anymore, but they were trying to get the store started up by selling things from a little house Daddy had built for them." Anna pointed down to the dock. "It was gone by the time I was born. But it used to be right down there, next to the river."

"What happened to the building?"

"Daddy took it apart and used the lumber to make the outhouses." Anna laughed. "I remember him saying that it hadn't been much bigger than an outhouse anyway."

"Because Babette was a partner in the store, they were able to build bigger and better, and they could afford to stock it with good merchandise. Babette used to help to buy for the store. That's how she met Bernard, her second husband. He didn't really like Babette working for the store though. And it wasn't long until Daddy paid Babette back every penny of her investment with interest. I remember him saying it wasn't good for friends to owe friends for anything except friendship. And Babette was one of our closest friends. Like an aunt to me."

"She's a lovely woman."

Anna looked out over the dusky blue light now blanketing the river. "You know, Hazel, I am almost perfectly happy right now."

"Almost?"

"I just wish that things were different between Lauren and me."

Hazel nodded. "There might not be much you can do about that, dear. Speaking from experience, daughters sometimes take time to appreciate their mothers."

Anna sighed. "I'm afraid I might be reaping what I sowed."

"But you loved your mother."

"Yes. But I didn't really understand her. And I never made much effort to get back here to see her."

"But that was understandable. With a baby, a seriously ill husband, a controlling mother-in-law . . . what choice did you have?"

"If I'd been stronger, I would've figured out a way to come back. I would've brought Lauren. Maybe Adam too. Maybe he would've gotten well if he'd been here." Anna felt a lump in her throat.

"There are no sadder words than *what might've been*."

Anna just nodded.

"Except that you have to let them go, dear. As much as I love history—and you know that I do—we cannot wallow in the mistakes of the past. Look at your grandmother, Anna, she didn't wallow now, did she?"

Anna couldn't help chuckling. "No. Grandma Pearl was not one to wallow in anything."

"And neither are you."

"I hope that's true."

"How long does it take to get to the ocean?" Hazel asked suddenly. "I mean if I were to plan a trip to the beach. How long would it take me to get there from here?"

"Well, you know how long it takes to get down the river to Florence. Then it's another fifteen minutes or so by car. You have to go around the jetty, either south over the bridge, or north over to Heceta, to get to a beach." Anna was surprised. "You haven't been to the beach yet?"

"Not yet. I was so anxious to begin my work up the river, I never took the time." She stood. "When was the last time you were at the beach, Anna?"

"Oh," Anna stood too, "goodness, it's been quite some time. Probably before I was married."

Hazel turned on her flashlight beam now, shining it over toward her cabin and meandering that way. "One of these days, you and I will have to take a holiday and go to the beach," she called over her shoulder. "You know what they say about all work and no play."

Anna laughed. "I know what they say, but I'm enjoying my work so much that it almost feels like play to me."

Hazel stopped and turned and grinned. "I know exactly what you mean, Anna. Goodnight now."

Anna said goodnight, waiting until she saw the

light go on in the cabin before she turned off the porch light. Just like Daddy used to do for Grandma. Then instead of going into the house, she went inside the old store and looked around. This was part of her future inn. Or so she was telling herself. And that was what had motivated her the past few days to clear and clean out this space. She'd moved some of the shelving units into the back room and some of them were simply pushed up against the wall so that at the moment it was simply a very large open space. But she could imagine it differently. With some interior walls, she felt it could be divided into four rather comfortable rooms.

She imagined each with its own private outdoor entrance, and some new large picture windows to let in light. Two rooms would overlook the river, and the other two would look out toward the woods. Combined with the two extra bedrooms upstairs (not counting her own) that would make six rooms that could be rented, plus the cabin. What she couldn't quite figure out now was the bathrooms. She thought perhaps the back room, which was now used for storage, might be able to be worked into some sort of bathroom with showers. And since it already had a sink plumbed into it—something her mother had insisted upon for reasons of hygiene—that might simplify matters.

In the meantime, if she really did manage to

lure some poor unsuspecting guests up here, she hoped they would be good-natured outdoorsy types who wouldn't protest over using an outhouse. Or maybe this was simply a pipe dream. But she'd been going over her finances, budgeting for what she thought she might need, and unless she was overlooking something, she thought she might be able to do this. Or at least try.

She turned off the lights and the generator, then, using her own flashlight, went upstairs where she lit a kerosene lamp and sat down at the kitchen table to go over her notes regarding her inn. She was calling it The Inn at Shining Waters to honor her grandmother. As she went over the figures again, she felt hopeful enough to make the decision to order a few things, including a new mattress to replace the one she'd put in the cabin. Her plan was to get the spare bedrooms up here into shape for renting initially. She'd already cleaned them and removed all personal items. Next she would repaint them and replace the curtains and linens and things to make them look welcoming—like what she'd done in the cabin.

She would also order another pair of beds to go downstairs. Even without the additional windows, doors, and walls that she hoped to put in someday, she felt she could make the space habitable and comfortable for hunters or fishermen in the interim. The dark fir floors were handsome, albeit a bit worn, and the wood-burning stove still worked. With a braided rug and a couple of comfortable chairs, it might even be cozy. She would put up some plaid curtains and add some rustic touches to make it look like a hunting lodge.

As Anna got ready for bed, she knew she had an ulterior motive for doing all this work—something that would reward her efforts even more than the possibility of making an income. She hoped that once the place was nicely fixed up, she would be able to entice Lauren to come out here. If she could convince her that it had been transformed into a nice little river inn, complete with telephones and electricity, perhaps Lauren might even invite her friends to accompany her on a little summer vacation before going off to college. With recreational possibilities on the river and the nearby beach, it seemed entirely feasible. At least that was what Anna was telling herself—and that was what drove her to work so hard. She was doing it for Lauren as much as she was doing it for herself.

After breakfast was cleaned up, Anna made a list of things she wanted to get in town. Unfortunately, she'd been unable to start the engine on Daddy's old boat, but she planned to canoe over to Babette's. If nothing else, she could place a phone order for more groceries. Or perhaps Babette would be planning a trip into town and she could tag along with her. Or she might get lucky and spot Henry coming or going. She could wave him down and catch a ride, and perhaps, if he wasn't too pressed for time, he'd be willing to take a look at Daddy's old motor because Anna knew she would either need to get it fixed or replace it. One couldn't live on the river without transportation. And a dugout canoe just wouldn't suffice—especially in bad weather.

She had just changed her clothes and was going for her canoe when she heard an engine. But it wasn't coming from the river. She went over to the back of the house to see a blue pickup driving onto her property, right through the grassy meadow directly toward her garden, which was already showing signs of life. Angry that whoever was trespassing so recklessly might drive right through her garden, she ran over, waving her arms and shouting, "Stop! stop!"

The pickup truck stopped and to her surprise, Clark jumped out. "Is something wrong?" he called out with concern.

"Oh!" She hurried over. "I just didn't want you to drive through my garden." She pointed to where the young plants were just beginning to sprout. "I was afraid you couldn't see it because of the meadow."

He nodded. "You're right, I couldn't."

"What are you doing out here anyway?" She

felt her heart give a little lurch at the color of those eyes again: like the river on a clear October day—deep topaz blue.

"The power and light guys are on their way, as well as the telephone company. I scheduled them both for today. I was afraid they might've gotten here before me." He looked around a bit nervously. "They didn't, did they?"

"No. No one's been here."

Hazel was walking toward them now. "I thought I heard a vehicle," she called out. "What are you doing here?"

He explained and they hugged. "I didn't know you'd be coming out again," she told him. "But it's a pleasure to see you."

"I just wanted to make sure things were done right," he told them. "This is a lovely parcel of land and it needs to be protected as much as possible. However, that will take some work." He looked at his mother now. "It might be better if you ladies weren't here during the installation process. It will probably get loud and messy." He glanced uneasily at Anna. "And stressful."

Hazel nodded as if considering this. Now she pointed to the pickup. "Do you need your truck today, Son?"

He shrugged. "Not once I unload some tools and things."

"Maybe I could borrow your truck and take Anna to the beach."

"That's a great idea, Mom."

"But I—"

"Remember about all work no play," Hazel told her. "And wouldn't it be a lovely day to go to the beach?"

Anna considered this. "I suppose so. Do you think I could run a couple errands in town before we come back?"

"I don't see why not."

So Anna and Hazel hurried to get what they'd need and Anna told Clark to make himself at home. "We'll be back before dark," Hazel promised.

"How do you get to the beach from here?" Anna asked suddenly. "I've never been on the road back there before."

Clark explained which turns to take and just like that, with Hazel at the wheel, they were on their way. "Well, this sure wasn't what I expected to be doing today," Anna told her as they bumped along through the meadow and then through a dirty path that cut between the trees and eventually turned into an uneven gravel road.

"Here come the power and light boys," Hazel said as a big truck forced them to pull off the road to allow them access. Not long after that, the truck from the telephone company forced them off again. "I think Clark was smart to send us packing today," she told Anna. "It'll probably be rather hectic at your place."

"I'm glad Clark is there to manage all of it." Anna sighed. She didn't even want to think of what would be going on there or if she'd be coming home to a mess of cables and wires and poles everywhere. Suddenly she wondered if the modern conveniences were really worth the effort. However, if those things made it more comfortable for Lauren to come visit—then it didn't matter if a few lines and wires cut into the landscape. Just being able to pick up the phone and call her daughter—now, wouldn't that be worth everything?

14

When Anna noticed Hazel pulling a familiar-looking black notebook from the bag she'd brought down to the beach, Anna shook her finger at her. "You said all work and no play," she reminded her.

Hazel just laughed as she opened up Daddy's old notebook of stories. "This is part work and part play. Besides that, it's just plain good reading."

Anna smoothed out the blanket she'd brought for them to sit on, wishing she'd had a good book to bring along with her. But she'd long since finished the one she'd picked up at a bus stop on the way to Florence a couple weeks ago. Maybe she'd find something to read in town while doing errands later. For now—and for a change—she would do nothing.

They'd already walked up and down the beach, admiring the white frothy surf, spotting fishing boats not far off, collecting a few shells and even a couple of sand dollars. They'd even removed their shoes and waded in the cold water. Anna had gone out far enough to get the bottoms of her rolled-up pant legs soggy.

As she unrolled her still-damp pant legs, she thought perhaps she really was due for a nice little rest. Lying back on the warm woolly blanket, she closed her eyes, letting sun soak into her as the sound of the waves lulled her into a delightful stupor.

"Nothing quite like the ocean to revive your senses," Hazel said as Anna sat up and rubbed her eyes.

A slight breeze was blowing now, and the sun had moved down the sky a bit. It looked to be around two perhaps. Anna checked her watch to see it was close to three already. "Goodness, I've been asleep for quite a while."

"It's this restorative sea air." Hazel took in a deep breath. "Good for what ails you."

"But I'll bet you're getting hungry." Since they hadn't had time to pack any food, they had planned to get lunch in town.

"I know you still want to do your errands," Hazel said as she stiffly pushed herself to her feet. "Perhaps we can find something quick along the way to munch on."

Anna agreed and they packed up their things and, after stopping for hot dogs at the Heceta Beach camp store, were soon on their way back into town. As Hazel drove, Anna told her about how she planned to move forward on getting the rooms in the house ready for the inn. "I've decided to call it The Inn at Shining Waters," Anna told her, trying the name out loud to see how it felt and sounded.

"The Inn at Shining Waters," Hazel repeated it slowly. "That's lovely, Anna. I know a name like that would get my attention."

"Do you think I'm being foolish?" Anna asked suddenly. "I mean . . . to start spending money—when my finances are already so limited—to develop the place into an inn?"

"I think you're being brave and entrepreneurial. Like I've told you before, you did a marvelous job getting the little cabin ready for me. And every time I turn around you've done some other clever improvement to the place. Like the rocking chairs out on the porch—so delightful. I think you have a gift for hospitality, Anna. And it is wise to use the gifts we have. I do not think you're foolish."

Anna felt a wave of relief. "That's why I wanted to do errands in town," she confessed. "I have a list of things I'd like to purchase for the

inn. And I couldn't wait to get started on it."
Now she rattled off some of the things she hoped
to find or order. "I realize we don't have much
time before the stores begin to close, but I'll
make the most of it. Then I'll arrange for Henry
to make a delivery."

"And we can probably bring some of the larger
things home in the back of the pickup," Hazel
said eagerly. "That is, if you find what you need
today."

Anna pointed to a furniture store. "Let's try
that first." She pulled out her list, skimming over
it as Hazel parked.

"And look—there's a secondhand furniture
store just two doors down," Hazel told her.

"Let's go there first," Anna said eagerly.

After some looking around, Anna managed to
discover a number of treasures, including a pair
of dark red, overstuffed club chairs. "I know the
color is a little strong, but I think they'll be
perfect downstairs by the woodstove," she told
Hazel. She also found a pair of matching twin-
sized bed frames in a honey-colored maple, some
bedside tables, a large dresser, several
mismatched lamps, and an old Oriental rug. "I
realize these things are rather old-fashioned,"
she told Hazel after she'd paid the man, "but I
think they'll be perfect for my inn."

"I have no doubt about that."

As the salesman and another employee loaded

her purchases into the back of the pickup, Anna and Hazel went over to the new furniture store. "Look at the prices," Anna whispered to Hazel. "So much more than what I paid for the used pieces."

Hazel nodded. "I'll say. And not any better quality if you ask me."

Anna had to agree. All the modern furniture had a flimsy look and feel to it, as if it wouldn't last more than a few years. However, she knew that Lauren loved this new look and if money were no object, Anna would have done the whole house in this contemporary style if that would ensure that Lauren would fall in love with the place and feel at home on the river. But money was an object. Truth be told, Anna was slightly relieved because she actually liked the substantial feel of the used pieces she'd chosen and she couldn't wait to see how they all looked when she put them together in her inn.

The only reason Anna found herself in the new furniture store was because she was determined to purchase new mattresses. The idea of sleeping on used mattresses, unless she knew who'd used them, was not appealing.

"I wonder," she asked the salesman, "if you would consider giving me a discount if I were to buy four new mattresses?"

"Four?" He looked surprised. "What are you doing? Running a boarding house?"

She smiled and told him about the inn she was opening. "I'll need one full-sized mattress and three twins."

"I'm sure we can work something out to make everyone happy." Then he introduced himself as Carl Edwards, the owner. And before long, he was showing her his selection of mattresses, explaining why some were better than others. She made her choices and paid for them, and he promised to see they got delivered next week. She felt slightly giddy at the amount of money she was spending, but continued to tell herself it was an investment in her future.

At the dry goods store, Anna picked out what seemed to be sensible linens. She suspected that Babette would suggest something more elegant if she were here, but for now, these durable white sheets and towels would have to suffice. Until she replaced her mother's old wringer washer—and she had no idea when that would happen—strong durable linens would be the only way to go. Plus white would not fade when it was line-dried in the sun—it would simply smell fresh and clean. She also got a few new blankets and pillows. For the tops of the beds, she planned to use some of the lovely patchwork quilts her mother had made over the years, quilts that had rarely seen the light of day, but would now proudly add color and charm to each room.

Next they went to the hardware store where

Anna gave the owner, George, who happened to be an old schoolmate, a list of things she wanted delivered up the river.

"Would you like this to go on your account?" George asked.

"I don't have an account," she told him.

He nodded. "Oh, sure you do, Anna, it's the same one your folks had for as long as this store's been here. Ain't never been closed."

"Oh." She felt worried now. "Do I owe anything on it?"

"Nope. Not a cent."

She smiled. "Well, that's good to know. Just the same, I'll just pay cash for this order."

"No problem with that." He glanced over her list, asking for some clarification on a couple of items then promised to give Henry a call to arrange for the delivery. "You have a good day," he told her. "It's nice to have you back. Now don't be a stranger, you hear?"

She thanked him, assuring him that she had lots of fixing up to do on the place and would probably become one of his regular customers. Naturally, he seemed pleased by this.

Finally, they stopped at the grocery store, where she gave Mr. Greeley her rather large order, picked up a few items to tide them over until it was delivered, and paid her bill in full. Feeling emboldened by her success, she told Mr. Greeley her plans to turn the old store into an inn.

He rubbed his chin and smiled. "An inn, you say?"

"That's right. I'm starting out small, just a few rooms, but I plan to grow it over time."

"And here I was getting all worked up that you were out there turning your place back into a store again. I thought for sure I was going to lose some business."

She laughed as she tucked the receipt in her purse. "No. I have no desire to run a store. But I would like to see how I can manage running an inn."

He nodded. "That's not a bad idea. If I hear of anyone looking for a room on the river, I'll be sure to send 'em your way."

"I'd appreciate that."

She and Hazel each carried a grocery bag out to the pickup. "Goodness," Anna said when she saw the fully loaded blue truck. "I hope Clark won't mind that we put his vehicle to such use."

Hazel laughed as she placed her bag on the seat between them. "I'm sure he'll appreciate your industry, Anna. He puts this truck to good use himself."

"I hope everything's going well at home." Anna felt worried again. What if everything was torn up now? What if they'd trampled her garden, or placed power poles where they'd obstruct the view? Or ran helter-skelter? What if her lovely property had suddenly turned into an unattractive, unappealing place to live? Then who would want to visit there or pay to stay in a room? She could just see it in her mind's eye—a picture of chaos and destruction where peace and tranquillity once reigned.

She glanced back at the pickup bed, filled with all she'd purchased. What a fool she'd been to spend her money like that. She'd heard the saying "counting your chickens before they hatch" and now she realized that was exactly what she'd done. How foolish. As Hazel drove the truck down the highway, Anna felt like her dreams of a sweet little river inn were going up in a puff of electrical smoke and telephone wires. Oh, why had she allowed modernization to come?

"I can tell you're quite worried about something, dear." Hazel glanced over at her as she stopped to turn off the highway.

"Is it that obvious?"

"I noticed you clutching your purse handle as if holding on for dear life." Hazel turned onto the side road now. "Either my driving is worse than I imagined or you are fretting over something. Which is it, dear? I can slow down if you like, although we're almost to the back road where I'll have to go slow anyway."

"No, no . . . your driving is just fine, Hazel." Now Anna confessed the horrible picture she'd just imagined, with dozens of power poles and lines and wires and piles of dirt and destruction. "Sort of like the scene of a bloody battlefield after everyone's been slaughtered," she said sadly.

"Oh, my. I don't think it will be as bad as all that."

"I sure hope not."

Now, probably to distract Anna's overactive imagination, Hazel offered to tell her another one of Anna's grandmother's stories. "You might relate to this one just now," she began. "I'm sure you've heard it before, but it's good practice for me to tell it. It helps me to translate what your father wrote down."

"Which story is it?" Anna asked with vague interest.

"It's about the cave monster."

"The *cave monster?*" Anna frowned. "I don't remember a story like that."

Hazel chuckled. "Perhaps they felt it was too scary for your young ears."

"Well, my ears aren't young now," she declared. "I'd like to hear it."

"Good." Hazel cleared her throat, looking straight ahead as she held onto the steering wheel with both hands, turning onto the graveled road. "Long, long ago in the cave by the beach there lived a fearsome cave monster. He was big and hairy with long sharp teeth and claws. Every living thing within miles feared this cave monster, and naturally, the horrible cave monster only came out at night."

"Naturally." Anna smiled at how Hazel always put her own little touches on these stories. Perhaps that was what Grandma had done too. Maybe everyone did that in their own way.

"But when the monster came out at night, he always killed and destroyed and devoured anything in his path, wiping out seals and sea lions and beaver and otters—he'd tear them to pieces then eat them whole, flesh and hair and bone, nothing left. No living creature was safe when the cave monster roamed at night."

"No wonder Grandma didn't tell me this story. I probably would've had terrible nightmares."

"So one day the chief of the sea lions decided he'd had enough of the cave monster. He wanted to get rid of him once and for all. But he wasn't sure how to do it. So the chief of the sea lions went to see Old Otter, because everyone knew Old Otter was very wise. The chief of the sea lions asked Old Otter how they could get rid of the cave monster."

"And?" Anna waited.

"Old Otter told the sea lion chief to gather up all the seaweed in the sea and to have his sea lions braid it together to make a long, long rope. Then he said to tie this rope to the biggest spear they had and to throw it at the sun. Then, when it hit the sun, they were to all pull together to haul down the sun and hide it so that daytime looked like night."

"Was the chief sea lion able to do this?"

"Yes. He did as Old Otter said and pulled down the sun and hid it. Naturally, the cave monster thought it was nighttime, so he emerged from his cave and was about to start slaughtering everything he could find—but just then the sea lions released their hold on the sun and it shot back into the sky so it was light and bright and daytime again."

"And?" Anna was actually curious now.

"And the brightness of the sun caused the cave monster to go completely blind and as he tried to stumble back to his cave, the sea lion chief picked up the spear he'd used on the sun and killed the cave monster so that he could never wreak havoc among them again."

Anna clapped her hands. "Good! Because that cave monster sounded like a really nasty fellow."

Hazel nodded. "Isn't it interesting how the fear of darkness translates across all cultures? It doesn't matter what part of the earth one is from, that thing that goes bump in the night scares everyone."

"Perhaps because there have always been real dangers at night," Anna said. "There still are in some places today. Even on the river there are cougars, bears, bobcats—they all feed at night—

and you don't really want to come up on one unawares."

"That's true enough. But I suppose I was wondering more about the metaphor in general. Darkness can symbolize ignorance, a lack of enlightenment, and sometimes we are most afraid of what we don't know—what we can't see or hear or understand unsettles us. In the darkest hours of our ignorance, our imaginations and fears can run amok. Whereas, we don't usually feel the same way in the clarity of daytime—or when we're fully aware of what's going on. Does that make any sense?"

"Sure. It's like how I'm rather worried about what my property will look like when we get back. Because I honestly don't know what is entailed in getting the electricity and telephones set up. It's like I'm in the dark; therefore, I'm probably imagining the worst." At least she hoped that would be the case.

"Yes, that's a good example. But also, consider something more serious like racism, which I believe is the consequence of ignorance—and for some people the differences they see in others is a lot like darkness; they don't understand it so they are frightened. Right now there are white people in the Deep South who are uninformed and ignorant. They don't understand African Americans, or Negroes as they call them, so they become fearful. They imagine the worst about their dark-skinned neighbors—and it leads them to do the worst."

"Just like with white men and Indians," Anna said sadly.

"Unfortunately. Fear and misunderstanding are bred in the absence of enlightenment."

"So those people, the ones who live in ignorance of their fellow man, are not unlike the cave monster," Anna mused. "If they choose to live in darkness they set themselves up to become destructive."

Hazel nodded eagerly. "You are quite right, dear. It makes me wonder if there's a hidden meaning in the cave monster story. You see, I think these stories have truths in them on various levels. They are not merely fables to entertain listeners by the campfire, but they might contain the wisdom of the ages—if we really listened."

The cab of the pickup grew quiet now, except for the rattling noises as the truck bumped along the rutted road. Anna looked out at the trees and thick foliage, wondering what area of her own life was in darkness—what was it that made her most fearful? Of course, it was probably her fear of poverty. Beaten into her by her mother-in-law over the past twenty years, Anna couldn't begin to count how many times Eunice had warned her that without Eunice's money and provision, Anna and Lauren would've been destitute and homeless.

Suddenly, as if a light had gone on, Anna realized that Eunice had been the cave monster in her life. Eunice had used the darkness (in this case, Anna's ignorance) to frighten and control her daughter-in-law and, in essence, devour her soul, which was far worse than destroying her flesh and bones. Eunice was Anna's cave monster! She considered telling this to Hazel, except that Hazel seemed to be in deep reflection herself. Besides, Anna realized, she needed to deal with her own cave monster. But how was she to do that? What would Old Otter tell her? Spear the sun and hide it until Eunice came out? Or perhaps she was being too literal.

Anna felt that if she continued to grow strong and independent and capable to provide for herself, she would reach the place where she never needed to depend on or be fearful of Eunice again. Perhaps Anna was already at that place but simply didn't realize it. Anyway, it was food for thought. And it made for a good story. Perhaps one day Anna would have a notebook full of her own stories to tell. Although she wasn't sure who she would tell them to . . . or who would want to listen.

15

To Anna's huge relief, her property didn't look a bit like a war zone when they got home. She could see tire tracks through the meadow and there were a few dirt piles, but all in all, not much had changed. In fact, as they got out of the pickup, she wondered if any of the improvements had actually been completed. Of course, she had mixed feelings about this. On one hand, she'd be relieved to keep everything just as it had been. On the other hand, she had been looking forward to a real telephone conversation with her daughter.

Clark, with what appeared to be a tool belt around his waist, came over to greet them. "How was the beach?" He frowned at the back of the truck now. "Don't tell me you ladies found all that on the beach?"

Hazel laughed. "Aren't we good beachcombers?"

"No," Anna assured him. "Those are things for my inn."

He nodded with a curious expression. "I see."

"And you're just in time to help unload them," Hazel told him as she removed a grocery bag from the cab.

"Were the men able to put in the electricity and telephone?" Anna asked as she reached for the other bag.

"Your phone is hooked up. The electrical work is done, but I still need to finish some things up before we actually power up the house."

"Really?" Anna looked around in surprise. "Where are the electric lines and wires and things?"

"You mean you *wanted* to see wires and lines?" Clark opened the tailgate of his pickup.

"Well . . . not really, but I assumed that was the price one paid for modernizations."

He chuckled. "Not when I'm the contractor. I had the power company bring out a trencher." He pointed to where a narrow trail of dirt went along one side of the meadow. She hadn't even noticed it before. "That's where all your electrical wires and telephone lines are: underground."

Anna's face broke into a huge smile. "Oh, that's perfect! Thank you for thinking of that, Clark."

He grinned. "You didn't think I'd let anyone spoil this beautiful place you have here, did you?"

"Your mother assured me there was no reason to worry." She sighed. "But I just didn't have any idea how you'd do it. I am so relieved!"

"And I'm starving." He pulled one of the nightstands out of the truck. "If I unload this is there any chance I can get something to eat?"

"Dinner will be ready in about twenty—make that thirty minutes—but if you're really hungry come on up and I'll find something to—"

"Thirty minutes is perfect." He nodded to the back of the pickup. "Where does all this go anyway?"

"Just put it down there for now." She pointed to the space she'd just cleared out. "Thank you!" Then she hurried on up the stairs and began to unload the groceries. Hoping Clark would stay for dinner tonight, she'd gotten some nice rib-eye steaks and a few other things.

"Need any help?" Hazel asked as she emerged from the bathroom.

"No, I think I've got it covered. Clark is staying for dinner—and it sounds like he's ravenous. It'll take me about thirty minutes to get it on the table."

"And you really don't need help?"

Anna tossed her a confident smile. "I'm fine, Hazel. Trust me, I'm used to this. Sometimes my mother-in-law would plan a dinner party for eight and only give me a couple hours' worth of notice. Thirty minutes for three people is a piece of cake—just don't expect cake."

Hazel laughed. "Then, if you don't mind, I'll just sit here and put my feet up."

"Make yourself at home."

Anna was actually thankful to work in the kitchen alone. Having no distractions was always the fastest way for her to get things done. She used to try to put Lauren to work, hoping she'd learn how to cook a little, but Lauren usually dragged her heels and as a result everything ended up taking longer. Now if Babette was here, it would be different. Babette knew her way around a kitchen and usually she was telling Anna what to do. But when it came to the basics, Anna had it down.

While the steaks were broiling, she boiled potatoes for mashing, finished making a chopped lettuce and tomato and cucumber salad, heated some canned green beans, and put bread and butter on the table. She opened a jar of bread-and-butter pickles and put them in a pretty dish. Then she opened a can of peaches, arranged the yellow halves on a lettuce-lined plate, filled their centers with dollops of cottage cheese, and topped them with maraschino cherries. Nothing fancy, for sure, but at least it was quick.

She was just putting the heated platter of steaks on the table when Clark came in. "Boy, does something smell good in here. I washed up in the sink downstairs, but do you want me to take off my boots, they're a little—"

"No, no," she told him. "My father never took off his boots. These wood floors sweep up easily. And everything is ready."

"Wake up, Mom," he nudged Hazel. "Time to eat."

"Oh, my!" She sat up with wide eyes. "Wasn't that fast!" She walked over and looked at the table. "My, my, Anna, but you are a wonder!"

Anna laughed as they sat down. "Everything happens fast when you're asleep."

As before, Clark offered to say a blessing and as soon as he said "amen" Anna handed the steak plate to him. "The big one is for you."

"That's massive," he said as he forked it and lowered it to his plate, "but I have a feeling I'll have no trouble making it disappear."

Hazel and Clark visited, talking about their day, the time spent at the beach, and what they'd accomplished. And for a moment, Anna just sat there, listening and soaking it in—it felt almost like being a part of a family again. So much so that she actually got a lump in her throat and had to chew her bite of steak for a long time just to be sure she could swallow it.

As they all finished up, Anna apologized for not having made dessert. "This morning I had planned to make a chocolate cake, but our unexpected outing derailed that idea."

"As delicious as that sounds, I couldn't have eaten another bite anyway." He smiled at her. "That was one of the best meals I've ever eaten, Anna."

"Seriously?" She found this hard to believe. "Thank you. But, really, it wasn't anything fancy."

"Poor Clark," Hazel said, "he's been living on bachelor food for a long time."

"I'll admit my cooking isn't the greatest," he

told them, "but I eat in some pretty good restaurants too. And when I say this was one of the best meals I've had, I mean it."

Anna chuckled. "Well, you have to admit you said you were starving. Even a bad meal can taste good if you're hungry enough."

He shook his head. "No, Anna, I mean it. This was great. You're an excellent cook."

Hazel laughed. "I have to concur with him, Anna. And I've eaten enough of your cooking to know what I'm talking about."

Now Anna was embarrassed, feeling as if she'd been fishing for compliments, although that wasn't the case. Anyway, she thanked them and stood, beginning to clear the table. "Would anyone like coffee?"

They all agreed that coffee sounded good. "How about if I serve it outside," she offered. "We'll take another chair down and we can sit on the porch and enjoy the balmy evening."

So while Clark carried a chair down, Anna made coffee and, even though everyone claimed to be full, she remembered there were still a few lemon cookies left from what Babette had brought by a few days ago. So she put these on the tray as well, and then carried it all down to the porch where Clark and Hazel were already sitting.

"What a lovely ending to a lovely day," Hazel said happily. "Can you believe we had two gorgeous sunsets in a row, Anna?"

"Speaking of sunset," Anna said suddenly, "what are your plans, Clark? Did you get a room in town?"

"Not yet, but I plan to."

"But aren't you worried about driving your truck back in the dark tonight? That road seems challenging enough in the daylight. I can't imagine navigating it at night."

"And what if the cave monster comes out?" Hazel asked dramatically.

"Cave monster?" Clark sounded confused.

"It's a story," Anna explained. "But, really, I wouldn't like to think of you out on that road in the dark. You're welcome to stay here if you like. There's plenty of room."

"I suppose you could have the cabin," Hazel suggested. "You might be more comfortable there. And I could stay with Anna in the house."

"Oh, I don't want to put you out of your cozy cabin, Mom."

Anna knew that they were all uncomfortable with the idea of him spending the night in her house with her. The truth was, Anna was probably the most uncomfortable. But if she really planned to run an inn, she would have to get over it. She decided to just be open about it. "I do want this place to be an inn someday," she began carefully, "but I suppose I'm a bit uneasy about, well, having men—even nice ones such as yourself—staying in the house with me." She looked to Hazel for help. "Is that a bit silly on my part?"

"I can understand your concerns," Hazel told her. "Especially if you had strangers here. This is an isolated place, Anna. You'll need to keep that in mind."

"But I did want to set up some beds and things down here." Anna pointed to the room behind them. "I obviously don't have it all ready yet, but I might be able to get it set up for you, Clark, if you don't mind roughing it a bit."

He laughed. "I was actually thinking about just camping out under the stars tonight."

"Wouldn't you rather have a comfortable bed?"

He shrugged. "I suppose that would be nice."

"Why don't you help Anna set things up in there," Hazel suggested. "That way you won't have to sleep on the ground or drive all the way back to town."

"Sounds good to me, if Anna is OK with it."

"That'd be great. You can help me bring a mattress down from upstairs," Anna said suddenly. "There are new ones coming, but that one up there is perfectly fine. It was from the spare bed in my old bedroom and it rarely got used."

Suddenly, they were all up and moving. "You should turn in, Mom," Clark told her. "I can tell you're tired and you've had a long day."

"That's right," Anna agreed. "We can handle this. We'll have a makeshift room set up for Clark in no time."

"I am feeling a little worn out." Hazel rubbed her back as she stood. "And I must admit I'm relieved not to give up my little cabin. I'm getting quite comfortable in there, Anna. I might just take up permanent residence here if you don't watch out."

"That would be perfectly fine with me," Anna assured her.

While Clark walked his mother to her cabin, Anna went in and turned on the overhead light in the room where Clark had unloaded today's purchases. It was such a big space, she wished there was a way to make it more cozy. She moved some things around, pushing the two red chairs over by the old woodstove, laying out the carpet, which actually looked rather homey. Then she dragged the headboard to one of the beds, setting it near one of the windows at the front of the room. That might work. She slid one of the bedside tables over next to it and even set a lamp on it, although there was no outlet to plug it into there. But it did make it look a bit less like an empty storeroom.

"Looks like you've made a good start," Clark told her as he came in and looked around.

"Just playing house," she told him. "And feel free to put up the bed wherever you like."

"I like it right there." He pointed to the window. "I can even have fresh air if I want."

"Someday I'd like to redo this whole space." She waved her hands. "But not for a while, I'm afraid." She smiled at him, then suggested they move the mattress down and finish setting up. They went upstairs and he followed her into what had once been her room. Since returning to the river, she'd been sleeping in her parents' old room since she liked the light in there and how its window looked out over the river. She pointed to the only mattress remaining in the room. "That would be the one."

Before she could remove the bedding, Clark picked up the whole works, cradling it in his arms. "Then I'll just be on my way."

"Don't you want me to put on some fresh sheets and things?"

He laughed. "I don't care. Unless there's something special about these things and you want them left up here."

"No, of course not."

"Then I think I'll just take my bed and wish you goodnight."

Anna felt unsure now, as if she wasn't being a very good hostess. "You don't need any help?"

"No. I'll just put that bed frame together and put this mattress on it, and I'll be asleep before you know it."

"Would you mind turning off the generator down there?" she asked. "When you're done with the light, that is."

"No problem."

But as she was cleaning up in the kitchen, she realized that he would have no source of light whatsoever once the generator was off. What if he got up in the middle of the night and stumbled over some of the things piled up down there? So she grabbed one of the kerosene lamps and some matches and shoved a flashlight in her jacket pocket, hurried down, knocking quietly on the door. She explained her concerns about his lack of light and he opened the door to show her that the bed frame was already assembled. "It looks nice and solid too."

She smiled. "Oh, good, I'd hate to think of it collapsing on you in the middle of the night."

He laughed. "So would I." Now he lifted up the mattress and slightly disheveled bedding and put it onto the wooden frame. "There. That should be just fine."

"If it's too cool down here, feel free to make a fire," she told him.

"Thanks, but it feels just about perfect."

She just looked at him for a long moment. "Are you always so agreeable?"

He seemed to consider this. "Nope." He shook his head. "I can be downright cantankerous sometimes."

She tilted her head to one side. "I'm not sure I believe you."

"It's true. If one of my subcontractors doesn't deliver the level of workmanship I expect, I can get quite disagreeable."

"Well, that's understandable. You want a job done right."

"I appreciate quality." His face lit up with a smile. "And what I said about dinner tonight was absolutely true, Anna. That was quality."

"Well, thank you." She felt her cheeks warming again. "And thank you for ensuring the quality of work around here today." She clapped her hands together. "And that reminds me—I have a phone now. I could even call my daughter." She glanced at her watch. "And it's not even too late—for her anyway." And hopefully Eunice would've gone to bed by now; she often did.

"Don't let me keep you."

"Thanks again. And sleep well. Breakfast is usually around eight, if that's OK."

"Perfect."

She hurried up the stairs, planning out what she'd first say to Lauren, how she would carefully invite her to visit, painting a lovely picture of how nice it would be, and how Lauren could even bring her friends along if she liked, as soon as Anna got things set up—and that would be as soon as possible. Anna couldn't wait to hear her daughter's voice. She hoped Lauren would be glad to speak to her mother by now too. After all, wasn't absence supposed to make the heart grow fonder? Oh, how Anna missed her little girl!

16

Anna found the newly installed phone on the kitchen wall near the refrigerator. She couldn't believe she hadn't even noticed it there before. With trembling fingers, she placed the call, not even bothering to reverse the charges this time. And to her relief, Lauren answered with a cheerful *hello,* almost as if she'd been expecting someone to call her.

"Hello, Lauren, this is your mother. How are you, darling?"

"Mom?" Lauren sounded slightly irritated now. "Where are you?"

"I'm still here at my parents' home on the river. Didn't your grandmother tell you that I called not long ago? I told her I planned to stay a bit longer?"

"You mean you're *still* there?"

"Yes, I just got the telephone working again, and I had one installed in the kitchen too. That's where I am right now. I can't believe how well it works, honey. You sound as if you're in the very next room."

"Well, I'm *not* in the very next room. And neither are you. I cannot believe you're still there, Mom. Why haven't you come home by now?"

"Didn't you get my letter explaining all that?"

"Yes, but I didn't think you were serious. Do you really plan to stay down in that backwater place? How can you possibly stand it?"

"It's actually quite lovely here, Lauren. There are boats out running the river and I've even done some canoeing myself. And I've been visiting with friends. And I went to the beach today and it was so beautiful. I even waded in the ocean, then I took a nap in the sunshine. It's not always warm and sunny like that on the beach, but it was today."

"Oh, fine. So you're off lollygagging at the beach and playing on the river and I'm stuck here doing *all* the housework."

"You're doing *all* the housework?"

"Who do you think does your work when you're off on some never-ending vacation?"

"You mean you're doing *everything?*" Anna could not even imagine this.

"Well, not everything. How could I possibly do everything and have time for a life, which I barely do now anyway, thanks to you."

"Thanks to *me?*" Anna couldn't help feeling indignant. Who did Lauren think she was cleaning up after anyway?

"Because you're not here to do it, *Mom.*"

"And you think I should be there to clean up after everyone?"

"Well, it's your job, isn't it, Mom? That's what Grandmother says. She says if I should be mad at anyone, I should be mad at you."

"Oh." Why was Anna even surprised.

"Do you know what I am doing right now?" Lauren's voice was tight and angry and Anna imagined her down on her knees scrubbing a filthy toilet.

"No, dear . . . I uh can't . . ."

"I am folding laundry."

"Oh. Well, what's so terrible about that?"

"Folding stupid *towels!*" Now her voice had a high-pitched mimicking sound. "First you fold the towel the long way, in thirds, so it will hang on the towel bar nicely, and then you fold it in half and in half again, so it will sit in the linen cabinet nicely. Everything needs to be nice and neat and straight—in the stinking linen closet where no one even looks. Have you ever heard of anything so completely ridiculous in your life? They are just towels for Pete's sake, who cares how they are folded or if they are folded at all?"

Anna remembered when Eunice had taught her to fold towels "properly" too. But she'd been doing it for so long, she never even thought about it now. However, she'd been about the same age as Lauren and her initial reaction had been similar back then.

"I'm sorry, Lauren."

"That's all you can say, Mom? That you're sorry? What about me? I feel like Cinderella—I mean Cinderella *before* the prince, back when she had to do everything herself—and I don't have any little mice to help me."

"If it's any comfort, I do understand." Anna did understand . . . only too well. "And I know how you feel, but—"

"You know but you don't care, *do you?*" Lauren sounded like she was on the verge of tears now.

"I do care, Lauren. I honestly didn't realize that you'd get stuck with all the housework after I left."

"Well, who did you think was going to do it?"

"I thought maybe your grandmother would help out. Or hire someone."

"She keeps saying you're coming back. You are, aren't you, Mom?" The pleading in Lauren's tone sounded genuine now, like she really did want her mother to come back. The question was why did she want her to come back?

"I don't know, Lauren. If I did come back, some things would have to change. Big things. And I'm afraid your grandmother wouldn't agree to it."

"What kinds of things?"

"For starters, I can't keep being your grandmother's slave. I'd need to be respected as a member of the household—not like an employee, one who isn't even paid." Anna sighed. "Really, I don't think any of that will ever happen anyway, Lauren. Your grandmother is too set in her ways."

"But if she agreed to those things? Would you come back then?"

Anna wanted to say no, she would never come back. But there was Lauren to think about. How could she burn that bridge? "If you could get your grandmother to change that drastically, Lauren, I'd be willing to discuss it with her. But the last time I spoke with her, I didn't get the impression she was open to that sort of a relationship."

"Well, I'll talk to her, Mom. I'll make her see that she needs to be nicer to you. I know she's been unfair to you. And now she's doing the same thing to me. She can't keep treating people like that. She needs to understand that."

Anna smiled. "Well, darling, if anyone can make your grandmother understand that, it might be you."

"I should go now. Susan is supposed to call and the line will be busy. But I will talk to Grandmother."

Anna looked at the phone now, seeing the number in the white circle. "Let me give you my telephone number, in case you need to reach me." She told her the number and Lauren insisted she needed to go to take Susan's call.

"Good luck with your grandmother," Anna told her as they said good-bye. "I'll be curious to hear how it goes."

She hung up the phone and returned to cleaning up the dinner things. She wanted to get them done before the generator was shut down, but just in case, she lit a kerosene lamp and set it by the sink. But the electricity went out just as she started to wash the dishes. Of course, this had no effect on the hot water and, she decided, washing dishes by kerosene lamplight was rather nice. She hoped the dishes would come out clean. However, she told herself, even after the electric was hooked up, she might have to wash dishes by kerosene light from time to time. Just for the fun of it.

She chuckled to think of Lauren complaining about folding the towels. What Lauren didn't have the sense to appreciate was that those towels had been tumbled soft in an electric clothes dryer. What if she'd had to wash the towels in a wringer washer, like Anna had been doing lately, then lug them outside in order to hang them to dry? How would Lauren like to remove the towels from the line later, attempting to fold them in thirds after they'd become stiff as a board?

As Anna watched the dishwater draining out of the sink, she wished she'd gone ahead and invited Lauren to come out here for a visit after all. Maybe Lauren would've been tempted by the lure of escaping the drudgery of folding towels or other forms of menial housework. Although it was impossible to imagine Lauren or Eunice stooping to such drudgery as scrubbing floors or cleaning toilets. Not only did they lack the skills, they lacked the wardrobe. Despite glossy advertisements, high heels and housework did not mix.

Anna hated to think what the house might look like by now, or how long it would take to get it back to shipshape, the way Eunice had always insisted it must stay. The kitchen alone would be a fright. And even though Eunice had told Anna in no uncertain terms to *never ever* use the automatic dishwasher (Eunice insisted the dishes never came out clean enough) Anna would lay bets that that particular appliance was in full operation now.

Anna rose early the next morning. Partly because she wanted to get a head start on the day and partly because she was concerned that Clark or even Hazel might wish to take a morning shower and she wanted to be sure to be finished with her own morning grooming before either of them came up. This business of only have one fully operable bathroom might put a damper on her plans for an inn. Although Hazel hadn't complained about her lack of facilities and had only bathed up here a couple of times, claiming that too much showering was hard on old skin (Babette said the same thing), so maybe Anna didn't need to be too up in arms quite yet.

But it did feel good to be clean and fresh—and neatly dressed—and ready for the day. She realized she'd taken more care than usual today and although she didn't want to consciously think about it, she knew the reason for this effort had slept in the old storeroom last night. Of course, it was difficult for her to attempt to look very stylish. She'd long since given up on that. It hadn't helped that Lauren, once she'd become a teenager, made it perfectly clear that Anna was far beyond help in that area anyway.

Fortunately, not many people here on the river (including Babette) were overly fashionable. Most leaned toward the practical. Although sometimes, like today, Anna wished she had something more feminine to wear than her crisp white shirt tucked into her neatly belted jeans with loafers. However, she had tied a red and blue scarf around her neck. It was somewhat jaunty and might even pass for fashion in some places, like the river.

"Don't you look pretty this morning," Hazel said as she poured herself a cup of coffee.

"Thank you." Anna smiled nervously. Maybe the scarf was a bit much.

"Clark said he slept divinely last night."

"Divinely?"

Hazel pursed her lips. "Perhaps he said 'heavenly.'"

"Oh, that's good."

"And he's already bathed and—"

"Bathed?" Anna paused from turning the bacon.

"In the river." Hazel chuckled. "I told him he might be taking after his great-grandfather after all, and he said that maybe it was about time."

"Oh." Anna wasn't sure how to respond to that. Instead she peeked into the oven to check the status of the huckleberry muffins, which hadn't even risen yet.

"I don't know if Clark's had a chance to tell you anything about his wife—I should say ex-wife—but she was not an easy woman by any means."

"I see . . ." Anna cracked eggs into a bowl with her back to Hazel. She was extremely curious to hear this, but didn't want to seem overly eager. Although she did wonder why Hazel was going on so about Clark.

"The truth is, I had my doubts about Roselyn right from the beginning." Hazel came over to the stove now, speaking in an intimate tone as if worried Clark might walk in on her disclosure. "And I suppose I've always been extra protective of my boy. You may have wondered why his name is Richards and mine is Chenowith. Well, Richards was my maiden name. I assume you know what that means."

Anna turned down the flame under the bacon and barely nodded.

"It was something of a scandal back then, but I considered myself a progressive girl. Quite independent, going to college, breaking from tradition. Clark's father and I never married. Neither of us was ready for that. I was in my third year of college . . . and well, I had other plans, or so I thought. My mother helped me with Clark until I finished school—several years later. Of course, I did marry eventually. I suppose I felt sorry for Clark. He was six and wanted a father, so I settled for a conventional life. Not that it turned out so well. Anyway, long story short, I've always felt protective of Clark, or maybe I was overcompensating for his early years, always trying to mother my male child." She chuckled. "Silly considering what a big boy— rather man—he grew up to be. Hardly needs his mama watching out for him. But old habits are hard to let go of."

Anna glanced at her watch. It was getting close to eight, and she wasn't sure where Hazel was going with this story. As if reading her thoughts, Hazel rushed on as Anna poured the eggs into the hot cast-iron pan, stirring them gently to scramble.

"As I was saying, Roselyn was difficult. Beautiful, yes, but in her case pretty came with a price. She and Clark married shortly after his graduation from law school. Roselyn's father was a judge in Seattle and Roselyn fully expected Clark to practice law for a few years then follow in her father's judicial footsteps. To be fair, I think Clark thought that was how it would turn out too. For that matter, so did I. But as you know, the war changed everything. Unfortunately, Roselyn never adjusted to the shift in plans. She nagged, begged, even threatened trying to get Clark to practice law. When Marshall came along, I really hoped she was settling into being the wife of a builder, but she was still clamoring after the life she felt she deserved."

"That must've been hard on everyone . . . especially the child." Anna pulled the muffins out of the oven and set them on top of the stove and finished scrambling the eggs. Everything was almost ready, but she was trying to absorb this story.

"I know you probably think I'm meddling to tell you this," Hazel said apologetically. "Maybe I am, but for some reason—maybe it's just wishful thinking on my part—I felt you should know these things."

Anna turned and smiled. "I appreciate it, Hazel."

"Here, let me help you with something there." Hazel came over and began putting the bacon on a plate. "You see, I could tell last night when Clark mentioned your fine cooking skills, you'd gotten his attention. Now, I don't know what that means or if it's just this mother's imagination, but it's the first time I've seen anything close to that since the early Roselyn days. And out of respect for you—and devotion to my son—I felt you needed to know a bit of his history, and I'm not sure he's comfortable speaking of it." She set the bacon plate on the table. "And that's all I'm saying about that."

"All you're saying about what?" Clark had just come through the door. Both women turned to see him and Hazel looked caught off guard and possibly speechless.

"About children," Anna said quickly. She placed the basket of muffins on the table and smiled. "I've been stewing away about my daughter all morning." She went back to the stove and as she spooned the scrambled eggs into the serving bowl she'd been warming, she told them a bit about last night's conversation. She was surprised at how candid she was being, but Hazel seemed relieved. And it did feel good to air her troubles—a bit like giving a dirty throw rug a good shake before hanging it in the sunshine.

Anna set the scrambled eggs on the table with

a clunk. "I can't tell if Lauren wants me to come back because she sincerely misses me or simply wants me to play housekeeper again—but I'm afraid it's the latter. You see, my daughter can't stand to get her hands dirty."

"Oh, my," Hazel said as Anna sat down. "That girl sounds like a handful to me."

Without asking this time, Clark bowed his head, as did the women, and after he finished saying grace, he asked a special blessing on their children.

"Thank you," Anna told him as they started to eat. "Maybe I should do more praying about Lauren and less fretting."

Now Clark confessed that his Marshall was becoming more and more of a handful for him too. "Teenagers these days." He shook his head. "I don't understand them at all. Sometimes I wonder if it's because they've had life too easy— everything is handed to them."

"Not like you kids," Hazel said sadly. "Growing up in the Depression, having your lives torn apart by the war."

"But the war hurt the children too," Anna pointed out. "Maybe it's because we've tried to make it up to them. I often feel guilty for what Lauren missed out on—like having a normal healthy father—so I suppose I might indulge her a bit more than I should. And I know her grandmother lavished her with things—too many things. Poor Lauren; no wonder she's so spoiled."

"That could be true with Marshall too," Clark admitted. "I'm sure that both his mother and I, and even his stepfather—we all probably overindulge him."

Hazel held up her hand as if giving testimony. "I'm guilty of that too. But goodness me, that boy just gives me that look—" She turned to Anna now. "He's quite a handsome boy, you see, and being the softy grandma that I am, I just can't help but give in to the lad."

"Well, the lad is almost a man now," Clark reminded her. "Or so he seems to think. He's only seventeen but he's certain he knows more about everything than everyone else."

"That's my Lauren too. Only she's eighteen. I keep hoping she'll grow out of it."

"Maybe after college," Hazel offered.

"Here's the latest," Clark said dismally. "Marshall is now trying to imitate James Dean."

"Who's that?" Hazel asked.

"You're kidding?" Clark looked at his mother like she had two heads.

Even Anna was surprised. "I don't get out much, Hazel, and I rarely see a film, but I must admit that I know the answer to that one. Of course, that's only because I have a teenaged daughter." So she explained about the handsome young actor who'd worn black motorcycle jackets and tight jeans and drove too fast. "He remains iconic amongst the young crowd."

Hazel laughed loudly. "Well, now. Tell me what is wrong with that? He sounds like an adventurous fellow."

"Mostly it's wrong that James Dean died so young," Anna explained.

"Oh?" Hazel frowned. "He's dead?"

Now Clark explained how he was tragically killed in a head-on collision. "Shortly after he got a speeding ticket, although it seems it was the other driver's fault."

"Oh, dear."

"And I suppose the idea of Marshall behind the wheel, since he's a driver now, and wearing his new leather jacket and thinking he's the next rebel without a cause . . . well, it does make a parent feel concerned. Although Roselyn seems to be taking it in stride."

"Goodness me, I certainly don't want Marshall to end up like poor James Dean." Hazel shook her head. "You say he's still a teen icon?"

Anna nodded. "Lauren was fifteen and very impressionable when James Dean died. She was devastated and it took her a long time to get over it. Even now if you mention his name, Lauren will get very melancholic."

"Marshall was only thirteen at the time, but he still thinks of James Dean as a hero."

"Oh." Hazel shook her head. "I had no idea

about James Dean or any of that. I must've been out of the country when all that happened."

"It was about four years ago," Clark said. "Weren't you in South America around then?"

She got a thoughtful look. "As a matter of fact, I think I was."

Anna was relieved that the conversation shifted from troubled adolescents to Hazel's global excursions, which were extensive. Most of Hazel's trips were work related, but it was apparent that she had a bit of a wanderlust as well. "I've been on every continent," she said finally, "but I still have a few places I'd like to see."

"I've never been like my mother," Clark admitted. "I get comfortable in one place and, if it's a good place, I don't want to leave."

"As long as he can build something," Hazel said fondly.

"That's true."

After the meal was finished, Clark politely thanked Anna, complimenting her again on her fine cooking abilities. It was pleasant to hear his praise, but as she cleaned up the breakfast things, she wondered if he saw her beyond a good cook and housekeeper. Oh, she knew that fairly adequately described her life. Certainly that's what her mother-in-law had trained her to be. In fact, it seemed that Eunice had spent the past two decades trying to obliterate Anna's spirit by reducing her to the role of domestic servant.

As she scrubbed a dish, just like she'd done thousands of times before, Anna could relate to James Dean's *Rebel Without a Cause*, except that Anna thought she had a cause worthy of rebelling against. After all, didn't she deserve a life beyond cooking and cleaning? What was she getting herself into with her dreams to run an inn? Wasn't that just like signing up for more of the same . . . or worse? What if she was jumping from the frying pan into the fire?

Yet strangely, as she took her time to clean up and put things away, she found a sense of solace and comfort in doing these familiar everyday things. Was it that she actually enjoyed menial tasks? Or perhaps her pleasure came from knowing she was not doing this service for her mother-in-law—who could never be pleased—but for herself. Not only that, but she could do these things when and how she liked—or not at all if she so chose. And it was her business if she decided to do these tasks for others. As long as she was happy and content like she felt now while drying a platter and looking out over the sparkling river, why should she doubt herself? Why not simply enjoy it?

Because, for all she knew, she might end up back in Pine Ridge kowtowing to Eunice and Lauren again—although she hoped not. To the depths of her being she hoped not. She recalled her ancestors now, remembering how her great-grandmother and her people made those long treks up and down the beach, north to the reservation and south back to the river. But Grandma would always end the story by stating that although the distance coming and going was the same amount of miles, the trip back home felt easier. Because they were walking in freedom, those were "happy miles."

17

While Clark worked on getting the electricity fully connected, Anna put some additional effort into the first floor of the inn. Her motives were twofold. She wanted to make Clark as comfortable as possible in case he wished to stay another night. But she also wanted to continue improvements in the hopes she might entice Lauren to come out here with some of her friends. Anna felt certain that if—and it was a rather large if—Susan and some of the other girls could be lured out here for a seaside vacation, Lauren would quite naturally be on board.

Anna had just finished putting some of her recent purchases onto the shelves against the wall, getting them out of the way, and was now standing in the center of the room and imagining what might be when Clark came into the room.

"Excuse me," he said, "I didn't realize you were in here."

"It's all right," she assured him. "I was doing some organizing, and I got sidetracked with a little daydreaming."

"About your future inn?"

She smiled wistfully. "I hope I'm not just entertaining a foolish pipe dream."

"I don't see why." He looked around the room. "This structure is sturdily built, and with the right improvements, I think potential guests would enjoy a visit on the river. Even without all the amenities, I'm enjoying it myself."

Encouraged by his optimism, ideas began spilling out of her. She told him about how she thought the space could be divided into four separate rooms with new windows and exterior doors. "So that people would be free to step outside and enjoy the river and the fresh air, but with a feeling of privacy."

"That's a terrific idea." He nodded. "In fact, you could save yourself some money if the doors doubled as windows."

"Doors as windows?" She was confused. "Oh, you mean glass doors."

"Sliding-glass patio doors are all the rage these days. They would really open up the view as well as provide access."

"Sliding-glass patio doors." She was trying to imagine this. "It makes sense, but I'll bet they're terribly expensive."

"Not like you'd think. And compared to

installing both a window and a door, you might actually save money. Plus, I sometimes get a good deal on them. Would you like me to look into it for you?"

She frowned. "I wish I could say yes . . . but, well . . . you see, my finances are rather limited."

He smiled. "Most people's finances are limited, Anna. Perhaps you just need to work out a budget for your upgrades. I might be able to help you with some estimates."

"Perhaps *limited* was overly optimistic." She grimaced. "My finances are seriously lacking." Suddenly she was besieged with real doubt, wondering if she had bitten off more than she could chew.

"I see." Clark's mouth twisted to one side now, almost as if he wanted to say something, but didn't quite know how to put it.

"I probably seem a bit foolish to you," she admitted. "Taking on a project like this without the funds to see it to completion. This is all so new to me, I'm sure I'm doing it all wrong." She glanced over to the sets of sheets and towels she'd purchased. Really, what had she been thinking? Simply having linens would not turn this place into an inn.

"I don't know that you're doing anything wrong, Anna, but I do know that to make this place into a viable inn will require some sort of a plan and a budget. I'm not sure what the building codes are here, but I know to add more bathrooms, which I assume you'll have to do in order to accommodate guests, will require another septic system and drain field, not to mention the actual construction of the bathrooms. Plus, I was giving it some thought, as a contractor, and I'd recommend you consider something like a detached bathhouse. I know it might sound rustic, but your property is a bit rustic, and building a detached building, perhaps with a covered walkway, might provide you with more comfortable facilities. And if you placed the bathhouse on the east side, it could also be easily used by someone staying at the cabin. Kind of like a camp."

"That's a great idea."

He pulled out his little notebook now, jotting some things down. "I could give you a ballpark estimate of what it would run."

She just nodded, swallowing hard as she realized that no matter what figure he quoted, it would be too much.

"For the bathhouse alone, and keep in mind this isn't an actual estimate . . . ," he looked down at his notes then back at her as he told her an amount.

Feeling slightly sick to her stomach, she helplessly held up her hands. "Oh, Clark, I don't know what made me think I could possibly do something like this in the first place. I don't have that kind of money. The truth is, I never will."

He looked slightly stumped as he closed his little notebook and slipped it back into his shirt pocket.

"But I do appreciate your expertise," she told him. She felt bad now. She hadn't meant to suggest that his estimate was unfair. She sighed and looked around the room. "I suppose I need to be realistic. This place will probably never be much more than it is right now." She brightened. "But I can still make the best of it. If nothing else, this can turn into a spacious guest room down here. I plan to paint the walls and—"

"I hope you don't think I was trying to shoot down your dreams." He looked uneasy. "I just didn't realize you were working with no budget whatsoever."

"I suppose I should've made that more clear."

"But banks will carry improvement loans, Anna. I assume this property is owned free and clear by you?"

"It is."

"Then it's possible you could use the equity in your property to secure a loan to complete the improvements."

She considered this. "I'm not very experienced in these things, but I always assumed that to get a loan you need to have a source of income, so that you're able to make the payments on the loan."

"That's true."

"And although I'd like to believe the inn would bring in some income . . . in time . . . it could be quite some time, or it's possible that the inn could be a great big flop. If that happened, I'd be unable to make loan payments and I'm afraid that could put my entire property at risk. Wouldn't the bank take away my property if I couldn't make my loan payments?"

"That's correct."

"That's a risk I can't afford."

"I understand, but I'm sure your pension would easily cover a loan payment—at least until you got the inn up and running properly."

"I don't get any sort of pension," she said quietly.

He frowned. "Why not?"

"I'm not sure exactly, but my mother-in-law often told me that any money coming my way had long since been eaten up by my husband's medical expenses."

Clark looked confused. "Are you sure about that?"

"I'll admit I'm not terribly smart regarding these things."

"But you said your husband served in the war, correct?"

"Yes, as an officer."

"And he was injured in the line of duty?"

"That's right."

"And he died a while back?"

She just nodded. "Then not only are you entitled to a pension, but I'd think Social Security as well." He scratched his head. "And if your husband was an officer, I'd think he would've had some additional coverage as well. But you say you're not receiving anything?"

"Not a penny."

"Did you ever?"

"No. I lived with my mother-in-law. She took care of all the household finances. And I took care of everything else, including my husband."

"So he wasn't hospitalized?"

"No. But the doctor did visit regularly. I know that was quite costly."

He firmly shook his head. "Not *that* costly."

"Well, there were my daughter's expenses too." Anna was studying him closely now. She could tell by his expression that he was skeptical about what she was saying. "And my mother-in-law's house is rather, well, *grand*. I suppose it's terribly expensive to maintain and we had the, uh, the privilege of living there with her." She nearly choked on the word *privilege*.

He pressed his lips together and scratched his chin, as if thinking hard. "Do you mind if I ask how your husband's family became wealthy. I assume they are wealthy if your mother-in-law lives in a *grand* house."

She explained about the family-owned lumber

mill and how her husband had been running it before the war and how he was supposed to continue the same afterward. "Except, as you know, a lot of things changed after the war."

"For clarification's sake, is your husband's father deceased?"

"Yes. Mr. Gunderson passed when Adam was a boy. That's why Adam was expected to run the lumber mill."

"Did Adam have siblings?"

"No. He was an only child, and like Lauren I'm afraid he was a bit spoiled too."

"Anna, I don't like to be intrusive, but this is just not adding up. If your husband's family owns a lumber mill, if he's an only child, and if he died from injuries received during the war, you should not be penniless."

"Well, I'm not exactly penniless." She stood a bit straighter. "My mother left me a little something." Of course that little something was shrinking fast. "And I do have this land."

"I'm sorry." He rubbed his chin. "That must've sounded insulting. I didn't mean to insinuate you were broke."

She smiled now. "The truth is, my resources are dwindling. That's why I need to get this inn up and running as soon as possible. Just having your mother renting the cabin is truly a godsend."

"Have you questioned your mother-in-law

about your financial situation? Have you asked her to explain why you receive no pension or stipend or anything?"

"When I question this, she's quick to remind me of how much she's given Lauren and me. She points out how she took us in, and how we'd be destitute without her. And I must admit Eunice keeps Lauren dressed in the finest. Also, she bought her an expensive convertible and has offered to cover all of Lauren's college expenses. I could never do any of those things."

He just nodded, but his expression was doubtful.

"You think I've been foolish, don't you? Allowing my mother-in-law to chart my course without really knowing what's going on." She bit her lip.

"I'm not sure what to think."

"Well, you're right to think I've been foolish. The more I consider everything, the more I'm sure that I've been extremely foolish."

He looked directly into her eyes now. "I think you've been very trusting, Anna. And I think you've been so put upon that you probably never had a chance to question if you had any other options. I will control myself from expressing my opinions about your mother-in-law. But I'm curious, wasn't there anyone else around—family or friends or someone—who could help you to figure these things out?"

Anna remembered the time she'd been on her way to see the lawyer in Pine Ridge. She told Clark about how Eunice had convinced her it was a complete waste of time and money. "And, as usual, Eunice reminded me that I couldn't afford to pay for a lawyer anyway." Anna shrugged. "Which was true."

"But some lawyers would work pro bono on a—"

"That must be Henry!" The sound of a boat engine rumbled as she hurried to open the front door. "He must have brought my deliveries from town." Relieved at this interruption, she hurried down toward the dock. She knew that Clark had probably made some valid points just now, but it was very unsettling to think about those things.

She waved and greeted Henry as he maneuvered his boat alongside the dock. Clark stepped up, grabbing the rope and securing it like he'd been doing it all his life.

"Boy, am I glad to see you," Henry said to Clark. "I was feeling sorry I didn't bring a boy along to lend a hand. Getting all worked up that Anna and me was gonna have to unload and haul all this merchandise into the house ourselves." He jutted his thumb back to where a stack of well-wrapped mattresses were piled. "Looks like someone's gonna be sleeping good tonight. Does that mean you're gonna stick around a while?"

"I hope so," she told him as they started unloading.

It didn't take long, with Clark's help, to get everything taken to the right places. Anna hurried into the kitchen as the men carried the last mattress up the stairs and into Anna's old room. Gathering the leftover huckleberry muffins into a bag, she went out and handed them to Henry. "Thank you so much," she told him.

He opened the bag and sniffed. "Well, thank you!"

As they walked back down the stairs, she took the opportunity to explain to Henry why she'd purchased "all them beds" as he put it.

"A river inn's a good idea," he told her.

"Of course, it won't be open right away," she said as they stopped on the dock, waiting as Henry climbed back into his boat and Clark untied the rope. "But I'll let you know when it does open." Even as she said this, she felt serious doubts. In all likelihood the inn would never open. Not without bathrooms; not without money.

"You do that, little lady, and I'll help get the word out for you." He waved as he put his engine into reverse and backed away from the dock.

"They say word-of-mouth advertising is the best kind," Clark told her as they walked back to the house.

She sighed. "Not that I'll be needing it. I mean since it's feeling more and more unlikely that this place will become an inn."

Hazel was walking toward them now. Anna looked at her watch and was surprised to see that it was nearly one. Where had the morning gone?

"I'm sorry, I lost track of the time. But I'm on my way up to start lunch right now," Anna assured her. "It should be ready in about twenty minutes or so."

"No hurry," Hazel told her. "I thought I'd take a little walk to stretch my legs."

"And I'll get back to what I was doing," Clark said. "If all goes well, your house will be fully connected to power before sundown."

"That's wonderful," Anna told him. "I won't miss the sound of that generator growling one bit." Of course, she might miss doing the dishes by kerosene lamplight, although she supposed she could continue that tradition if she really wanted. Or perhaps, if times got hard and she was unable to pay a power bill, she would be forced to. That made her curious as to how much a power bill would be. And there was telephone too. Perhaps Clark was wise in suggesting she make a budget. There was so much she didn't know or understand about finances. All those years of allowing Eunice to handle so much had probably crippled her more than she realized. Anna remembered how she'd been grateful for

Eunice's help early on. With a toddler and sick husband to care for, plus the housekeeping in general, it had been a relief not to juggle finances as well. But now she realized that even if her ignorance had been blissful at times, it had probably been rather expensive in the long run.

18

Readjusting to her mother's old methods of doing laundry had been a challenge at best. Even with the electricity fully connected, the old wringer washer felt archaic compared to the automatic machine Anna had been accustomed to using in her mother-in-law's sleek laundry room. The late model GE appliance with all its dials, buttons, and settings, combined with its matching clothes dryer, may have spoiled Anna forever.

Still, she reminded herself as she rearranged the soggy sheet to go through the wringer again, she'd rather wrestle dripping sheets and towels through the wringer and peg them on the clothesline than return to her old life with Eunice. In fact, she'd rather wash her clothes in the river, pounding them on the rocks like Grandma had done than to go back to Eunice's "modern conveniences." Of course, Anna realized that rainy days, which were common in this part of the country, could put even more of a damper on this already tedious chore. Plus if she ever had real paying guests here beyond Hazel, who was easy to please, she would need to provide them with fresh linens on a fairly regular basis. How was she going to handle that?

"Hallo?" called a familiar voice.

"Babette!" Anna yelled back. "I'm in the laundry shed!" She stepped out of the lean-to her father had built long ago and waved.

"Oh, there you are." Babette came over and joined her. "Hard at work too."

"I don't know how Mother managed to do laundry out here for so many years." Anna swiped her forehead and caught the last of the sheet, carefully setting it in the basket to hang later. She turned off the wringer and shook her head. "This is hard work."

"Oh, your mother, she never use this old machine after your papa die, only once in a great while."

"How did she do her laundry?"

"She wash her clothes in the kitchen sink and she hang them in the house to dry. Then when it ees a bright sunny day, she come down here to wash sheets and towels sometimes. But she no like this old machine either. She call it the *Monster*."

Anna laughed. "I'll have to call it that too."

"Your handsome handyman ees here, no?"

"Clark is still here." She carried the heavy basket out to the clothesline. "He's putting up a lamppost this morning, between here and the cabin, to make it a little safer at night. We think we've had a bear roaming about here lately and the light might help to keep him out of harm's way."

"Ees the electricity working now?"

Anna nodded as she gave a sheet a snap then flung it over the clothesline. Babette handed her a clothespin. "Even the cabin has power now. Can you imagine what Grandma would say?"

Babette chuckled. "Maybe ees good she ees not here to say anything."

"But I think she'd approve of what I'm doing." Anna snapped a pillowcase now. "I think she'd like the idea of making this place open to others."

"Oui. I think she like eet too. Your grandmamma, she liked people. Always wanting to help. You know, Anna, I wrote down some of her herbal medicines. Do you think your friend Hazel would be interested?" She handed her another clothespin.

"Why don't you ask her?" Anna reached for a towel. "In fact, why don't you stay for lunch?"

"I would like that. And perhaps I can ask your handyman some questions."

"Of course."

Babette helped Anna hang the rest of the wash then continued up to the house with her. Then, without asking or being asked, Babette rolled up her sleeves and began helping with lunch preparations. As always, Anna enjoyed working with Babette and she appreciated the cheerful chatter and hearing the river news that her French friend was so expert at collecting.

"The Flanders' baby ees so beautiful," Babette told her as she sliced a tomato, one that she'd brought from her own garden. Makes me wish I had children so I can be grandmamma."

"I still feel sad that my mother didn't get to see Lauren more."

"Ees no good to live in the past, Anna. Your mama, she love your letters, the photographs you send, eet make her happy."

"Hello!" Hazel called as she came into the house. "Something smells good in here." She greeted Babette and peeked at the sauce she was stirring then sighed happily. "I feel as if I have fallen into a fine feathered nest," she told them. "Someday The Inn at Shining Waters will be so popular that there will be a long waiting list for guests."

Anna laughed. "I hope you turn out to be right." She didn't mention that the idea of running a successful inn seemed more impossible now than ever.

"I was telling Anna," Babette said to Hazel, "I wrote down some recipes for herbal medicines from her grandmamma. I thought perhaps you would like to see."

"Oh, Babette, I would love to see them. Would you mind if I copied them down?"

"Not at all."

"I'd like to copy them too," Anna told her.

"I will bring them with me next time I come."

Now Babette began to reminisce about the early days on the river, telling them about when Anna's parents lived in the small cabin that later became the back room of the store. "We were so young and happy, Oscar and Marion, Bernard and me." She sighed as she turned off the flame beneath the sauce. "So long ago."

"I sometimes forget that my parents lived in that small room," Anna admitted as she poured coleslaw dressing over the chopped cabbage.

"Because you were only a baby when your papa built the big store."

"Since we are talking family history," Hazel began, "I still have some unanswered questions about timelines. Perhaps you and Babette can help to fill in some blanks for me."

"Certainly," Babette assured her. "I am happy to help."

So they agreed that following lunch they would sit down with Hazel and share whatever they could to help her with her thesis. Before long, Clark joined them and as they ate lunch, Babette explained the project she needed doing at her house. "Ees this something you can do?" she asked hopefully.

He nodded. "Sure. But I have a suggestion. Instead of remodeling your bathroom, have you considered building an additional bathroom?"

Babette's mouth twisted to one side. "Another bathroom?"

"Adding another bathroom increases the value of your home, plus it allows you to have the use of the older bathroom while the addition is in the works. Lots of people are finding that two bathrooms are handy."

Babette giggled. "But eet ees only me in the house."

He smiled. "Yes, but if you have guests or if you sell."

"Or," she held up a forefinger, "if I marry again."

Anna was surprised. Would Babette really remarry? At her age?

She shook her finger at Anna now. "Do not look so shocked, chérie. There ees man in town. You never know." She chuckled. "Where there ees life there could be love."

Hazel laughed loudly. "I like the way you think, Babette."

Clark cleared his throat, almost as if uncomfortable—and Anna certainly was—then he mentioned that it looked like deer had gotten into her garden.

"Oh, dear," she exclaimed. "Did they eat everything?"

"Not everything, but I think they enjoyed themselves."

"My mother used to have the same problem. In fact, she used to have a fence, although that seems long gone."

"Your mama did not garden the past few years," Babette explained.

"Oh."

"Well, we can put up a fence easily enough," Clark assured her.

Anna just nodded. She wanted to ask how that was possible when she was quickly running out of funds, but she didn't want to discuss her finances in front of everyone. And perhaps a fence wasn't as costly as she thought, or perhaps there was fencing material on the property somewhere. Besides that, it would probably be worth the investment to protect her garden. She had hoped to put up some of the produce at the end of summer, in order to save money on groceries when winter came. She thought of the big chest freezer in her mother-in-law's garage, usually less than half full. Something like that would come in handy now that she had electricity. Still, she reminded herself, as the others discussed the local wildlife, she knew that her grandmother had made do with very little. Certainly, Anna could do the same if necessary.

"Is much hunting done around here?" Clark asked. And immediately, Babette began telling stories of her late husband Bernard, and how he and Anna's father had been quite adept at hunting and fishing.

"I remember the year they got the elk." Babette shook her head. "So much meat!"

Anna nodded. "I remember that too. It was during the Depression and between you and Mother, plus Daddy's smokehouse, I don't think much was wasted."

"And your grandmamma, she used the hide and antlers too."

"It's too bad people don't know how to live like that anymore," Anna said sadly. "I mean the ability to hunt and fish and grow your own food, make your own clothes."

"Some people do," Hazel said. "But I suspect it won't be long before most people in our country depend on others for everything they need."

After lunch, Clark thanked Anna and excused himself. She wanted to ask him how much longer he thought he'd be staying with them. Not because she wanted to be rid of him—nothing was farther from the truth—she simply wanted to figure out how much she needed to order in the way of groceries. As greatly as she appreciated his handyman skills, especially since he took the initiative to continue with improvements he felt necessary, her budget, if she could call it that, was stretched a bit to feed another mouth.

With the lunch things cleaned up, Babette and

Anna went over to the cabin to answer Hazel's questions. "Eet ees like an office in here," Babette said in surprise as she looked at the typewriter and papers and recording machine.

"This cabin has been very handy for me," Hazel told them as she pointed to the chairs she'd arranged by the kitchen table. "And with electricity, I'm happy as a clam." She nodded to her machines. "Such time-saving devices." She turned on the recording device. "You don't mind if I record your words, do you? It saves me from having to take notes." They both agreed this was fine, then Hazel began to question them. She started by asking for dates regarding births, deaths, marriages, and other things. Mostly Anna had to estimate, but Babette was more helpful with some things.

"I assume your grandmother had some schooling," Hazel said.

"Yes," Anna confirmed, "she attended school on the reservation. I think for most of her childhood she went to school. But her reading and writing skills were somewhat minimal. At least that's what it seemed like to me. If she ever had something that needed to be read or written, she relied on Daddy, and later on, she would ask me to help her."

"Do you suppose her vision was impaired?"

Anna considered this. "I think you could be right. I remember she would peer at books as if trying to see them."

The questions continued, and many of them made Anna think. For instance, she had never considered what Grandma Pearl might've gone through in her young adulthood. "I know she married my grandfather when she was about seventeen," Anna explained. "They had met on the reservation."

"And they came here to live?"

"I don't think they did that. Not right away. I remember hearing that they both worked in town. I think at a fish cannery. Although later my grandfather worked in logging. Until he was killed in an accident."

"Oh, no, chérie," Babette said. "Eet was not an accident."

"What?"

Babette shook her head. "No one spoke of eet, but your mama, she tell me her papa ees killed."

"Killed?" Anna questioned. "How do you mean?"

"Murdered."

Anna felt a wave a shock. "What?"

With wide eyes, Babette nodded. "Oui. I am sorry to tell you. But eet ees true."

"How did it happen?"

Babette now told them how Pearl's first husband, the one who didn't drink, was a good man, a hard worker—he had built the cabin they were sitting in—but that he had been killed while working for a logging company. "Your grandmamma, she was very pretty," Babette told Anna. "Like you, but not so tall."

Anna just shrugged.

"Women were scarce back then," Babette continued. "Your mama, she tell me that her papa was killed so that another man can marry your grandmamma."

"I've heard stories like that before," Hazel confirmed.

"But your grandmamma, she no marry the bad man—the one who murder her husband."

"But she did marry a white man," Anna pointed out. "Her second husband, the one who drank."

"Oui. He was not a bad man, he just drink too much."

"Oh."

"That must've been sad for your mother," Hazel said to Anna. "To lose her father so tragically."

Anna just nodded, trying to take this in.

"Eet was hard on her," Babette said. "I think eet ees why she build a wall."

"Build a wall?" Hazel queried.

"To separate her from the Indian. Marion want to live like white woman. She attend white school. She dress like white woman. She feel safe."

"I see." Hazel nodded, making some notes.

"I think I see too." Anna sighed.

They continued to talk, piecing together Anna's family history as if it were one of her mother's patchwork quilts, until the recording machine began to sputter—indicating that they had filled up an entire tape.

Anna looked at her watch. "Time for me to go begin dinner," she announced.

"And time for me to go home," Babette added.

"Unless you'd like to stay for dinner." Anna smiled.

"Lunch and dinner? All in one day?"

"Why not?" Anna slipped an arm around Babette. "You are my family."

Babette beamed. "Oui. I stay for dinner. But you must let me go and get something to bring!"

"Great." Anna nodded. "And if you want to stay late, you can spend the night, just like you sometimes did with my mother."

"Oh, chérie!" Babette hugged her. "I am so glad you are home!"

Despite her impending sense of poverty, Anna felt happy as she started dinner. And once again, she realized she would rather be poor and happy than rich and miserable. Really, that was all there was to it! And if she had to hunt and fish and grow her own food just to survive here on the river, she was more than willing to do so. In fact, she decided, as she vigorously mixed biscuit dough, that she would get up early tomorrow morning, just like Daddy used to do, and get out the fishing pole and tackle and take out her canoe and catch some fish—and she would do it all before breakfast time.

19

To Anna's surprise, Clark managed to get a fence up before dinner the following day. She walked around admiring his workmanship of solid posts and wire fencing going all around the perimeter of her garden. "How did you do this?" she asked as they walked back to the house.

"I've gotten rather good at snooping around the property and finding materials and things. As you can see the wire is a bit rusty. It was nearly buried in the outbuilding by the meadow, and the poles were piled out in the back. I suspect your father got it quite some time ago."

"Well, you are like a real pioneer," she told him. "You have no idea how much I appreciate it, but I do hope I'll be able to cover the bill. Perhaps you'll consider allowing me to make installment payments."

"And then I'd have to have you bill me for lodging and food." He smiled. "Don't you see this is like a working vacation for me? And getting to spend time with my mother like this has been worth a lot."

"Still, I'm sure I owe you—"

"Let's not talk about that." He pointed over to the dock now. "I'm curious if that boat is operable."

242

She sighed, shoving her hands into her jeans pockets. "Not at the moment. I keep meaning to ask Henry to take a look at the motor. But there's just been so much to do."

"Do you mind if I take a look?"

"Not at all."

"I noticed you went out fishing this morning."

"Yes. But without luck. Not that I'm giving up."

"Well, I got a little envious. I was wishing I could go too. I thought if that boat was running, I might try my luck."

She waved her hand. "You are welcome to it." Excusing herself, she explained she needed to get back to the house to work on dinner.

"Mind if I join you?"

She tried not to look surprised. "Not at all."

As they went into the house, he told her that he'd made a rough drawing of a bathhouse. "I'm trying to come up with an economical but functional plan," he explained as he followed her into the kitchen.

"That's nice," she said a bit stiffly as she washed her hands.

"I know . . . I know . . . you're worried about the money." She simply nodded as she dried her hands then reached for an apron.

"I want to talk to you about that too."

She looked at him. "I thought you said you didn't want to talk about money."

"I don't want to talk about you owing me money," he clarified. "But what if someone owed you money?"

She gave him a skeptical look as she checked the pot on the stove, turning the flame up just a bit. Since today had been cloudy and cool, she had decided to make stew, or what Babette would call beef bourguignonne. She was even using the bit of Babette's leftover Burgundy from last night to flavor the broth.

"Hear me out," he said as he pulled out the kitchen stool and sat down. So while she attended to dinner, he explained his plan to go to Pine Ridge and speak to the attorney about what Anna might possibly have coming to her. She couldn't quite believe her ears, but she felt a tiny bit of encouragement to think that someone wanted to look out for her financial interests— that is, if she had any.

"I'd hate to waste your time," she told him as she sliced into a loaf of bread that she'd made earlier.

"I feel fairly certain that it won't be a waste of anyone's time," he assured her.

"What makes you so certain?"

"Remember, I did graduate with a law degree," he reminded her.

"Yes . . ." She nodded as she began to set the table.

"And I was in the service. I learned a bit about

the benefits and insurance plans that were available to war widows."

"But I wasn't a war widow."

"Not technically. But I still think you have a case to make."

"You know I can't pay you for your service," she told him.

He held up his hands. "I expect no payment."

"And how can I let you do this for free? Already, you've done so much for me. I know I'll never be able to repay you and—"

"There you go again," he said.

"Put yourself in my place."

"OK. If you'll put yourself in mine."

She frowned.

"I've had a great time being out here on the river, Anna. It's been like . . . I can't even explain it . . . like a healing experience."

She stopped setting the table, looking curiously at him. "Really?"

He nodded. "Really."

"It's like that for me too."

"And for my mother." He sighed. "How do you put a price on that?"

"I don't know." She set another plate down.

"If it will make you feel better, we can keep an account. I'll charge you for my work to be paid by free stays at your inn."

"Really?"

"Absolutely. It would be a completely fair

trade." He chuckled. "Probably more than fair because I suspect your inn will grow in value after a few years. So, really, I'll be making a pretty good deal."

She stuck out her hand now. "You want to shake on that?"

He grinned and reached for her hand. "You bet I do!"

As they were shaking hands, Hazel walked in. At first she looked surprised but then she simply laughed. "Caught you two, didn't I?"

Embarrassed, Anna pulled her hand away and Clark quickly explained their little deal. Then he went on to tell his mother about his plan to see if Anna might have more funds coming to her.

"Yes," Hazel said eagerly. "I have been wondering about the very same thing myself. How is it possible that her widow's pension and everything could've possibly been used up?"

"The problem is that I'll need Anna to come to Pine Ridge with me," he told Hazel as Anna ladled out the stew.

"Why is that a problem?" Hazel asked.

"You'd be here alone."

"Oh, pish posh, that's not a problem."

"Wait a minute." Anna set their bowls on the table. "What are you saying, Clark?"

"That you'll need to come and talk to the lawyer too. I'm sure he'll have lots of questions and—"

"But I can't just up and leave this place," Anna told him.

"Of course, you can," Hazel assured her. "I'll be here to see to things. If there's anything that needs seeing to."

"But who will get your meals and—"

"I will get my own meals." Hazel waved toward the kitchen. "I know how to cook. And maybe Babette will come over and join me for dinner and—"

"But you are my guest," Anna protested. "I can't just abandon you."

"We are talking about your life," Hazel said firmly, "and your livelihood. I insist you do as Clark is recommending. Go to Pine Ridge and straighten things out, Anna. Good grief, what if you are entitled to money? What if your mother-in-law has been deceiving you somehow? Do you want to simply sit back and allow her to take everything? And what about your daughter? Don't you owe it to her to look into these things?"

Anna set down her own bowl of stew. "Now that you put it that way, I suppose you're right."

"Of course, I'm right."

So it was settled. On Monday, Clark would call the attorney at Pine Ridge first thing in the morning and make an appointment to discuss Anna's financial affairs.

"Oh, I'm so thrilled," Hazel said. "It's almost as if you are practicing law, Clark."

"I'm not practicing law, Mother. I don't have a license to do that. I'm simply assisting a friend."

"Well, yes. I understand that. But it is exciting just the same."

On the following Monday Clark and Anna put their bags in the back of his pickup and set out for Pine Ridge. Feeling nervous about seeing Lauren and Eunice again, Anna had dressed in her best suit. It felt strange to wear hosiery and good shoes again and she could tell that Clark was looking at her curiously. "You look nice," he'd said as he helped her into the pickup.

"Thank you," she'd replied a bit crisply.

"But just for the record, I think you always look nice." He grinned and started the engine.

She made nervous small talk as Clark drove them down the bumpy back road to the main highway. She wanted to appear relaxed and comfortable, but all she could think about was how her mother-in-law would probably intervene in their meeting. She could imagine Eunice swooping in, talking fast, and convincing everyone, including Clark, that Anna was a half-wit who didn't know up from down. "Hasn't she told you that I've taken care of everything for her?" Eunice would declare in an aggrieved tone. "Hasn't she explained that I've given her a beautiful place to live, food to eat, fine clothes to wear, that I've provided generously for every possible need for both her and her daughter? And now she expects something more from me? How ungrateful!" Then Anna would want to slip out the door with tail between her legs and run.

"I'm worried I've painted the wrong picture of my mother-in-law," Anna began uneasily.

"How so?"

"Well, I may have made her seem like an evil, selfish, witchlike sort of woman."

Clark laughed.

"And now I'm concerned you'll meet her and think that I've been unfair."

"Why would I think that?"

"Because my mother-in-law is very smooth," Anna explained. "She is well spoken, well groomed, and well liked in the community. She is used to getting her way, but she does it in such a way that no one really seems to notice."

Clark nodded. "I'm well acquainted with people like that."

"Oh." Anna looked down at her hands in her lap now. She had on a pair of summer weight gloves, something Eunice would approve of, but they felt constrictive and uncomfortable and, feeling aggravated at herself for wearing them, she peeled them off, tucked them in her handbag.

"A lot of people couldn't understand why my marriage failed," Clark said quietly.

Anna turned to look at him. His eyes were directly forward, looking intently at the rough road ahead. He had an attractive profile, high forehead, straight nose, strong chin. She felt it was the sort of face she could enjoy looking at from all angles and that it would probably remain handsome into old age.

"Your description of your mother-in-law reminds me a bit of my ex-wife."

"Oh?"

He nodded, adjusting his grip on the steering wheel. "Roselyn was very smooth too. She still is. And like your mother-in-law she's a smooth talker too. And trust me. No one is quite as stylish as my ex-wife. All her friends, and she has plenty of them, say so." He made a sad smile. "I'm sure we looked a bit mismatched at times."

Anna didn't know how to respond to that.

"Even so, people were surprised when Roselyn left me. I'm sure many of them reached their own conclusions. And I've never been particularly concerned, but I suspect that based on appearances, I look to be the reason our marriage fell apart." He sighed.

"Your mother told me a bit about it, Clark. I hope you don't mind."

He shrugged. "No, not at all. It's not something I enjoy rehashing. But what you said about your mother-in-law . . . well, it struck a familiar chord with me. Roselyn was an expert on keeping up appearances when others were looking. But when it was just her and me and Marshall, well, she let her hair down so to speak."

Anna nodded. She could imagine. "That does sound like Eunice."

"So I just want you to know I understand. And I know better than to go by outward appearances."

She sighed in relief. "Thanks for telling me that."

Now, and perhaps to change the subject, Clark told her about his childhood and young adulthood, sharing some interesting tales of wild youth and crazy experiences. He even told her about the time he'd built a tree fort in the backyard and, wanting all the comforts of home he'd "installed a toilet," which was simply an old toilet seat attached to an apple crate with a hole through the floorboards. "I'd yell 'look out below' whenever it was in use," he told her between chuckles. "I suppose that was my training to become a bombardier." They both laughed so hard that Anna had tears in her eyes. Not only did Clark's antics prove a good distraction from her worries, his stories helped to pass the time. And it seemed like the four-hour trip passed quite quickly.

"Our appointment with Mr. Miller isn't until three o'clock," Clark informed her as he drove into town.

Anna was staring at the businesses along Main Street as if she were a stranger, feeling as if she'd been gone for years instead of just a few weeks. Her throat felt dry and she was nervously twisting the handle of her handbag. Was this all a mistake?

"So I thought perhaps we could get some lunch. Do you have any recommendations?"

She couldn't help laughing. "You may not believe this, but the last time I ate in town was before the war."

"Then I'd say it's about time you gave it another try." He pointed to the Checkerboard Café. "What do you think about that place?"

"I'm sure it's perfectly fine." As he parked, she looked around to see if there was anyone she recognized nearby. Not that she knew so many people in this town. Although she did know Lauren's and Eunice's friends—only by name and from waiting on them at the house. The truth was, Anna had very few friends of her own.

"May I tell you something," she asked suddenly, "before we get out?"

"Certainly." He turned off the engine then looked at her.

"This is difficult to say." She took in a deep breath. "But my mother-in-law didn't approve of me, probably for many reasons, but also because of my—my Indian heritage."

"Oh." His expression grew serious. "I'm sorry."

"Eunice never could accept that her son married a . . . *a half-breed*. I hate those words, but that's actually what she called me. That and *squaw*. Even in front of her friends. Her bridge club would be there and she would say things like, 'Oh, let my little squaw get that for you, Gladys.' Then she would laugh and act as if she was being funny, like she meant no harm, and like it didn't hurt me. I think it even made some of her friends uneasy. But she did it just the same."

Clark frowned. "What a cruel woman."

"As a result, I didn't spend much time in town, except to go to the library. But I wasn't comfortable being out and about. I'd order groceries and other things by telephone. And if I did go to town, I would try to avoid the sorts of places where I'd see any of Eunice's friends. Or even my daughter's. I know it was cowardly on my part, but once it became a habit, it was hard to stop."

"So I assume this is making you fairly uncomfortable right now, being in town like this."

With eyes cast downward, she nodded.

"Oh, Anna," he said in a compassionate tone. "I'm so sorry for all you suffered here. It's hard to believe anyone could be so unfeeling. But you must understand that it's your mother-in-law with the real problem, don't you?"

"I try to tell myself that. But I would be lying to say it hasn't taken a toll on my self-esteem."

"How could it have not?" He reached over and took her hand.

Surprised, she looked up at him. His deep-blue eyes caught her off guard and she felt herself catch her breath.

"I think you're an amazing and wonderful woman, Anna. I'm sure your husband felt the same way. I'm just sorry your mother-in-law couldn't see who you really are. It is her loss."

She forced a shaky smile. "Thank you."

"I don't know what to say that could help you to be strong, Anna, but I hope you'll try. And don't forget that I'm here with you. I'll be strong for you if you need it."

She thanked him again and he squeezed then released her hand. Now, holding her head high, she waited for him to walk around and open the door for her. Her worst fear was that she'd run into Eunice and some friends and it would be incredibly awkward and possibly humiliating for her. But they went into the café and nothing like that happened. Even so, she had very little appetite and it was hard to make small talk as she focused on slowly eating a bowl of vegetable beef soup.

"It's strange," she told him as they waited for the check, "but I don't know if I would've fully realized how unhappy I'd been here if I hadn't gone back. The difference between being here and being back on the river feels like the difference between darkness and light."

"Sometimes it's good to face our fears," he said. "It can whittle the bullies down to size." Then he paid the bill and asked her about guiding him on a short driving tour of the town. Eager to escape public eyes, she gladly agreed. The cab of the pickup felt reassuring and she relaxed a bit as she pointed out the highlights of the rather lackluster lumber town. And finally, he was parking in front of the office of Joseph P. Miller, Attorney-at-Law.

"Eunice isn't going to be at this meeting, is she?" Anna asked as Clark helped her out of the pickup.

"No. And I made it clear to Mr. Miller that I'm not here as your attorney, but if we need to find someone else to represent your case, we will do so. However, I hope it doesn't come to that. Mr. Miller sounded like a reasonable man."

Not only was Mr. Miller a reasonable man, he was no longer representing the Gunderson family or the lumber mill. He explained that a new attorney had that responsibility now. "I can't say I'm sorry either," he told them. "Mrs. Gunderson came into my office last spring and, due to some demands she wanted to make, I decided it was time to part ways." He held up his hands with a weary expression. "I plan to retire next year and

I was just getting too old for some of her shenanigans."

"So have you had a chance to go over my questions and concerns?" Clark asked.

Mr. Miller set a manila file folder on the table. "I have." He nodded to Anna now. "Do you remember how I tried to get you to come to my office that time?"

She explained what had happened with Eunice.

"I suspected as much. In fact, that was part of the discussion that led to your mother-in-law seeking out another attorney. About a month ago, I sent a registered letter to you and when it was returned, I learned that you had left the area with no forwarding address."

"What?"

He shrugged. "Your mother-in-law hasn't been cooperative in locating you."

"Which is why we are here," Clark stated.

It didn't take long before Mr. Miller made it clear that not only was Anna owed back money from a number of sources related to Adam's military service, she had also inherited money from his estate following his death. He stated all this in a matter-of-fact way, but by the time he handed her an envelope containing a rather large check, Anna felt confused and a bit light-headed. For a moment, she wondered if this was all simply a dream—a very abstract but pleasant dream.

20

"I wish I could say that I understood everything that transpired in Mr. Miller's office," Anna said as they drove through town. "But the truth is, I felt a bit overwhelmed."

"That's to be expected," Clark said as he slowed for the one traffic light in town. "Not only are you inexperienced in the world of finances, you're also under a lot of emotional stress. Considering all that you've been through with your husband's mother, I think you're holding up remarkably well." He glanced at her. "And you're sure you want to go to her house?" He chuckled. "Face the lioness in her den."

Anna nodded. "I want to see my daughter. And I'd like to pick up the rest of my things, if you don't mind."

"Not at all."

She directed him to the white-columned house at the top of the hill. "Go ahead and park the truck right in front," she instructed him. "I don't care if Eunice doesn't like it."

"That's my girl." He nodded.

She took a deep breath, telling herself she could do this.

"Do you want me to come in with you?" he asked as put the truck in park.

She turned, looking hopefully at him. "Would you mind?"

"Mind?" He grinned. "Not at all."

"And do you think it would be OK—I mean if things should get ugly with Eunice—if I made it seem as if you are my attorney?"

He nodded. "If you don't, I probably will."

She smiled shyly. "Thanks, Clark. You have no idea how much I appreciate your friendship."

As he went around to open her door, she slipped on her gloves, felt to see if her hat was properly in place, and even checked the front of her dove gray suit in case there was something from lunch on it. But it looked tidy. She'd sewn this suit last spring, wanting something presentable to wear to Lauren's graduation. Eunice had questioned Anna about the suit, asking where she'd gotten the funds to purchase such an expensive suit. Anna had explained it was only the price of yard goods and buttons as well as a carefully chosen Vogue pattern. But she'd felt proud that Eunice hadn't realized it was homemade. Especially since Eunice often made fun of Anna's housedresses, hastily sewn and not very fashionable.

Hooking the strap of her black handbag over her wrist, Anna held her head high and walked up to the front door and, for the first time in her life, she rang the bell. It had always been her job to answer the door, although it was never for her; it felt strange to be on this side now. She glanced at Clark, then decided to ring again, bracing herself for the angry face of her mother-in-law. But instead it was Lauren who answered. *"Mom?"* she exclaimed. "What are you doing here?"

Anna opened her arms and hugged her daughter. "Oh, Lauren, it's so good to see you. You look so pretty too." She held her at arm's length, taking in the pink-and-white striped sundress with a wide flowing skirt. Lauren's blond curls were pulled back in some new hairdo. "You seem older, darling."

Lauren laughed. "I am older. Remember I'm almost a college coed now." She glanced curiously over Anna's shoulder. "Who's that?"

Remembering Clark, Anna did a quick introduction, explaining about how Clark's mother was an anthropologist doing research on the river. "Is your grandmother home?"

"Not right now." Lauren led them inside. The house looked just about the same, although it wasn't neat as a pin like it would've been if Anna had still been living there. She noticed dusty surfaces on furniture, dust bunnies on the hardwood floors, and windows with smudges. Not that she cared.

"That's probably good," Anna said as they sat down in the formal living room. "I wanted to talk to you first anyway."

"You'll have to make it quick, Mom." Lauren

glanced at the mantle clock. "Donald is picking me up in about ten minutes."

"Donald Thomas?" Anna felt worried. Donald Thomas was a few years older than Lauren, and had a reputation when it came to the local girls. Anna had overheard conversations among Lauren's friends and didn't understand why Lauren would want to be involved with someone like that. Then she remembered that Eunice and Donald's mother were good friends. Perhaps that was a factor.

Lauren nodded in a pleased way. "Yes, Donald and I just started going out. He's home from college. He's been at Oregon State, and when he heard I'm starting there in the fall, he sort of took me under his wing." She giggled in a coquettish way.

"What happened with Lou Anne?" Lauren remembered how another girl had been practically engaged to Donald.

Lauren waved her hand. "She's yesterday's news, Mom."

"Oh." Anna knew this wasn't the time to express her concerns. Perhaps there would never be a time since Lauren didn't usually take her mother's advice too seriously.

"Susan," Lauren called over her shoulder. "I'm downstairs." Lauren turned to Anna. "Susan's here today. She's dating Gordon Myers. The four of us are driving up to the lake together."

Susan joined them now. She was dressed similarly to Lauren in a full-skirted sundress, although hers was red-and-white polka-dots. Neither of the girls seemed appropriately outfitted for a day at the lake. Although Anna knew she was probably out of touch when it came to fashion—at least that's what Lauren and Eunice usually said. Anna smiled and greeted Susan, introducing her to Clark, then she redirected her attention to Lauren.

"Since you're in a hurry, I'll get right to it." She quickly explained that she was here to collect her things. "I plan to live permanently at my parents' house and I'd like—"

"What do you mean?" Lauren demanded.

"I mean I'm planning to stay on the river, Lauren. I wanted to—"

"How can you do that to me?"

"You'll be in college soon, Lauren, and I'm sure you'll be busy with—"

"But there's the rest of the summer, *Mom.* And even after school starts, I'll still be coming back here to visit sometimes. You know, on weekends and holidays. And I might bring friends with me. I want you to be here, Mom."

"You could come to visit me on the river," Anna suggested. "Even bring your friends if you like."

Lauren laughed like this was ridiculous.

"I'm fixing the place up," Anna explained. "I'm making guest rooms and—"

"*Mom!* You would seriously expect me to bring friends out there?"

Now Anna began to tell her how she was making it into an inn. How there were lots of things to do on the river, and how the beach was nearby.

"That sounds nice," Susan said pleasantly.

"Of course, you'd be welcome there too," Anna told Susan. "It's becoming a popular recreation area and—"

"But what about *me?*" Lauren demanded. "How can you just leave me here with Grandmother? I already told you how I'm having to do all your work with you gone. And it's just not fair."

Susan giggled and rolled her eyes.

"Lauren," Anna said gently, "I don't understand why you think it's *my* work."

"Because you've always done it. And Grandmother says it's how you pay your way."

"But I'm not even living here now, honey. Why should I still be paying my way?"

"Because that's just how it is, Mom." She made a pout. "If you loved me, I'd think you'd understand that. I'd think you'd want to be here. It's your responsibility."

"Oh, Lauren," Susan teased. "You're starting to sound just like your grandmother."

Anna suppressed the urge to laugh, and Lauren's scowl just deepened.

"Lauren." Anna looked into her eyes. "I'd really love to have you come stay with me on the river. I think you'd be surprised at how nice it is there. It could be a very fun vacation for you. And, like I said, you can bring some friends." She turned to Susan. "I'd love to have you come too, Susan. We could have such a good time."

"It's really a lovely area," Clark told the girls. "I suspect it's going to become a popular vacation spot in the future. And the inn your mother is opening is very unique and quite comfortable."

"I think it sounds great," Susan said. "I'd like to go see it. To be honest, I'm getting a little sick of Pine Ridge. And Gordon likes to go fishing." She looked at Clark. "Is it a good place to fish?"

"The best," he assured her.

"Come on, Lauren," Susan urged her. "Your mom's offering us a free vacation and you're acting like a spoiled brat."

Just then the doorbell rang and Lauren hopped up. "That will be the boys."

Anna stood too. "You will think about this, won't you, Lauren?"

Lauren's lower lip jutted out. "I'm still mad that you're leaving us, Mom. I think that's unfair."

"Don't worry," Susan said offhandedly, "I'll talk some sense into her."

Anna attempted to hug Lauren, but it was like hugging a porcupine. "I love you, honey."

"We gotta go, Mom." Lauren hurried off and the two girls grabbed up their bags and things, then burst out the front door without even inviting the young men to come inside. Not that Anna was surprised. Lauren had seldom bothered to introduce her friends, not even to Eunice. And if Anna tried to intervene, it usually resulted in an unfortunate scene. Usually, Eunice would defend Lauren's bad behavior, saying that she'd already met the person in question. It always felt like the two of them were pushing Anna farther away, keeping her on the outside of their inner circle.

Anna sighed as the front door closed. "I feel like such a failure as a mother."

"Don't worry. I'm pretty sure we all feel like that when our kids are this age."

"I guess I should go start gathering up my things," she said.

"Need any help?"

She started to say no. She didn't want him, or anyone, to see where she'd lived all these years, a small room by the laundry room—the maid's quarters. Then she realized she no longer cared. This wasn't her anymore. "Sure," she told him. "I'll see if I can find some boxes in the garage first. I used to keep some stored in there."

"This is a nice house," he said as they went through the formal dining room and then through the swinging doors into the kitchen.

Anna laughed to see what a mess it was in there. "It used to look a lot tidier than this."

"Looks like your mother-in-law might need to hire a real housekeeper."

After finding the boxes, Anna led Clark to her old room. "It's rather embarrassing," she admitted as she opened the door to the tiny room, "but this is where I lived."

Clark didn't say anything, but she could tell by his expression that he was uneasy in the small space.

"I'm sorry. If you'd rather wait out there, I can easily load these boxes myself and just—"

"It's all right, Anna. I guess I'm just a little dumbfounded. How many bedrooms did you say this house has?"

"Six."

"Yet you stayed here—in what I'm guessing is the maid's quarters."

"It was partly my own choice," she explained. "I used to have a room upstairs, back when Adam was alive. It was later on, when Eunice or Lauren was entertaining and there was a need for more room, I'd stay down here. Finally, I realized this was actually rather convenient. I could check on laundry or something in the oven without constantly running up and down the stairs." She held up her hands. "And I suppose it gave me some space . . . my little getaway from my mother-in-law."

He nodded. "That makes sense."

It didn't take long for Anna to get the boxes packed and for Clark to carry them out to the truck. He was just picking up the last box for her when she heard her mother-in-law's shrill voice. Calling out loudly, Eunice was demanding to know who was in her house.

"Oh, dear." Anna tossed an apologetic look at Clark and picked up her handbag. "Time to face the music."

"Who parked that utility vehicle in front of the house?" Eunice called out as she came through the kitchen. "I want it moved immediately. Take it around to the—"

"Hello, Eunice," Anna said calmly as she stepped into the kitchen.

"Anna?" Eunice clasped her chest with her hand. "Good grief, girl. You nearly scared me to death. What are you doing sneaking around here like this?"

"I'm sorry. Lauren let me in. Then she left with her friends—just a few minutes ago."

Eunice nodded, getting a slightly smug expression on her face as she slowly removed her white gloves. "I see you've returned to your senses then, decided to come back to where you belong. It's about time."

"No, actually, that's not why I'm here. I simply came back to see Lauren—and to pick up my things."

Eunice's countenance darkened. "What do you mean *pick up your things?*"

"I mean I'm going back home. To *my* home." Anna nodded to where Clark was just emerging from her room with a box in his arms. Without fanfare, she did a quick introduction.

Eunice scowled with displeasure. "What, may I ask, is he doing in your room, Anna?"

"That's not my room anymore," Anna said simply. "Clark is just helping me to move my things."

"Just like that you're leaving us?" Eunice set her alligator handbag on the kitchen counter with a thud, dropping her gloves on top. "What about your daughter, Anna? What about your responsibilities to her? Are you just abandoning her?"

"I told Lauren she is welcome in my home at any time. My home will be her home."

"What sort of home could that possibly be?" Her lips puckered like she'd bitten into a lemon. "That nasty backwater place with no electricity or plumbing or—"

"You're wrong about that," Clark injected. "Anna is making some very nice improvements to her property. It's turning into what I predict will one day be a destination place—a delightful river resort."

"I can only imagine." Eunice's tone was full of disapproval.

"Before I leave," Anna began slowly, "there's something I want to tell you, Eunice. We met with Joseph P. Miller today."

"*Oh?*" Eunice's icy blue eyes flickered, and unless it was Anna's imagination, her papery complexion grew slightly paler beneath the rouged cheeks.

"Mr. Miller told me that, uh . . ." Anna wasn't sure how to say this. "Well, he explained the financial situation to me. But I found it rather confusing. His account is much different from yours, Eunice." Anna glanced at Clark helplessly.

"I'm Anna's legal counsel," he told Eunice. "Along with Mr. Miller, I'll be representing Anna in the matter of her husband's estate."

"*What* estate would that be?" Eunice's eyes narrowed as she looked at Anna. "I've told you over and over that *anything* that once belonged to Adam is long since used up. You know that, *Anna*."

"That may be what you told Anna, but it's not correct," Clark calmly said.

"Well, that is perfectly ludicrous." She turned to Clark, laughing drily. "Now I don't have the slightest idea what that daft Joe Miller has been telling you, but you should know that I have dismissed Joe as the family attorney. I honestly think the man is getting rather senile in his old age. Everyone in town is concerned about the poor old man's state of mind. I heard he forgot where he parked his car at the supermarket last week. Can you imagine?"

"You seem to be somewhat forgetful too, Mrs. Gunderson." Clark's tone was gentle but firm. "Mr. Miller sent a registered letter to Anna. He sent it to your home, but it was undeliverable. And when he inquired as to Anna's forwarding address, you told him you had no idea where she'd gone to. Did you forget?"

"Why didn't you tell him where I was?" Anna asked. "You knew I was at my parents' home. You could've told him that."

"I don't have the address of that backwater old shack on the river! I doubt that mail even goes out to the sticks."

"I've sent letters to Lauren, right here at your house," Anna told her. "Every single one of them has my return address—surely you must've noticed."

"As if I pay the slightest bit of attention to Lauren's personal mail and such."

"Then things must've changed since I left," Anna told her. "You used to have a locking mailbox that only you were allowed to open."

Eunice made a pained expression. "Tell me, Anna, is this the thanks I get for taking you in like I did? After Adam died, you and Lauren had nothing and I let you remain with me. But this is how you show your gratitude! My friends told me I was a fool for opening my home and my heart to you, but I didn't listen. Despite our differences, I allowed you and Lauren to be part of my household. For years I've covered all your expenses. I've treated Lauren as if she were my own child, even though I knew full well that she, like you, was part Indian. But this is how you repay me for my generosity. I suppose I should've expected as much. I never should've trusted a—someone of *your background*."

Something in Anna snapped. "Why don't you go ahead and just say it, Eunice? Say it like you usually do. Call me an Indian squaw, a half-breed. Just get it out into the open. I know you want to say it."

"You're right. You *are* an Indian, Anna. You were never in our class and you knew it. You will never fit into my world and you never should've trapped my son into marriage. It's no surprise that Adam took his own life—he finally came to his senses and realized what he'd gotten himself into by marrying a squaw. He regretted it so much that he killed himself." Eunice's features were twisted, as if hatred and bitterness had carved themselves into her face.

Feeling as if she'd just been slapped or kicked, Anna slowly backed away from her mother-in-law. Pushing past the swinging doors, she went into the dining room. She paused by the large mahogany table, holding on to the edge to steady herself, and took in a slow breath, trying to grasp what Eunice had just said. Adam's mother had known that he had taken his own life—although she'd never said a word. Eunice had known. And all this time, she had blamed it, like everything else that went wrong, on Anna.

"The truth hurts, doesn't it?" Eunice continued. In the dining room now, she came closer, her eyes still filled with hate. "Is it any wonder that I've despised you? If not for you, I'd still have my son right now. If not for you, Adam would be alive."

Everything inside Anna told her to run and hide like she used to do when Eunice attacked. But this time she remained fast. Holding her head high, Anna just stared at Eunice. "How can you possibly say that?" Anna quietly asked her. "You know as well as I do that Adam's war injuries took a great toll on him. That is why he . . . why he died."

"But he never would've gone into the war if he hadn't married *you*."

"*What?*" Anna blinked. "Adam went into the service because he *had* to go. He didn't even want to leave Lauren and me. And then he was wounded at Normandy. What you're saying makes no sense, Eunice."

"That's because you have no sense. I don't even expect you to understand."

Anna shook her head. She felt lost and sad and

sickened. How had Eunice's mind gotten so mixed up, so poisoned?

With the cardboard box still in his hands, Clark moved between Eunice and Anna, almost in what seemed a protective way. He stared at Eunice with a perplexed expression, and so intently that she actually stepped back. "If I hadn't just witnessed this—with my own eyes and ears—I'm not sure I would've believed that anyone could be so cruel and unfeeling, but as Anna's legal counsel, I'm taking this whole thing into consideration."

"Do not try to intimidate me, young man."

"As I said, Mrs. Gunderson," Clark's words came out evenly, but as sharp as a well-honed hunting knife, "I represent Anna's legal interests, as does Mr. Miller, and if necessary, we will resolve this matter in the courtroom with a judge to determine who is at fault."

"Are you threatening me?" Eunice demanded. "In my own home?"

"I'm simply stating the facts, Mrs. Gunderson. We're prepared to do whatever is necessary to see that Anna gets what is hers."

"Nothing is hers," Eunice spat out the words. She tapped the cardboard box in Clark's arms. "That's probably not even hers. In fact, I should go through those things to see if Anna has stolen anything from me. I wouldn't put it past her."

"I've taken *nothing* from you." Anna stepped

up to Eunice and, looking down on her realized, perhaps for the first time, that she was several inches taller than her mother-in-law. "But you have taken all you're going to get from me. It's humiliating to admit, but I let you walk over me for years—I allowed you to make me into your doormat. But my spineless days are over, Eunice. I got my strength back—I found it at the river—and I will never, never give it away again."

"Get out!" Eunice pointed toward the door. "Go, you ungrateful half-breed, I hope to never see your squaw face again. Get out of my house! Good riddance! *Go!*"

"Don't be deceived into believing you can get rid of Anna completely," Clark informed Eunice as he and Anna walked toward the foyer. "We still have money matters to settle with you and, as I already said, we're willing to resolve them in court."

"Fine," she snapped. "Take me to court. See if I care!"

He turned around. "Just so we are clear, Mrs. Gunderson. Mr. Miller has already produced plenty of evidence—enough to prove our case outside of a courtroom, but if you force us to stand before a judge, we will make sure that you not only pay back Anna for all you owe her, including years of pain and suffering, but you will also be held responsible for all the legal costs as well. It will be costly."

"Well!"

"Now if you will excuse us," Clark said politely, "we have a long drive to make."

With no more words to say and with shaking knees, Anna walked out of the house. It wasn't until she was seated in the cab of the truck and Clark was out on the open highway that tears began to slip down her cheeks. She retrieved a handkerchief from her handbag and turned to the side window in an attempt to conceal her quiet sobs. But she sensed Clark glancing toward her and she suspected her emotional display was making him uncomfortable. She wanted to reassure him that she wasn't as devastated as it might seem, but the lump in her throat seemed to swallow her words. Instead, she gave him a watery smile. "I'll be OK," she murmured.

"I know." He reached over and put his hand on her shoulder, clasping it gently in his grasp. "You are a *strong* woman, Anna, a *very strong* woman. I think your grandmother would be extremely proud of you today."

21

For the following week, Anna distracted herself from fretting over the ugly scene with her mother-in-law by investing all her energy into renovations at the inn. With the check from Mr. Miller, a payoff from Adam's life insurance policy that had been sitting in an investment account unbeknownst to Anna, she now had the funds and freedom to get the inn into great shape. She knew she should be deliriously happy about this, she should be having fun, but instead she felt as if a heavy storm cloud was hanging over her head. A black cloud named Eunice.

She was glad to discover that Clark wanted to stay on to help with the renovations. The quality of his work and his construction expertise were invaluable. Already he'd begun to put up walls to divide the downstairs space into rooms. He had wisely recommended making three rooms instead of four. Two would be bedroom-sized and one would be a suite with a bathroom where the old back room used to be. And he'd lined up a plumber to come out and do the preliminary work or "the rough plumbing" as he called it. He was also suggesting that Anna might build additional cabins like Pearl's Oyster Shell, to give guests even more privacy.

"Are you sure you really want to spend this much time here?" Anna had asked with concern one evening. As much as she wanted and needed his help, she felt guilty about keeping him from his other business responsibilities. Surely he had other commitments he should attend to, big houses to build, important customers waiting for his return. "I'd hate to think that my little projects might be taking you away from something more important."

He frowned. "Are you trying to get rid of me now?"

"No," she said urgently. "Nothing could be farther from the truth. I just wondered if you can really afford to stay on here, like this."

Clark had simply smiled. "I can't afford not to stay."

Anna could barely admit it (even to herself) but she suspected that Clark might have feelings for her—unless it was just hopeful thinking on her part. And she knew she had feelings for him. However, this was all so new to her—this possibility of a future romance—it was so strange and wonderful and confusing. Most of all, she didn't want to rush anything. She'd been rushed into a relationship once before, and that hadn't turned out too well. So, attempting to repress her feelings, she was determined that history not repeat itself. Not with her. This gave her one more reason to throw herself into the work of getting the inn ready for occupancy.

As Anna worked, she realized that she wanted everything to be perfect in her inn. Not perfect in the way that Eunice had always wanted things done—with everything spotless, impeccable, brightly shining, impressive, and new. No, Anna simply wanted this inn to be perfect as in *just right*. She wanted to offer guests the sort of place where anyone and everyone would not only be comfortable but also be able to have an unforgettable river experience that would leave them feeling renewed, rejuvenated, and refreshed.

However, there was another motivation in getting the inn in order, something she longed for but tried not to obsess over: she hoped Lauren would come for a visit. She'd already written Lauren, specifically asking her to come out before it was time to go off to college. She'd pointed out that since July was coming to an end, summer vacation was limited. Anna had suggested the last two weeks of August for Lauren's visit—encouraging her to bring several girlfriends with her. She'd even written a little note to Susan (in care of Lauren) reminding her of the invitation. And she felt hopeful.

In her determination to transform what had once been a somewhat rundown but comfortable family home into an inn, she removed all personal items (except for the few special Siuslaw pieces from her grandmother). She packed up her parents' belongings, taped the boxes closed, and temporarily stored them in the attic. Then she thinned out most of the furnishings until she had what felt like a fairly blank palette. Then she studied the paint chart she'd picked up at the hardware store and tried to make a decision.

For as long as she could remember, all the walls in the house had been painted a pinkish brown color that felt heavy and depressing. She'd always assumed her parents had gotten a good deal on a bad color of paint. However, she wasn't fond of the popular shades of this era. She found all those aqua, pink, or yellow tones—the colors found so liberally in her mother-in-law's house—to be off-putting. She considered painting everything white, but that seemed a bit stark.

Finally, she settled on a creamy shade called "Sandy Beach." It was light enough to brighten the rooms and contrast with the old-growth fir floors, but still a friendly color—almost the same shade as a doeskin cape her grandmother had kept in a trunk. Anna held the paint sample next to the arrangement of "artifacts" (as Hazel called them) on the dining table and it all seemed to fit. She had decided to use the baskets and other items as her inspiration for the interior design of all the rooms in the inn.

Anna had also laid out a couple of old Pendleton blankets that she'd found in the linen closet. Despite some moth holes, she was determined to put them to use somehow. Perhaps she'd sew the undamaged parts into pillows or piece them together for bedspreads on the twin beds. But she felt the Indian patterns and colors were perfect for the look she was trying to accomplish. She knew it might seem a bit backward or old-fashioned to certain people (like her mother-in-law) but Anna didn't expect those types to frequent an inn like this anyway.

"What have you here?" Hazel asked as she came into the house for lunch.

Anna laid the Navajo-design blanket over the back of the old sofa. "I thought I might use these things for the inn." She waved to the things on the table then showed Hazel the paint color, explaining her plans. "What do you think?"

Hazel ran her hand over a woolen blanket. "I think it will be perfectly delightful. In fact, this reminds me of some of the National Park lodges. Have you ever been to the Grand Canyon or Yellowstone or Yosemite?"

Anna shook her head. "I haven't been much of anywhere. The store kept my parents on the river most of the time. And once I left to get married, well, you know how that went."

Now Hazel began to describe the interiors of some famous inns and lodges and how blankets similar to these were used, as well as Indian artifacts, rustic wood carvings, and stone. "Of course, it was on a much larger scale, but the feeling was the same. They call it lodge style, I believe. But the rugs, blankets, tables, chairs, lamps, all the furnishings—everything has a rustic quality that feels like a celebration of nature and the great outdoors."

"Yes!" Anna said with excitement. "That's just

the kind of look I'd like to achieve here. Do you really think it's possible?"

"Absolutely. And if anyone can accomplish it, I'd put my money on you, Anna."

"Thank you." Anna glanced around the room. "Do you think guests will find it too quaint or old-fashioned?"

"I think guests here, just like at El Tovar, will fall in love with it."

"El Tovar?"

"The main lodge on the south rim of the Grand Canyon. It's spectacular."

"Oh." Anna went to check on the soup.

"I got the boat running," Clark announced as he came into the kitchen. "I cleaned all the spark plugs, changed the oil, and drained and replaced the gas. As far as I can tell, the engine runs as good as new."

"That's great," Anna said as she ladled out some clam chowder. "Maybe I'll run it into town today to pick up some paint and things. Anyone want to come?"

"Not me," Hazel told her. "I'm making good progress on my thesis right now. I want to keep my nose to the grindstone."

"I'd like to come," Clark said. "Just in case the engine decides to give you a problem. Besides, an outing would be nice."

"You know what you kids should do," Hazel said suddenly.

"Kids?" Clark frowned.

"Compared to me, you're kids."

"What should we do?" Anna asked.

"Go see a movie!"

"What?" Anna made a face. "I haven't seen a movie in years. Besides, aren't the movies these days just for the younger generation?"

"Precisely my point, my dear. You should go see a movie and remember that you're still young."

"A movie?" Clark nodded. "It might be interesting. What do you think, Anna?"

She giggled. "I don't know. I suppose it would be entertaining."

"Well, Mom, if it'll make you happy, maybe we'll look into it."

"And don't worry about the time," Hazel assured Anna. "I'll just warm up some of this soup for dinner. By the way, it's delicious."

"But what if there's not a movie we care to see?" Anna asked.

"Babette thought there might be a good Rock Hudson movie playing."

Anna laughed. "Babette adores Rock Hudson."

As it turned out, the Rock Hudson film wasn't going to make an appearance in Florence until October and the horror movie playing at the theater didn't interest either of them. But Anna felt relieved. She hadn't sat in a movie theater for years and the idea of sitting in the dark for a couple of hours next to Clark was a bit unsettling. Besides, this gave them more time for running errands—and she had a lot she wanted to accomplish before the stores closed.

"I hate to keep you in town longer than you'd like," she told him. "But my list is rather long."

"As a matter of fact, so is mine." He grinned. "I'm going to check out the lumberyard and several other places."

"When do you want to meet back up?"

He looked at his watch. "How about we stick around until the businesses close and then I'll take you to dinner."

"To dinner?" She was surprised.

"Why not? Mom expects us to take in a movie. We should go ahead and make a night of it. It won't even be dark until nearly nine."

She smiled. "That sounds nice." So she suggested a restaurant and they went their separate ways. As Anna went to the places on her list, she couldn't help contrasting the difference between being in Florence and Pine Ridge. Here she felt free and welcomed and happy—she was home. If she never went back to Pine Ridge again, she would be perfectly content.

After ordering paint, she went to the secondhand store again. This time her list was longer and she knew that anything she purchased would have to be delivered. But before she bought anything, she went to the new furniture store as well, just to look around. Then after some careful consideration, she returned to the secondhand store and selected the pieces she felt would best lend themselves to the lodge look she wanted to accomplish, and when she told the store owner what she was trying to achieve and how she planned to use Pendleton blankets and Indian artifacts, his eyes lit up.

"I've got a bunch of those Pendleton blankets in the back room," he told her. "I don't keep them out here because I'm worried about moths."

Soon she was looking at a fine selection of interesting blankets. Not only that, but he had some hand-woven Navajo rugs that would be useful as well. She felt he was really catching the vision for what she wanted as he pulled out a couple of rustic-looking lamps that someone had just brought in.

"You know, this whole camp style was real popular right after the war," he said, "but now a lot of folks are getting more modern with their furnishings, so I'll probably see more of these older pieces coming in. Would you like me to keep an eye out for them?"

"I'd love that," she told him. And after completing her purchases, she gave him her phone number. Then she returned to the new furniture store to look again. Anna felt the saleswoman was getting annoyed with her, since she seemed unable to make up her mind. Anna wished the owner, Carl Edwards (the one who'd given her a deal on the mattresses), was around to help. But it seemed the impatient saleswoman was her only option today.

A leather sofa had caught her eye the first time she'd come into the store. Neatly arrayed with some other modern pieces in the front of the store, as if to show it off, it was the most expensive item she'd seen in the store. And although the long, low sofa was more of the new modern style, the fact that it was brown leather gave it a feeling that she thought might work into her overall plan. Imagining it paired with the Navajo rug she'd just purchased, and combining both with her father's old wooden coffee table, which she was keeping, just might work. Plus she'd seen a handsome pair of rust-colored club chairs and ottomans that she felt could add to a comfortable seating arrangement.

However, the prices on these new furnishings were a bit staggering. She knew she could easily afford them, but being unaccustomed to spending this kind of money, it made her jittery. She slowly strolled through the store, looking at some other pieces with possibilities and wondered what to do. She reminded herself that this would be an investment in the inn and her future, and that she had plenty of money. Also, she told herself, this would be the first time she'd ever purchased brand-new furnishings for her own home. Real quality that would probably last for years to come. So, really, what was wrong with that? What was making her so fearful?

Of course, the image of Eunice popped into her head just then, sourly shaking her head, pointing her finger, telling Anna she'd been wasteful, and that she owed everything she had to her, and that she'd better come home right now and clean Eunice's house! Anna knew that was perfectly ridiculous, but the image was hard to shake.

"If you're working on a budget, we have some *bargains* in the back room," the woman told Anna. "Markdowns on some, uh, damaged or dated pieces."

Anna's first reaction was to feel slightly insulted by this suggestion. She could tell by the woman's tone and expression that she doubted that Anna was a serious buyer. But hearing the words *dated pieces* sparked Anna's curiosity. So she said she'd like to see them and followed the smartly dressed woman to the back of the store. Wearing a narrow, black pencil skirt and pale blue sweater set, the woman's high heels clicked on the floor with importance, almost as if she was in a hurry, although there were no other customers in the store.

In comparison, Anna realized she probably looked like a hick (or a backwater bumpkin as

Lauren might say). She hadn't bothered to change from her serviceable green corduroy trousers, loafers, and plaid blouse. But at least she was comfortable, and riding a boat down the river hardly called for high style.

The woman pushed open the door and Anna studied the random pieces arranged willy-nilly in the back room. Some of them were just plain ugly, but a couple of things were actually in the old camp style that she was going for. Without second-guessing herself, she pointed to several pieces. "I'll take that and that and those."

The woman nodded in a slightly smug way. "I thought you might like these old things." She pulled off their tags and smiled. "Would you like them delivered or did you plan to pick them up yourself?"

"Delivered."

"Fine. I'll write them up for you."

"Thank you." Still thinking about the leather sofa, Anna went back into the showroom and was just heading for the leather sofa when the owner stepped in.

"Hello there, Anna," Carl called out, tipping his hat.

"Hi, Carl." Relieved that he remembered her name, she went over to him and asked how he was doing.

"I'm just fine. Anything I can help you with here today?"

She smiled. "Well, your saleswoman showed me some bargains in the back room and that was helpful, but I'd like to consider something else as well."

"What are you looking for?"

She pointed to the brown leather sofa. "I'm thinking about that."

He nodded with his hat in his hands. "I could tell you were a woman with fine taste, Anna. Just by looking at you." Now he told her a little bit about the sofa and its quality construction. "This piece will probably last until your great-grandchildren come along."

She laughed. "That I'd like to see." Now she showed him the other pieces she was considering and he told her a bit more about them, showed her some things she'd missed, and before long he was writing up a very large order. Meanwhile the saleswoman was helping an elderly woman pick out a new bedroom lamp, but glancing back at Anna with a puzzled expression. Anna hoped she wasn't calculating her lost commission.

"And since you're buying so much today, I'm going to offer you a ten percent discount," Carl told her. "What do you think of that?"

"I like it." Anna carefully wrote out the check, trying not to cringe at the large amount. "Thank you very much."

"I can't wait to see your inn, Anna." He gave her the receipt. "Are you going to have some sort of open house to let the locals see what it's like?"

"That's a great idea, Carl." She nodded and closed her purse. "I'll make sure you get an invitation." Then she thanked him, smiled at the saleswoman, and left.

Now instead of feeling nervous and jittery, she felt exhilarated—and strong. She knew it was probably silly to feel this way, like she'd just won some small battle with her mother-in-law, but she did. Unfortunately, she knew that this was far from the last battle. Because Anna knew that, whether imaginary or real, her run-ins with Eunice were far from over.

22

By the time she met Clark for dinner, Anna was feeling a bit giddy. Besides purchasing the furniture, she had also ordered new appliances for the kitchen, including a freezer chest, and a new automatic washer and dryer as well. And although there was still an amazingly large balance in her checking account, she couldn't believe how much money she'd spent today.

"You look flushed," he told her after they were seated at a table. "Are you feeling well?"

She quickly explained what she'd been doing and how unnerving it was to spend so much money so quickly, but he simply chuckled and said, "Good for you."

She gave him a nervous smile. "I'm sure that's easy for you to say since you deal with large projects on an ongoing basis, but this is all new to me."

"Well, I'm sure you're making wise choices."

"I am learning a lot," she confessed. "I probably ask far too many questions. But I want to use my funds wisely. The inn will be my livelihood and I want it done right."

Now he told her about some of the things he'd found today. "The good news is that I might've actually been a little high on some of the estimates I gave you," he said finally. "The prices on lumber and a few things aren't as high here as I'd figured they'd be."

"You said 'good news.' Does that mean there's bad news too?"

He laughed. "No. Don't worry. I didn't mean it like that. Sometimes good news is just that— good news."

She sighed in relief. "I must seem like a neurotic worrywart to you, but I'll be glad when this part is over—the buying and building and setting up part I mean."

His smile faded. "You mean the part where I'm involved."

Now she was flustered. "No, that's not what I'm saying. I do enjoy your involvement, Clark. And I truly appreciate everything you're doing. It's just that all these preparations are a bit stressful."

"Then take a deep breath and just enjoy them." He grinned. "Most women don't have a problem spending money on their homes."

"That's probably true. I know my mother-in-law didn't think twice when she had rooms redone in her house. Of course, she had an interior decorator to pick everything out for her—and then other workers would come in and complete the project. Then she would complain if something wasn't done perfectly, so much so that it seemed she didn't even notice all that had been done right."

"I've had clients like that before. My rule is that I only work with them once."

"That would be tricky in a town as small as Pine Ridge. Not too many wealthy customers to choose from. Eunice Gunderson gets most people to do what she wants."

"Yes, I suspected as much. All the more reason you should be thankful to be away from her clutches, and why you should enjoy doing what you like with your own place. This is your big chance, Anna. Why not have fun with it?"

She nodded. "You're right. I should."

"Sometimes it's more about the journey than the destination."

She studied him closely. "How did you get to be so wise?"

He laughed. "I think I got my best training in the school of hard knocks."

"You and me both. But I'll take your advice. I'll focus on the journey. Although I am looking forward to the destination. I'm so excited to see what it'll be like when everything is done and operational. Oh, I know it will be work to keep the inn running, caring for guests, and preparing food, but I honestly can't wait to get started." Now she told him about Carl's idea for an open house. "I have no idea when I'll be ready for that." She glanced curiously at him. "Do you have a time frame?"

He got a thoughtful look. "Well, the rooms in the main building will be done soon—hopefully in time for Lauren and her friends to visit. Although I'm not sure about the bathhouse, but I hope to have it fully running by mid-September."

Anna felt a twinge of disappointment. "So it won't be done when Lauren and her friends come."

Clark's eyes lit up. "Unless I have some help. How would you feel about having my son, Marshall, come out to give me a hand? He's worked with me before and knows his way around a construction site."

"Do you think he'd come out here?"

"I know he's trying to earn some money before school starts. And he works hard when he's not distracted." Clark chuckled. "Lately it's the girls that distract him, but I don't think that will be a problem out here."

"Would he mind the rustic conditions?" she asked.

Clark shrugged. "Might be good for him."

Anna wasn't too sure about that, but she did like the idea of getting the bathrooms done in time for Lauren and her friends—especially since she knew that Lauren didn't like rustic conditions either. And one bathroom in the house, plus the outhouse outside, probably wouldn't please her pampered daughter. More than anything, even if it was slightly shallow and shortsighted, Anna wanted Lauren to arrive at the inn and be pleasantly surprised, perhaps even impressed. It seemed a possibility.

23

Two days later, Marshall arrived on the boat with Henry—along with all the furnishings Anna had ordered in town the other day. "Right handy that I had to give this young man a lift up the river," Henry told Anna as she met the boat. "We'll need an extra hand to unload all these things."

Anna quickly introduced herself to Marshall, apologizing for having to put him to work so quickly. "If we just get the things unloaded onto the dock, Henry can get on his way. He probably has more deliveries to make."

"Your lumber order won't be ready to pick up

until after one," Henry told her. "You're my number one customer today, Anna."

"Well, if you can help us with these things, I'd love to have you stay for lunch."

He grinned. "You got yourself a deal!"

They were just unloading the second chair when Clark joined them on the dock. "I'll take it from here," he told Anna. "You just direct us as to where these things go." He grinned at Marshall as he helped to set the chair onto the dock. "Hi, Son, good to see you made it."

Marshall gave his dad a slightly aggravated look, then paused to remove his black leather jacket. But before he could set it down on a pier, Anna grabbed it. "Here," she said with a smile, "let me put that someplace safe for you."

"Thanks."

She smoothed her hand over the leather. "It's a very nice jacket."

Now he smiled and she saw how much he resembled his father.

Anna directed them and as they were bringing up the last load—the brown leather sofa that went in the living room—she went to check on lunch. Fortunately, she'd put a roast in the oven that morning. She'd planned to use it for a couple of meals, but realized she'd be lucky if it filled up everyone for lunch today.

"What're you doing with your old furnishings?" Henry asked after they put the sofa into place. All the new furnishings were still wrapped in packing blankets and cardboard, and Anna was eager to see how they looked, but knew she needed to get lunch served first.

"I'm not sure," she told him as she mashed potatoes. "I want to save a couple things, like Mother's old rocker and Daddy's desk, but the old sofa and chairs . . . I haven't really thought about." She looked at the crowded room. "Do you know anyone who could use a few things?"

Henry grinned and rubbed his chin. "Well, you know, my place ain't terribly big, but if I got rid of a few old things, I might be able to take 'em off your hands, if you like."

She nodded eagerly. "I would love that, Henry!"

"All righty, boys, you wanna help me load them up in my boat?"

"You got it," Clark told him.

Shortly after they left with the old sofa, Hazel came into the house. "Something smells delicious in here," she said as she came into the kitchen to take a peek. "Ooh, roast and potatoes and gravy—and it's not even Sunday! You're spoiling us, Anna."

Anna just laughed. "Well, those guys deserve a little spoiling. They're doing a lot of hefting and hauling today."

It was fun to set the dining room table with five places. It made Anna wonder how it would feel to be running a real inn. She realized that serving new and various groups of people each day would require some planning and preparation on her part, but she felt she was up to it. She hoped she was up to it.

After they were seated at the table and Clark's usual blessing was said, he explained to Marshall and Henry what his general construction plan was. "We'll finish up the rooms downstairs first, then the bathhouse, and when those are complete, we'll move on to building the first four cabins."

"Four new cabins?" Henry looked impressed.

"Yes," Anna told him. "We plan to keep them simple—with a small bath and kitchenette."

"The permit allows for up to twelve cabins." Clark poured gravy over his potatoes. "But it might take a while for the inn to get that busy. However, if business picks up, and if Anna is game, I'll come out and build the other cabins next spring or summer."

After lunch, Marshall went on the boat with Henry. The plan was to help Henry unload the used furniture at his shanty, then to help him pick up and load the lumber.

"Do you think Marshall minds playing delivery boy today?" she asked Clark as she set a fresh pile of bedding in one of the downstairs bedrooms. It was next to the room where Clark was staying and she wanted to get it ready for Marshall.

"He seemed happy to go." Clark paused from where he was fitting in a sliding glass door. "Hopefully he'll be equally happy to stick around and help me too."

"That looks great," she said as she admired the view from the wide opening. "You were absolutely right about these glass doors. You can even see the river from here."

Clark stood and looked out. "It's nice, isn't it?"

"I still have to pinch myself sometimes," she admitted. "This all feels a bit dreamlike when I think of where I was a couple of months ago."

"Well, with Marshall here, I hope to hurry things on a bit." He pulled a screwdriver from his tool pouch. "Any word from your daughter yet?"

"Yes," Anna said happily. "Lauren and her friends are all coming in just two weeks."

"Two weeks." He nodded and continued installing the sliding door.

"I've decided that even if the bathhouse isn't finished, we will just make the best of it."

"I'll do what I can," he told her. "With Marshall's help, it might happen."

She left him to his work and continued getting the room ready for Marshall. She wanted the boy to feel as at home as possible. The downstairs rooms were nearly finished now. With just the sliding doors to be finished and some touch-up painting, they would be ready for real guests before long. Plus she'd been working on the upstairs bedrooms as well. And after she got Marshall's room arranged, she planned to put the living room together. She could hardly wait to unwrap the furnishings up there. And later this week, the appliances would be delivered. Everything, it seemed, was falling into place.

For the next two weeks, everyone at The Inn at Shining Waters was kept very busy. Marshall and Clark focused on the construction, finishing up the downstairs rooms and the bathroom in the suite, as well as getting the bathhouse nearly completed. Meanwhile Anna did the painting and cleanup, as well as fixed meals and kept things running smoothly. It was hard work with a tight deadline, but Anna knew it would be well worth it once Lauren and her friends arrived on the third Saturday of August.

All the bedrooms, both upstairs and down, were in great shape now, with fresh new linens and interesting albeit slightly woodsy furnishings and rugs. Each room had its own unique look, with Pendleton blankets on the beds, rustic lamps and headboards, comfortable chairs—all the things she hoped would make her guests feel at home. Even the living room had come together nicely. Across from the stone fireplace, the leather couch and Navajo rug were flanked by the rust club chairs and her mother's old wooden rocker. This, combined with some unique end tables and lamps and the Indian artifacts added here and there for interest, made for a surprisingly pleasing effect. Hazel had proclaimed that portion of the house "the Lodge at Shining Waters." She told Anna that from now on she had to call it the lodge.

Also, with the appliances installed and running, life began to run a bit more smoothly and easily for Anna. She almost thought she could keep up—even with a houseful of guests. Not only that, but with Babette's help, she'd come up with a simple yet interesting menu that was actually fairly easy to shop for as well.

"I have brought you something special," Babette told her a few days before her guests were scheduled to arrive. She held out a basket. "A surprise." She removed the linen cloth to reveal a number of tiny jars containing her wonderful lavender cream, as well as miniature soaps, all prettily packaged and tied with purple satin ribbons. "To put een your guest rooms and for you too." She nodded. "You like?"

Anna threw her arms around Babette. "I *love!*"

"And maybe . . . eef guest like, I will sell more." Babette laughed. "I can be business-woman too."

Everything seemed to be coming together just perfectly. So much so that on the afternoon before the big day, Anna even had time to take a short canoe ride. Although she now had three additional dark green canoes for guests to use, she still preferred the *River Dove*, and before long, she was peacefully paddling along. By now she'd gotten somewhat used to the logs in the river and she told herself that, in time, these logs would all be gone and that the river would return to its former glory. She was determined to do her part to make sure that happened. In the meantime, she would enjoy what the river still had to offer. As Hazel had so aptly put it in June, the river would help to heal Anna, and Anna, in time, would help to heal the river.

Anna knew she wasn't the only one enjoying the canoes lately. Marshall had grown fond of canoeing during the past couple of weeks. In fact, he'd even taken out her dugout canoe a couple of times, which was fine with her. Marshall also seemed to like working with his dad and he was really helping to speed things along, putting them ahead of schedule. It was fun listening to the two of them talk as they shared meals. It was obvious that Marshall admired his father and when Clark praised Marshall's efforts, the boy beamed. So much for wanting to be a rebel.

Hazel was enjoying having her grandson nearby too. They'd taken some nature walks together and Marshall seemed impressed with his grandmother's knowledge of so many things. Then every evening the four of them would gather after dinner—outside if the weather was pleasant, in the lodge if it was windy—and they would visit or play games and sometimes Hazel would tell a story, often one of Anna's grandmother's old stories, and even Marshall would listen with what seemed genuine interest.

So although the past two weeks had been busy and intense, they had been good. And now Anna was almost sad to see they were coming to an end. Marshall would be going home on Sunday. His mother claimed it was time for him to get ready to start back to school. And Clark sounded as if he was planning to go home for a week or two as well. Even Hazel was nearly done with her work.

If it wasn't for the highly anticipated visit from Lauren, Anna might actually be on the verge of feeling rather lonesome just now. As it was, she was too full to feel sad. It was one of those rare summer days of clear sky and sunshine and just a slight ocean breeze to keep things fresh. Anna hoped this weather would hold for Lauren and her friends during the following week. Setting the paddle to rest in front of her, Anna leaned back in the canoe. Taking in a deep breath, she simply relaxed, letting go of everything as the motion of the water gently swayed her, like a mother rocking her child, and the river's song was the soothing lullaby.

Anna closed her eyes, soaking in the sunlight

and the musky smell of both the living and the dying vegetation along the riverbanks, and the *shush-shush* sound of the water. Anna felt completely at peace on the Siuslaw, with the assurance that she was in the right place . . . at the right time . . . perfection. She couldn't remember a moment, unless it was in childhood or the day that Lauren was born, in which she had felt this perfectly happy.

Finally, she knew it was time to see about dinner, so she paddled back home and pulled the canoe up on the riverbank, turning it upside down, laid it next to the others, and headed up to the house. On her way she noticed a small pile of building scraps that she'd meant to put on the burn pile. Scooping them up she carried them over to the bonfire site she'd been making these past few weeks. To celebrate the girls' first night here, Anna planned to torch the scraps. Then they'd all enjoy a blazing bonfire. She hoped it wasn't too childish, but she'd even gotten marshmallows and the fixings for s'mores. She remembered how much Lauren had loved them at a summer camp she'd gone to a few years ago. One time Anna had even tried to make them in the oven for Lauren and her friends, but the result was a sticky drippy mess, which Eunice had frowned upon.

Clark came over to join her, tossing a couple pieces of scrap wood onto the growing pile. "Are you getting excited about your guests arriving tomorrow?"

She grinned. "I am. I feel like a kid I'm so giddy."

"Well, it's all coming together. We just finished the grouting on the last two showers on the men's side. It should be dry in a few days. In the meantime, I've got them taped off with a sign." He chuckled. "Not that the girls are apt to want to shower on the men's side."

"Even without those other two, there should be plenty of showers for everyone," she told him. "Even if everyone wants to shower at the same time."

"This is turning into a lovely piece of property, Anna. You should be very proud."

"Mostly I'm very thankful." She smiled. "I never could've done it without you. Not just the construction, which has been major, but without your help I never would've gone back to Pine Ridge and discovered the insurance money."

He cleared his throat. "Speaking of that, I returned Joe Miller's phone call this afternoon."

"Oh?" She tried to read his expression. "How did that go?"

"Sounds like your mother-in-law is digging in her heels."

She shrugged, kicking a scrap piece of cedar into the pile. "No surprises there."

"That's true. But Joe said that he hoped you

weren't counting on getting the remainder of your money too soon."

Anna pressed her lips together and just nodded. She'd warned herself this might happen, that it probably *would* happen. She'd told herself not to be a fool and not to expect any more money from Adam's estate. But she realized now that she'd still been holding out some hope, secretly wishing there'd be enough to get her through the first year—just in case her expectation of filling the inn with paying guests went unfulfilled.

"Joe said it could take six months, maybe up to a year, Anna, or longer even, just to get everything all sorted out."

Anna sighed. "I'd been afraid of that." She remembered how stunned she'd been at the size of the check Mr. Miller had given her. And yet it was disappearing quickly. Much faster than she'd imagined possible. After she paid Clark what she owed him, her bank account would be fairly well thinned out. Still, she reminded herself, it was more than she'd had a few months ago.

"It seems your mother-in-law tied up your funds quite neatly. Not only in her lumber mill, but in a number of other investments and annuities as well. Joe thinks that even in the best-case scenario, meaning if a judge comes down on Eunice, she'll simply claim she invested the money for your benefit. But at the moment she's still insisting that every penny from Adam's estate has been spent on Lauren and you, and she claims she can prove it. She also says that you granted her power of attorney long ago." He paused. "Do you recall doing anything like that?"

Anna tried to think. "Does that mean I signed something? A legal form?"

"Usually that's how it's done. Do you remember signing a document like that?"

Anna held up her hands in a helpless way. "I honestly don't know. As I've said, Eunice took care of all the finances and business. Sometimes she would have me sign something. Oh, she'd usually have some complicated-sounding explanation, which I never questioned. And early on, despite our differences, I trusted her about these things. I had no reason not to. The truth was, I needed her to handle those things. Especially when Lauren was small and Adam's illness was so demanding and I felt overwhelmed with everything. Not just caring for Adam and Lauren, but all the cooking and cleaning—well, it was all I could do to keep my head above water."

"I think we can get the judge to take that into account—in case you did sign something authorizing Eunice to handle your finances. We can explain how you were unaware as to what you were signing—and that you trusted your mother-in-law was looking out for your best interests. It's a natural assumption."

"Meaning this will go to court then?"

"It's probably the only way we'll recover what's yours, Anna."

"Oh, dear." She picked up a stick and threw it to the top of the debris.

"Sorry to be the bearer of bad news."

She forced a smile. "It's not your fault, Clark. I just appreciate how helpful you've been in unraveling this mess." She wanted to add that she would understand his need to bow out of the legal business after he finished up the work here. She couldn't expect him to continue offering her legal advice after the four cabins were completed in November, but she couldn't manage to say those words just yet. The idea of him permanently leaving, returning to his old life, made her sad. She turned from the burn pile and, saying she needed to start dinner, began walking toward the house. Clark went with her.

"Anyway," he continued, "I wanted you to know that we can set up a payment plan for my construction bill—it doesn't even need to start until after you're on your feet with guests and everything, I'd be perfectly happy to wait until a year from now to—"

"No!" She stopped walking and firmly shook her head. "Absolutely not. I wouldn't dream of it. You've already given me a more than generous deal on your fine work. And when I think of all the wonderful improvements you and Marshall have done"—she waved her hand toward the charming cabin-like bathhouse—"I can hardly believe it. No, Clark, I plan to pay you this week for what you've done, as well as for the additional four cabins. I plan to pay you *in full*. I've budgeted for this already."

He nodded, then looked down at his feet as if feeling uneasy.

"And hopefully the guests will come as expected, and I'll make good money, and I'll be ready for you to build even more cabins next spring." She tried to exude confidence. "In fact, one year from now I expect my inn to be fully booked."

"I wouldn't be a bit surprised."

"I've already worked out the budget for that too," she told him as they came to the house. "And I really believe it's doable."

"Is that your telephone I hear ringing?" he asked as they stopped.

"Yes. Excuse me." She dashed up the steps and into the house, breathlessly answering the phone. *"Hello?"*

"Mom?"

"Yes." She paused to catch her breath. "Lauren, darling, how *are* you?"

"Not so great." Lauren's voice sounded strange.

"Are you sick?"

"No . . . it's not like that."

"What then, darling?"

"I won't be able to come visit you."

"Why not?" Anna's heart sank as she sat down on the kitchen stool.

"It's just not going to work out." Lauren's tone grew sharp now. "You never should've expected that it would."

"Why?"

"Because what you're doing is wrong, Mom. Just plain wrong!"

"What on earth are you talking about?"

"Taking money from Grandmother like you're doing—and after all she's done for us. I can't believe you'd do that to her, Mom!"

"Lauren Marion Gunderson, what in the world are you talking about?"

"*You,* Mom. I'm talking about you! Grandmother says you're suing her for everything—that you want to take away her house and the cars and that I won't be able to go to college and—and—*oh,* Mom!" Lauren burst into sobs.

"Lauren, that is *not* true. I swear to you that's not how it—"

"Grandmother told me you'd deny everything. But don't bother trying to fool me. I heard Grandmother talking to the lawyer and I know what's going on. I just never thought my own mother could do something so low." She choked back another sob. "Anyway, I can't come see you now. *Not ever!*" She hung up with a loud bang.

Anna just sat there with the dial tone buzzing dully in her ear. What was going on in Pine Ridge? She called back, hoping to get some explanation and the chance to defend herself, but this time Eunice answered. "What do you want?" she demanded angrily.

"To speak to my daughter, please."

"What daughter?"

"My daughter *Lauren,*" Anna declared. "Please, let me talk to her now."

"You have no daughter. You have turned against us. You are a stranger to—"

"Eunice!"

"Do not call this telephone number again, *do you hear me?* And if you do call here, if you continue to harass us, I shall have my attorney file a restraining order and then you will be arrested and put in jail where you probably belong. You are not to be in contact with us—not me and not Lauren. You are dead to us now. Do you understand?"

"But I just want to speak to—" Again she was cut off. With shaking hands, she replaced the receiver and tried to understand what was happening, tried to make sense of what seemed to be utter nonsense.

24

Anna tried to conceal her heartbreak during dinner. She planned to let her friends know about her disappointment—later—because she knew that if she opened the dam right now all her emotions would come raging out and ruin the meal for everyone. And so she was quiet.

"This has been a great couple a weeks," Marshall said as he helped himself to another piece of chicken. "I feel kinda silly for the way I was acting about coming out here before." He laughed. "Like I was being sent to prison—but the truth is this place is like paradise."

"Even though I worked you so hard?" Clark spread butter on a biscuit.

"I don't mind working hard." Marshall sat up straighter. "Not when I'm getting paid."

"And the benefits aren't bad." Clark grinned at Anna. "Besides the great food, you've got canoes and fishing and the great outdoors."

"I just hope I get to come back and help with the other cabins—maybe you can plan to build them during spring break, Dad. Then I could come with you."

"We'll see what we can do." Clark glanced at Anna again.

"Maybe if I'm not ready for the cabins in the spring, you can come back to help with them in the summer," she told Marshall. "Or just to visit." She smiled. "You know you're welcome here anytime—and I mean as my guest, not as a customer."

"That'd be swell."

"I can hardly believe that I'm nearly done with my thesis," Hazel told them. "All I need to do now is some editing and I've decided that I can do that at home."

"So when are you leaving, Grandma?"

"Maybe with you and Clark on Sunday." She smiled at Anna. "I'm sure you won't mind having a few less mouths to feed while your daughter and friends are here."

Anna set her fork down on the plate of barely touched food. "I'm sorry," she said quietly. "Will you please excuse me?" Then she stood and hurried to her room, closing the door behind her. She sat down on the bed, wringing her hands as tears silently slipped down her cheeks. She wished she'd gone outside instead of getting stuck in her room, which suddenly felt claustrophobic. She considered going out again, bolting for the door, but she did not want her friends to see her like this. She felt powerless and miserable, and totally incapable of running this inn. Really, what had made her think she had the strength to do such a thing? She thought she was strong, but in reality, she was weak. Very weak.

Anna remembered something her grandmother used to say. "When I am weak, I am strong." The first time Anna heard it she'd been confused, asking what it meant. Grandma Pearl said the words were from God's Book. "It means when I run out, when I am empty and weak, God can fill me. I must be empty first."

As she cried alone in her little room, Anna felt as if she was being emptied. And yet the tears continued to flow—as if there were a deep well inside of her, full of sadness and loss and disappointment—and it was all pouring out tonight. After a while she fell asleep. Upon waking she realized it was dark out. The house was quiet. Her guests must've gone to bed.

Feeling like a very bad hostess, she crept out of her room and turned on the light. To her surprise, all the dinner things were cleared up. She wondered what they must've thought of her— perhaps they were glad to know they'd all be going home on Sunday. Or perhaps they'd decided to go home Saturday. Really, there was nothing to keep them here any longer.

These thoughts only brought more sadness and once more the tears began to flow. She thought about her grandmother's words again. Anna had no doubts she was being emptied, but she wondered what it took to get filled back up, like Grandma had said, with God.

"Ask and the Creator gives," Grandma used to

say. Sometimes she'd say this in reference to good weather or catching a big fish or finding a bountiful spot to gather blackberries or pickleweed. But tonight Anna decided to take this to heart. She would ask the Creator to give her what she needed—and she would ask him now. And so she prayed for strength. "Give me your strength," she prayed. "I feel I've run out of my own. I am empty. Please, fill me up." It was a very simple prayer—but from the heart—and when she finished, she felt her sense of peace returning to her. And she felt energized.

She decided to go into the kitchen and get things set up for breakfast in the morning. Sometimes she did this at night. Then she decided to set the table and—thinking that her guests, frightened off by tonight's behavior, might be considering an early departure—use the good china. After the table was set, she noticed the tiny crystal vase that her mother loved to fill with violets in the springtime. Her mother loved violets—everything about them, their velvety petals, the rich color of purple, but most of all the smell. And that reminded Anna of one of her mother's favorite sayings.

"Forgiveness is the sweet fragrance of violets on the heel that crushed them," Mother would sometimes say with a twinkle in her eye as she arranged the delicate blooms in the tiny vase. But Anna had never quite understood the meaning of this saying. Her thinking was that no one should go around trampling on violets, especially not on purpose, and certainly not in order to walk around with sweet-smelling shoes. That was wasteful and wrong.

But she considered it now. *Forgiveness . . . like the smell of crushed violets . . . on the feet that trampled over them.* She felt that Eunice had trampled over her—many a time—and especially so today. Did that mean Anna needed to release something that smelled as sweet as violets to Eunice? Never mind that Eunice didn't deserve such a gift. But how was that even possible? Was Anna supposed to send Eunice some perfume?

Anna set the vase in the center of the table and just stared at its sparkling cut surface as it reflected the light. Just like that, Anna understood perfectly. She needed to forgive Eunice—whether or not Eunice deserved it. And Anna realized that when she forgave Eunice, it would be like releasing the sweet smell of violets on the heel that had crushed her. Simple enough . . . just not easy. Once again, she prayed, asking for God's help—and believing that he could show her how to forgive someone who had walked all over her.

Anna awoke feeling refreshed and at peace the next morning. She was still sad that Lauren wouldn't be coming to visit, but she felt hopeful that someday—maybe not too far in the future—Lauren would come. With breakfast preparations already in process, Anna slipped outside and went around to the shady corner where Mother's little patch of violets used to grow. Slightly overgrown with grass and weeds, Anna pushed back the weeds to see that there were still some violets growing there. She picked a tiny bouquet, then went back into the house to put it in the tiny vase.

She was just stirring huckleberries into the pancake batter when she heard someone come in. "Good morning," she called out cheerfully.

"Good morning," Clark said gently. "How are you feeling this morning?"

"Quite well." She smiled brightly.

"Oh, that's good to know. I was worried that you'd taken Joe Miller's news a lot harder than I'd expected you would."

She waved her hand. "No, no. I wasn't upset over that. Well, perhaps a tiny bit, but no, that's not what was troubling me last night." Now she confided to him about her disturbing conversation with Lauren. "It was hard enough to hear she's not coming today. But to find out that she thinks I'm robbing Eunice of everything . . . well, that was difficult."

"It sounds as if Eunice is poisoning your daughter's mind."

Anna pressed her lips together, wondering how she could make him understand.

"Perhaps I should send Eunice a legal letter, warning her that she needs—"

"No," Anna said quickly. "Please, don't do that." Now she walked over to where the vase of violets was in the center of the dining room table and she explained to him about her mother's saying.

"I think I've heard that before." Still he looked a bit bewildered.

"So I have decided to forgive Eunice," she said as she walked back to the kitchen. "Even though Eunice doesn't deserve to be forgiven, just like the heel doesn't deserve to smell sweet, I will give it to her." She stopped at the big new stove, turning on the flame without having to strike a match.

Clark nodded with a thoughtful expression. "I respect that. In fact, I think it's not only very mature of you, but it's very wise as well."

"Wise?" She tipped her head to one side.

"I've learned from experience that when you withhold forgiveness from someone it puts you into a kind of bondage with them. It's like they own a piece of your soul if you remain bitter." He sighed. "I did that with Roselyn for a number of years before I figured it out."

"So you've forgiven her?"

He grinned. "The truth is it's kind of a process with me. I find I have to forgive her again and again. But hopefully, in time, I'll get beyond it altogether."

Anna smiled. "I think it might be like that for me with Eunice too."

"Well at least you've put the wheels into motion, Anna."

"There's something more too," she admitted as she dropped a pat of butter onto the cast-iron frying pan.

"What's that?"

"I've decided not to pursue any more money from Adam's estate."

Clark looked concerned. "But you've got it coming to you, Anna."

"That doesn't matter." She watched the butter melting.

"But what if you need it?"

"It wouldn't be worth it."

"But it might be quite a large sum of money."

"I don't care." She turned off the flame and folded her arms. It was a stance she used to take as a child when she wanted to be stubborn.

"But what if—"

"There are no what-ifs," she told him. "If I fight Eunice for that money, I will end up being the one who is robbed. It will steal my peace and it will destroy the joy of creating this inn and it will even take my daughter from me." She shook her head. "No, I've made up my mind, Clark. Even if it was a million dollars, it's not worth it."

He just nodded. "I understand."

"Thank you." She turned back to the stove.

"Do you plan to communicate that with Joe? Or would you like me to?"

"Would you mind letting him know?"

He chuckled. "Not at all. In fact, it'll be interesting to hear the old boy's response."

Now Hazel and Marshall were coming into the house. Anna called out "Good morning" to them, apologized for being out of sorts last night, and quickly explained what had been bothering her.

"Oh, dear!" Hazel frowned. "I know how much you'd been looking forward to having your daughter visit. I'm just so sorry, Anna. I realize how important it is to have family around." She put an arm around Marshall and squeezed him to her. "I've so enjoyed this time with mine so much—thanks to your generous hospitality."

"Maybe we can be like Anna's family today," Marshall offered.

"That's right," Clark said. "Think of us as your family, Anna. You've been putting up with us, making us feel at home—isn't that what family is all about?"

"I say we should officially adopt her," Hazel proclaimed. "In fact, I think I already did. I swear it feels like Pearl is related to me now. After living in her little house, reading her stories, experiencing her river—why, it's as if old Pearl is my ancestor too."

Anna laughed as she flipped the pancakes. "I

would be honored to be related to all of you. And I'll gladly take you up on the offer."

As they sat down to breakfast, Anna mentioned her concerns that she might've scared them all away last night. "Hopefully, no one will be leaving here earlier than Sunday."

"Not me," Marshall assured her. "Now that our work's done, I want to do some more fishing today and, if it's OK, I'll take the motorboat out."

"That's fine," she told him.

"And I'm not ready to go yet," Clark added.

"I'm not going until the boys are ready," Hazel said.

"I want to catch a really big salmon," Clark told her. "I want something to brag about when I see Tom and Randy back at home."

"That's great." Anna felt relieved. "I want to light that bonfire tonight, just like I'd planned to do for the girls and, well, I was hoping you'd all still be around to enjoy it with me."

"What a delightful idea!" Hazel clapped her hands. "A way to celebrate our time together— and to bond our friendship."

Anna knew it wouldn't be quite the same without Lauren here. But, all things considered, it might be even better. Sometimes Lauren could be rude and demanding and rather spoiled. Perhaps Anna wasn't missing out on so much after all.

Still trying not to fret over her absent daughter, Anna carried the folding lawn chairs over to the bonfire area, arranging them in a semicircle that looked past the burn pile out across the river. She remembered when her dad used to have fires like this, usually in the fall, and how she always looked forward to them. Her plan was to enjoy this one and, since not much landscaping maintenance had been done the past few years, there would be more than enough cuttings for another fire in the fall.

Having heard the news of Anna's disappointment, Babette joined them for dinner and brought along dessert and a bottle of her best Burgundy. After dinner, all three women lingered in the kitchen to clean up. "Looks like it's cooling off out there," Anna said as she noticed the fog rolling in. "We might want to bundle up a bit before we go out."

Shortly before sundown, they all gathered around the pile, waiting as Marshall held up the lit torch that he'd put together to ignite the fire.

"I feel like this is a dedication," Hazel said ceremoniously. "I think we should all say something about the establishment of Anna's inn."

"Oui!" Babette agreed. "Like a toast!"

"You start it off, Marshall," Hazel urged him. "Then light the fire."

"Here's to The Inn at Shining Waters and all the glorious enormous fish that will be caught by the people who come to stay here!" Now he threw the torch onto the pile and everyone cried, "Hear! Hear!"

"Here ees to all the lovely guests who come to The Inn at Shining Waters," Babette said. "May they eat well and laugh a lot and make reservation to come back again and again!"

Anna laughed. "Hear! Hear!"

"And may those guests all be as blessed and refreshed as I have been during my stay," Hazel said. "May their souls and their spirits be restored and renewed."

Everyone agreed and now Clark spoke up. "Here's to Anna, the Queen of Shining Waters, may she be greatly blessed just as she greatly blesses others."

She thanked him, but now everyone was looking at her. "I'd like to say something too." She smiled shyly. "Here's to my new friends, who are becoming like family. Thank you all for helping me get to this place. I will treasure you always."

"Hear! Hear!"

The fire began to take hold and they made themselves comfortable in the lawn chairs, visiting and laughing and eating s'mores and even singing a couple of old camp songs led by Marshall and Babette.

Then Hazel stood. "Before I turn in for the night, I'd like to tell a final story—one that I transcribed recently."

"Please," Babette said eagerly. "Tell us!"

"I found this one particularly touching because it seems that it's a true story about something that really happened to Anna's grandmother."

"Really?" Anna was intrigued.

"That's my best guess. Perhaps you've heard it before." Now she began to tell about a time when Pearl was a girl. "I'm guessing she was about sixteen," Hazel clarified. "They were on their way home from the reservation and Pearl must've been a pretty girl—perhaps like Anna here, only younger. Somewhere along the way, perhaps even on the reservation, Pearl had caught the eye of a young man named John."

"My grandfather," Anna said.

"Yes. And the reason I know your grandmother was attractive, well, besides the old photo you showed me, is because there were quite a few young women traveling in the group—and it seems the men were rather limited in number so John could afford to be choosy. Apparently John was very interested in your grandmother. Trying hard to get her attention and not succeeding. But she was being coy or playing hard to get, or perhaps she was simply shy. So one morning John went out to forage for food and he returned to camp with a big bag of oysters. And as he shucked the oysters, he found a number of pearls."

"Yes!" Anna exclaimed. "I do remember this story."

"Perhaps you'd like to finish it." Hazel looked hopeful. "I'd love to hear your version."

Anna nodded then, following Hazel's example, she too stood. "I hope I can get this right. Like Hazel said, my grandfather, John, was finding some pearls as he shucked the oysters. So he gave these pearls to the other girls traveling with them. But he didn't give a single one to my grandmother—whose name happened to be *Pearl*."

Hazel chuckled. "And Pearl was none too happy about it either."

"In fact, she was downright angry about being slighted like that." Anna folded her arms as if she too were mad. "Pearl glared at John, then stomped off down the beach until she found a rock where she sat down and pouted alone." Anna suddenly remembered how her daughter acted like that sometimes.

"Then what happened?" Marshall asked eagerly.

"John went and found Pearl and asked her why she was so angry."

"He did not know?" Babette looked skeptical.

"Maybe he did. Anyway, Pearl demanded to know why John had given the pearls to all the other girls, but had given none to her. Especially after he'd acted so interested in her. She told him he was a mean, mean man."

"What did he say about that?" Marshall asked.

"John told her that the pearls were worthless."

"Worthless?" Babette looked shocked.

"It seems the pearls were misshapen and flawed and not fully formed," Anna explained. "John told my grandmother that he'd hoped to find at least one smooth, lovely pearl to present to her. But he'd been disappointed to find none of them were good enough for her. He explained that it would be wrong to present a less than perfect pearl to a perfect Pearl." Anna chuckled. "And that was how my grandfather captured my grandmother's heart."

Anna sat back down and looked into the snapping and crackling fire, watching as a pitchy piece of wood popped, shooting a shower of sparks into the darkened sky. This day had not turned out as she had hoped it would . . . but perhaps it was still a perfect day.

25

Life on the river became strangely quiet after Anna's guests departed. No more hammering or sawing, no big deliveries arriving from Henry, no more happy chatter around her big table at mealtime. While a part of her welcomed the slower pace and solitude, another part of her felt somewhat lonely. She kept herself occupied by adding the final touches to the rooms in the inn, working in her garden, putting up produce, and getting herself geared up for all the guests she hoped would soon be coming her way. And every single day, whether it was sunny, foggy, misty, or drizzling, she took out her canoe and experienced the river. Really, it wasn't a bad way to live. Still, she found herself longing for something more.

"You need advertisements," Babette told Anna one morning. Babette had surprised her by dropping by with pastries. "In newspapers and magazines."

"I'm not sure I can afford that. Not just yet."

"Can you afford not?" Babette stirred cream into her coffee.

Anna sighed. "You're probably right. I guess I should look into it."

"Why not let me help you, chérie? Do not forget, I was once businesswoman."

Anna remembered how Babette was naturally gifted at business, and how her parents had been dismayed when her second husband insisted she quit the store.

"You leave everything to me." Babette smiled with confidence. "Your guests, they will come."

"Don't forget I've only got five rooms and a cabin available right now." Anna explained how she wanted to have an open house. "But I thought I should wait until the other four cabins are built, and that won't be until late November."

"Too bad your clever carpenter ees gone. When will he return, chérie?"

"I'm not sure." Anna missed him too. "Clark had business to attend to. He said it might be up to a couple of weeks before he comes back."

Babette leaned forward. "He ees handsome, no?"

Anna smiled.

"His eyes light when he sees you, Anna. I think he ees in love."

Anna laughed nervously.

"Why ees this humorous, chérie? Do you not find him attractive?"

"Of course, he's attractive." Anna waved her hand dismissively.

"Not your type?"

"Oh, Babette."

Babette held up a forefinger. "Aha, I see eet een your eyes, Anna. You care for Clark. Eyes do not lie, chérie."

"Even if that's so, what difference does it make? Clark has his work, his life, his home— and they're not here on the river."

"Perhaps not yet."

As they cleared the coffee things, Babette continued to babble on about Clark, saying what a fine man he was and how she was certain that he had deep feelings for Anna, as if by simply saying this made it so. And even if it were true, it only made Anna uncomfortable. Because she felt certain she wouldn't be able to tear herself away from the river, not even for someone like Clark. She had no desire to live in a city. As much as she cared for Clark, she would hate to be forced to make that kind of a decision.

Linking arms with Babette, Anna walked her down to the dock. "Looks like we're going to get some more weather." She nodded toward the western sky where gray clouds were gathering.

Babette pointed in the opposite direction. "Who ees that?"

Anna turned to see the small motorboat coming toward the dock.

"Eet ees Danner's boat," Babette observed.

"Dorothy!" Anna exclaimed when she recognized the redhead at the helm.

Sure enough, it was Dorothy waving as she pulled into the dock. Anna hurried to secure her boat as Dorothy hopped out. The two women squealed and hugged.

"I can't believe it!" Anna exclaimed as she studied her old childhood friend. "You've hardly changed a bit."

Dorothy laughed. "Other than putting on about forty pounds!"

"You were always too skinny," Anna told her.

Dorothy looked closely at her. "The years have been kind to you."

Anna chuckled. "I don't know about that."

"Well, you look just the same to me."

Babette hugged Dorothy now, promising to see her later. "I must hurry home to miss the rain."

Dorothy frowned at the darkening sky. "Maybe I should head back home too."

"Oh, please, stay," Anna begged. "We need to catch up."

"Oui," Babette called out as she started up her engine. "You stay with Anna, Dorothy. You must see her inn."

So Anna gave Dorothy a quick tour of the renovated cabin, the bathhouse, and downstairs rooms. All the while they asked questions and exchanged information, trying to make up for the last twenty years in less than twenty minutes. Of course, Anna didn't tell Dorothy everything—not because she didn't want her friend to know, but simply because Anna didn't want to add sadness to this unexpected and happy reunion.

Big fat raindrops were just starting to pelt them as they hurried up the stairs. "Now, you'll have to stay awhile," Anna said as they rushed into the house.

"Oh, Anna!" Dorothy exclaimed as they went inside. "This room—it's just lovely. Everything you've done in your inn is so inviting and warm.

I wish I could stay with you during my whole visit on the river."

"You're more than welcome to stay." Anna laughed. "It's not like I have anyone else here right now."

"You should see how crowded my parents' little house is right now. Both my girls came with me. They're crammed into my old bedroom. And I'm sleeping on the couch."

"Bring them over here if you like." Now Anna showed Dorothy the other improvements and how the upstairs bedrooms were ready for guests too.

"Everything is just perfect, Anna." Dorothy sighed. "So comfortable, and yet it's unique and interesting too."

Anna thanked her, explaining how she hoped the inn would reflect some of her grandmother's ideals. "Things like quietness, wholeness, healing . . . the serenity of the river. And, really, you're welcome to stay here."

"You honestly mean that?" Dorothy's blue eyes looked hopeful.

"Of course." Anna turned on some lamps and lit a fire in the fireplace, explaining how her own daughter and friends were supposed to have been here, but that they had canceled at the last minute. "So, truly, I'd love to have some company."

Before long it was settled: Dorothy called her

parents' house and explained the plan and, after visiting for several hours, fixing some lunch, and waiting for the rain to stop, they set out to fetch Dorothy's preteen girls. Jill and Joanna already had their bags packed and seemed thrilled at the prospect of staying in an inn. Even Dorothy's parents seemed relieved, and Anna invited them to come over to share some meals.

The next few days passed far too quickly. Anna loved hosting her friend and the girls. They did all the things she'd hoped to do with Lauren and her friends—boating, swimming, fishing, and lighting campfires—but on the last night there, after the girls had gone to bed, Dorothy confessed to Anna that her marriage was in serious trouble. She had discovered that her husband had been involved with another woman. "I'm just devastated," she said sadly. "I don't know what I'm going to do—to stay or to go. Either option feels hopeless to me. I came out here hoping to figure things out."

Anna didn't know what to say.

"I'd leave him, but I can't imagine being on my own at my age." Dorothy frowned and shook her head. "I don't have any job skills or source of income. I feel so helpless, and hurt, and then I get angry."

"Do you still love him?"

Dorothy's mouth twisted to one side. "I shouldn't. But I suppose I do."

"Do you think he still loves you?"

"He says he does."

"Do you think you can ever forgive him?"

Dorothy held up her hands. "I don't know. He swears he'll never do it again. But how can I be sure?"

Now Anna told her about her mother-in-law and then she explained about the violets and how it wasn't easy, but how she was trying to forgive Eunice. "It's like a friend of mine told me, forgiveness is a process. But I'm working on it. In fact, I've been thinking about this very thing this past week. Like I mentioned, I want this inn to be special, a place of healing, and I feel certain that forgiveness has a direct link to healing."

Dorothy slowly nodded. "I sort of understand that. Constantly being angry at Ralph makes my stomach hurt. I honestly think it could be giving me an ulcer. You should see how I go through the Pepto-Bismol."

"I wouldn't be surprised if it was making you ill. Bitterness is like a sickness."

They talked late into the night, and before Dorothy went to bed she decided she was going to attempt to forgive her husband. "I think it's what I really wanted to do all along," she admitted, "but I just didn't think he deserved it. Now I'm going to remember those violets."

Anna thought of Lauren as she got ready for bed. Although she'd already forgiven her daughter, she wasn't too sure that her daughter had forgiven her. What if Lauren's bitterness made her sick? Anna didn't want to see that happen. Tomorrow, after Dorothy and the girls were gone, Anna would attempt to call her daughter again.

To Anna's relief, Lauren answered the phone. And when Lauren realized it was her mother, she didn't even sound angry. "I'm so glad I reached you," Anna said. "I was afraid you might've already gone off to school."

"No, school doesn't start for a couple of weeks."

"The reason I'm calling, besides wanting to hear your voice, is to tell you I'm sorry and that I hope you'll forgive me."

"Forgive you for what?" Lauren sounded truly oblivious.

"Well, I know that I hurt you by leaving—you told me that several times. Although I felt I had to leave."

"Yeah, I sort of understand that now. And I am going off to school. And I know that Grandmother can be a drag. You probably needed a break."

"And then you thought I was trying to take her money, Lauren. And I want you to know that's over with. Mostly, I just don't want you to be angry at me. It's not good for you and it's not good for us. I just want you to know that I love you, honey. I know I've made mistakes in being a mom, but I do love you."

"I know that, Mom. And Grandmother said that you'd backed down from your lawsuit. Although she thinks you might be trying to pull some sort of trick. You aren't, are you?"

"No, Lauren. Not at all. I told my lawyer friend to let Mr. Miller know that I don't want anything from your father's estate. I just want to be free to live my own life."

"So you're never coming home?"

"My home is here on the river, Lauren. I've really fixed the place up. I hope you'll come see it someday." Now she told her about how Dorothy and her girls had visited and had a good time. "I think you'd like it."

"I'll come see it . . . someday. Maybe after school starts—like for a weekend or during holidays."

"That would be wonderful, darling."

They talked a while longer, but then Lauren told her that Donald Thomas would soon be there to pick her up. "And I need to do my hair."

"So you're still dating Donald?"

"Yeah." She let out a happy-sounding sigh. "I think I might be in love, Mom."

As much as she appreciated being confided to, Anna had to bite her tongue. "Oh . . . really?"

"Yeah. And maybe when I come to visit you,

I'll bring Donald with me. He loves to go fishing."

"Sure." Anna felt uneasy, but was determined not to show it. "September is a good fishing month on the river."

"Great. I'll tell him that." Now they said goodbye and, although she was relieved to know that Lauren was no longer angry with her, Anna felt worried about the seriousness of this ongoing relationship with Donald Thomas. But perhaps she was just being judgmental. Maybe people could change, and maybe she was wrong about him.

Anna was surprised to hear the sound of a motor interrupting the stillness of a sunny afternoon, but it wasn't coming from the river. She dropped the hoe she'd been using and walked over to the other side of the house, and there was Clark's blue pickup driving through the meadow. An unexpected surge of joy rushed through her, and she felt her cheeks flush. *He was back!* Attempting to compose herself, she walked over to greet him, suddenly wishing he'd given her some notice. Today had been a gardening day and she was wearing an old pair of her dad's overalls with the legs rolled up like clam diggers, and her hair was in two braids.

"Welcome back," she called as he hopped out of the pickup.

"Anna!" He looked as if he too was caught off guard. "I didn't even recognize you just now. I thought you were a girl—someone who'd been hired to help out around here."

"I'm the hired help, all right, but the pay is meager." She laughed as she brushed dirt from her knees. "I was just working in the garden. It's really coming on now."

His looked intently at her, his deep-blue eyes shining brightly. "It's *so good* to see you, Anna. It feels like it's been a lot longer than a week and a half."

"I know." She glanced down at her dirt-encrusted fingernails, then shoved her hands into her pockets.

"So, are you full up with guests now? Is there a room available or will I need to pitch a tent this time?"

"Of course you can have a room. Unfortunately, I don't have any guests at the moment." As they walked toward the house, she told him about her friend's recent visit. "But she and her daughters just left yesterday."

"Oh." Clark nodded in a way that suggested he felt uneasy about something.

They were by the house now. "So go ahead and make yourself at home. Your old room is empty and waiting."

"Are you sure you want me to stay here?"

Now Anna felt confused. Had she

misunderstood? "You did come back to work on the other cabins, right?"

"Of course."

"Oh, good." She smiled.

"It's just that, well, I'm not sure about staying here alone with you, Anna."

She frowned. "Oh?"

"I, uh, I just wouldn't want it to look like, well, I wouldn't want it to seem—I mean your reputation—I hadn't even considered how it might appear."

"Oh." She nodded as a slow realization washed over her. This was a valid concern since folks on the river did like to talk. And a widow living out here alone with a divorced man would definitely cause some tongues to wag. It might even hurt business for the inn. But did this mean he'd be leaving again? Gossip or not, she didn't know if she could bear to see him go.

"I guess I didn't think this through." He set his bag down on the porch.

"I don't know what to say, Clark." She was truly embarrassed now. "When your mother was here, and Marshall . . . well, it was different then, wasn't it?"

"Yes, it was." He rubbed his chin and sighed. "I hadn't planned it like this, Anna, but . . . oh well, why not?"

"What?" She felt puzzled again.

Clark took in a deep breath, then reached into

his shirt pocket and cleared his throat. "I wanted to plan something more special, Anna, something old-fashioned and memorable." To her stunned surprise, he now removed a small, blue velvet box and got down on one knee, looking up at her with the most sincere expression she had ever seen. "The truth is I knew from the start that I would do this, Anna, I just had no idea how soon I would actually do it."

Anna felt slightly faint and a bit dizzy as she stared down at him. What on earth was he thinking? Why was he doing this?

"Anna, I love you." He looked directly into her eyes. "I know, you're probably shocked by this—I wouldn't blame you if you turned me down, but I love you, Anna. I love you so much that every day spent away from you was pure misery. I had no idea I could love someone this much, but I do. You don't have to answer me right now, because I can tell by your face you're in complete shock. But, I still have to ask you. *Dear Anna, will you marry me?*"

Her hand flew up to her mouth, but no words came out.

He looked worried now. "I know, I know. I'm doing this all wrong." He slowly stood, still holding the small box in his big hands. "I didn't mean to do it like this. I'm not usually the impulsive type. Not that this is an impulse, Anna. It certainly is not."

So many things were racing through her mind now. She had sworn she'd never jump hastily into marriage again. And she had promised herself she would never leave this river. But as she looked into his eyes, all she could think was that she loved him too.

"Oh, Clark," she finally said. It was all that would come out.

"I know my eagerness has probably overwhelmed you." He started to open the little, blue box now. "But since I've gone ahead and plunged right in, I might as well finish it. I really did have a plan . . . of sorts."

He opened the box and held it out for her to see. Anna's eyes grew large as she stared down at the biggest pearl she'd ever seen with a smaller diamond next to it. Set in what appeared to be platinum, the ring was beautiful. *"Oh, my!"* was all she could mutter.

"I was inspired by your grandparents' story. Thinking about how John couldn't find the right pearl for Pearl reminded me of another story. The story of a man who found an amazing pearl—the most magnificent pearl in the world—and he went home and sold everything he owned just so he could go back and purchase the incredible pearl. Well, Anna, that's how I feel about you. When I found you, I knew you were amazing, incredible, wonderful. I knew I would give up everything, I would sell everything, I would do anything just to have you say yes to me."

"Oh, Clark," she spoke quietly, looking from the pearl to his eyes, knowing that she was going to throw her earlier resolve to the wind. "I love you too. My answer is yes, Clark, most assuredly yes."

He wrapped his arms around her and, pulling her close, he kissed her solidly—and she kissed him back, intensely and with all the longing that had been building in her. It was a long wonderful kiss—and like a perfect pearl, she knew she would treasure it forever.

"Oh, my!" she exclaimed when he finally released her. She honestly thought she was seeing stars and her head felt light.

Now he took her hand in his and, ignoring her dirty fingernails, he slid the beautiful ring in place. "I had to guess at the size, but we can get it adjusted."

"It's perfect," she murmured, still feeling slightly dizzy and totally stunned. Was this a dream?

He kissed her again and this time it was an even longer kiss. Finally, he released her, grinning as he picked a piece of grass out of her hair, then stroked his fingers down her cheek. "How about if you clean up a bit and let me take you to dinner in town—and we can discuss this new development further."

She just nodded and, still feeling slightly off balance, dashed up the stairs and into the house. Part of her still felt worried, fearful, and unsure—but it was only a tiny part of her. The rest of her was happy, excited—*alive*—for the first time in years. She felt truly and fully alive. As she quickly showered and changed she realized that even if Clark wanted to get married tonight, she would eagerly agree. So much for her earlier reserve.

However, as they lingered over a candlelight dinner, they came up with a better plan. The wedding date would be soon, but to Anna's relief, Clark didn't suggest they elope tonight. Instead, they decided on the second Saturday in September. It gave them less than two weeks, but since Anna only wanted a simple but meaningful ceremony with just a few close friends and family, it would probably be sufficient. In the meantime, to protect Anna's reputation, Clark would take lodging elsewhere.

Once they got back to the inn, Anna called Babette, sharing the good news. Of course, Babette wasn't the least bit surprised and immediately offered to take Clark in during the interim. "And, chérie, you must let me be your mama for the wedding!" Babette went on to explain how she'd always dreamed of planning a wedding and how she would not accept no for an answer. So it was settled.

Clark kissed Anna goodnight, then got into the motorboat and headed down the river toward Babette's. Anna just stood there on the dock, soaking in the river sounds, and watching the running lights on the boat getting smaller. Finally, she looked up to see the stars shining brightly over the river and she realized that this day might very well have been the happiest day of her life. She hoped there would be many more to look forward to.

26

True to her word, Babette handled most of the wedding preparations. At first Anna tried to reel in her enthusiastic friend, pointing out how time was short and how neither Clark nor Anna particularly wanted this to turn into the event of the season.

"But eet ees good advertisement for the inn," Babette explained. "We will have your picture in the newspaper and perhaps others will want a wedding here too."

"I suppose that does make sense." Anna held out her hands, turning in a circle, so that Babette could see the fit of the dress. Babette had taken Anna's measurements and arranged with her friend Lois, a dressmaker in town, to sew the wedding garment. Anna had insisted on something simple, and Babette had given Lois a photo of a dress Audrey Hepburn had worn in a film. The result was a classic-looking design of creamy white taffeta with three-quarter length sleeves, a boat neckline, and full skirt that went nearly to her ankles.

"I like it," Anna proclaimed as she admired how the skirt swished back and forth in Lois's three-way mirror. "I feel like a princess." She giggled. "A middle-aged princess."

"Oh, phooey," Lois told her. "You aren't even close to middle-aged yet."

"But that ees not all." Babette smiled mischievously at Lois. "You have the other things ready too, no?"

Now Lois brought out several other items of clothing, holding them out for Anna to see. "A suit for your honeymoon," Lois said as she held up a sky-blue jacket and skirt. "And something to wear for a special night out." She pulled out a simple yet elegant black dress. "I don't know where you're going, but you could wear something like this anywhere."

Anna just stared at the lovely clothes. "I don't know what to say."

"Do not say anything," Babette told her. "Just try them on!"

After the fitting, Babette took Anna to lunch. "I am having so much fun with your wedding, chérie. I think your mama, she ees looking down from heaven and clapping her hands."

"I will never know how to thank you for all you're doing."

"No, no." Babette held up her hands. "We are family."

"Speaking of family, Clark and I have a final count on who we think is coming for sure. Clark only has nine guests, including Hazel and Marshall. I only have eight, including Lauren and her boyfriend and Dorothy and her family."

"So your mother-in-law, she ees not coming?"

Anna shook her head.

"I tell you she would not come."

"Even so, I feel better knowing that she was invited."

Babette opened her little notebook and took out a pencil. "That number combined with neighbors I've invited from the river and friends een town—eet ees about sixty guests." She smiled brightly. "Exciting, no?"

"Sixty!" Anna was shocked. "Who all have you invited?"

"Trust me, chérie. Some are old friends. Some are new. You will not be disappointed."

"Oh, Babette." Anna just shook her head. "Are you sure?"

"You have nothing to worry about. Nothing. Your mama-Babette, she ees taking care of everything. You only must be sure your rooms are ready for your overnight guests. That ees all I ask."

Lauren had been a bit shocked to hear her mother was getting married. But after a couple of phone calls, she seemed to adjust to the idea. Not only that, she began to confide in her mother in a way she'd never done before. Most of it had to do with Donald—and how much in love she was with him—but Anna was trying to be open-minded. In all fairness, she barely knew the boy. Perhaps he was all that Lauren believed him to be. Anna was looking forward to meeting him at the wedding.

The big day came quickly, and to Anna's dismay it started out as a gray one. Babette's plan had been to have the ceremony outside. Chairs and tables had already been delivered, an arbor was in place, and the weather forecast had been for sunshine.

"You know what they say," Hazel told Anna as she got off Henry's boat that morning. "Rain on your wedding day is good luck."

Anna laughed as she gave the older woman a hand. "Babette promised the sun will come out in time for the ceremony."

The two women hugged and Hazel put her hands on each of Anna's cheeks, looking deep into her eyes. "This is a very happy day for me, daughter-to-be!"

"Thank you. It is for me too—whether it rains or not."

"Don't you fret, Anna," Henry called out as he set someone's bag on the dock. "It's already clearing up out on the ocean. By the time I bring out your next set of guests, it'll be nothing but blue skies."

"How many trips are you making today?" Anna asked him.

"I got two more groups and Arnold Gasby's bringing the last bunch on his boat around four."

"And some guests will come in their own boats." Anna gauged the length of the dock as she went over to greet Marshall. He was helping Henry with the bags. "Would you mind overseeing the boats and the dock?" she asked him. "To make sure there's room for everyone."

"No problem." He made a slightly shy smile. "And in case you didn't hear, I was pretty excited when Dad told me his plans to propose to you." He chuckled. "I even got to go with him when he picked out the ring."

Anna hugged him. "I feel like the luckiest woman in the world right now."

"Looks like that's it for now." Henry was getting back on his boat, while the other guests gathered their bags.

"You won't be late for the wedding, will you, Henry?"

He winked at her. "You know I won't, Anna."

As Henry's boat pulled out, Hazel introduced Anna to the other members of their party, a small combination of family friends and relatives. Everyone seemed happy and congenial and Anna, delighted to play hostess, showed them to their rooms.

By noon, the skies, as Babette and Henry had predicted, began to clear. It was around one when Anna put out a simple buffet lunch for the guests. It was the only thing that Babette had allowed Anna to do, and when it was time to clean it up, others jumped in and told Anna to go take a nap. Of course, Anna felt anything but sleepy today. Plus she was anxious to see Lauren. But after Babette promised to get her when Lauren arrived, Anna agreed to retire to her room, where she dozed off.

The wedding was scheduled for five and Lauren arrived with the last group at a little past four. "I can't believe how much this place has changed," Lauren told Anna as they dressed for the wedding in Anna's room. The plan was for Lauren to be Anna's maid of honor. Marshall would stand with Clark. "It's really nice now, Mom."

Anna beamed at her daughter. "I'm so glad you like it—and so glad you made it finally."

"Grandmother wasn't too pleased," Lauren said as she pulled layers of pale blue taffeta over her head and into place.

"Yes, she communicated that to me." Anna helped fasten the back of Lauren's gown.

"No talk of that woman," Babette said firmly. "This day ees for happy only."

"Oh, you look beautiful," Anna told Lauren. "That color is lovely with your eyes."

Lauren smiled. "Donald likes me in blue, too." Anna just nodded.

Now Babette insisted that Anna tell Lauren the story about her great-grandparents and the pearl. And after Anna finished the tale and showed her daughter the ring Clark had given her, Babette pulled out a lovely strand of pearls and matching earrings—ones that Anna had seen her wear off and on over the years.

"Oh, Babette!" Anna shook her head. "No, no—I can't wear your pearls!"

"Oh, Mom, they're so perfect with your dress," Lauren told her as she admired the pearls. "You have to wear them."

"Remember they say something old, something new," Babette told her. "The pearls will be something borrowed . . . at least for today."

So Anna agreed and Babette fastened them around her neck.

"But what about something blue?" Lauren asked.

Anna hugged her daughter. "You are my blue. Your eyes and your dress." And, Anna thought, she also had the river for blue . . . and Clark's eyes.

"Perfect!" Babette proclaimed.

● ● ●

The wedding ceremony was perfect too. Anna knew it wouldn't be everyone's ideal of perfect. Someone like Eunice would surely turn up her nose at the homey gathering alongside the Siuslaw, the string quartet of high school kids playing slightly off-key, the flowers from local gardens along the river, or old Henry Ackerman wearing a crooked bowtie walking Anna down the "aisle."

But to Anna everything was absolute perfection. And when she and Clark exchanged vows, with the sparkling river stretching out beyond them, they both had tears of joy in their eyes. The dinner of salmon and roast beef was delicious and the wedding cake, baked by Dorothy's mother, was a bit lopsided, but very tasty. Everything about the wedding and reception was so delightful and so wonderful that Anna felt slightly guilty for not enjoying it more.

However, all she could think about on this special day was that she had just become Mrs. Clark Richards—a man she loved with every fiber of her being. A man who loved her equally—perhaps even more than equally. Clark loved her so much—and he loved her river so much—that he had chosen to relocate his life to her river. Their river now. And he'd assured her, again and again, that he was thrilled to do so.

After guests made a final toast to the happy

wedding couple and after the couple changed into traveling clothes, they were paraded by their guests down to the motorboat, which Lauren and some of the others had decorated with streamers and balloons, and Henry, acting as their captain, welcomed them aboard. Waving good-bye to their family and friends, the couple was now transported down the shining river as the sun slowly set, painting the sky in shades of pink and coral and lavender.

"Thank you for sharing your life and your river with me," Clark told her as he held her close in the back of the boat.

"Thank you," she told him, "for being the man I wanted to share it with."

"You know that you've made me the happiest man in the world, my Anna Pearl."

"That makes us a perfectly matched pair."

He pulled her closer.

"Listen," she quietly told him, "and you can hear the river singing its song."

He paused to listen, then smiled. "I think the river is happy too."

Discussion Questions

1. Anna's story begins on a somber note. Not much is going right in her life. And yet she still seems to have a smidgen of hope. Why do you think that is? Can you relate?

2. Not uncommon in Native American philosophy, the river is almost like a character in this story. Describe why you think Anna was so moved by it. Have you ever been moved by a geographical location? Explain.

3. Like many Americans in this melting-pot country, Anna's heritage is diverse. How do you think that was helpful or harmful to her?

4. Describe what you think Marion (Anna's mother) and Pearl's (Anna's grandmother) relationship was like when Marion was younger.

5. Anna remembers how her family had to "make do" during the Depression, lamenting that it's too bad people don't live like that today. What is something you'd like to "return" to if you could?

6. It required a full cast of friends to help Anna heal and take a proactive role in her own life. Which relationships did you think were most valuable and why?

7. Not much is mentioned about why Eunice is Eunice, but we know she has a story too (which you'll hear more about in book 2). Why do you think she was so bitter and bigoted and hateful?

8. Racial divisions aren't uncommon in our country (especially historically). So what was it that helped Anna, and those around her, to knock down those walls?

9. Lauren comes across as somewhat frothy and superficial. Why do you think she's like this? Do you think it's possible that she'll change? Explain.

10. In some ways, Clark is Anna's knight in shining armor. How did you react when he proposed to her? Do you think he should've done it differently?

11. Anna believes the river has healing properties. Some say Anna has a healing touch too. This is understandable in Native American culture, but what is your reaction to it?

12. Grandma Pearl's stories (which are compilations of the writer's imagination as well as some elements of authentic Native American stories) sometimes seemed relevant to the story. Could you relate to any of them? Which one and why?

13. Ultimately, Anna finds herself by returning to the river. Do you think there are reasons that we learn more about ourselves when we return to the places of our youth? Why or why not?

Center Point Publishing
600 Brooks Road ● PO Box 1
Thorndike ME 04986-0001 USA

(207) 568-3717

US & Canada:
1 800 929-9108
www.centerpointlargeprint.com